NOV - - 2021

THE
DANGERS
OF AN
ORDINARY
NIGHT

THE
DANGERS
OF AN
ORDINARY
NIGHT

A NOVEL

LYNNE REEVES

CROOKED
LANE

NEW YORK

Copyright © 2021 by Lynne Reeves

Published in the United States by Crooked Lane Books, an imprint of The Quick Brown Fox & Company LLC.

Crooked Lane Books and its logo are trademarks of The Quick Brown Fox & Company LLC.

Library of Congress Catalog-in-Publication data available upon request.

ISBN (hardcover): 978-1-64385-865-4
ISBN (ebook): 978-1-64385-866-1

Cover design by Kara Klontz

Printed in the United States.

www.crookedlanebooks.com

Crooked Lane Books
34 West 27th St., 10th Floor
New York, NY 10001

First Edition: November 2021

10 9 8 7 6 5 4 3 2 1

To Tom for the dance

Act One

Giddy in the unfamiliar feel of make-up and costumes on
this first warm evening of the year, they had forgotten
to be afraid.
—Richard Yates,
Revolutionary Road

1

The Swing of the Sea

THE HARVEST MOON is a spotlight leading June Danforth deeper into the woods. The girl is lost on the stark neck of land that occupies the coastline halfway between Boston and Cape Cod, with no clear memory of how she got there.

June remembers the audition—the casting director applauding her improvisation—and then leaving the high school with a friend. But the rest of the night is a blur, and the harder June tries to pin down specifics, like where Tali is now, the tighter her muscles get, the clammier her skin feels. Her train of thought is a twisted wreck. The only thing she's certain of is that something terrible is happening to them. She needs to keep moving. To find Tali.

June's ballet flats are at odds with the terrain. The rocks are bent on tripping her, and thorny branches grab at her hem, her collar, her sleeves. Tired of defending her clothes, June considers taking them off. She could leave the slippers on a rock. Hang her coat from a tree. But the offshore wind is a killjoy; it sings a warning: *"He will see them. He will find you."*

Seconds after picking up her pace, the air current chants louder: *"Someone is chasing you."*

June takes the dirt path and stumbles upon a board-walk. Each time she loses her footing, getting up is harder. Her hands and knees are scraped and bloody; everything stings. But she perseveres, and in no time she's rewarded. There's light visible in a distant set of windows. *Please be a house. Please be at home.* June disregards the "No Trespass-ing" sign. Whoever lives there will understand when she explains. How will she explain? She'll say she's sick. It's not a lie. After only a burst of sprinting, her stomach stabs and taunts. Her chest is tight. Her hair is drenched, though it's not raining. June doesn't sweat this much after taking the most grueling dance class. If only she could lie down. Curl into a ball. Just for the time it takes to figure out what's going on.

Then the growl of a wolf orders her to stop. His voice, high-pitched though human, says, "It's okay. You're trip-ping. But Jesus, you've gotta stop running."

The animal is covered in yellow-gray fur; his throat and belly shine white courtesy of moonlight. He's perched on a boulder near the water, his paws hanging limp over the edge. He's relaxed, as if to say she never had a chance of getting away from him.

"I don't get what's happening," June says. Is she even awake?

"I had no idea you never used before. You should've said something."

The creature points at June, or beyond her. His fingers are long and lean, with knuckles sprouting dark hair. A man's hand emerges from what she now realizes is merely a winter jacket. Part of her wants to turn and see what this wolf-man is pointing at, but the last time she dared look behind her, the gnarly trees wore mocking faces. With every word—his and hers and the ones echoing around her—the rush of the sea gets louder, pounding out a beat in her head. Or is that the start of a migraine? The rocky shoreline draws and pulls water over stone at the same time it distracts June, luring her to it. *"Come in,"* it says. *"The water is fine."*

Despite the vagaries of weather, wind, and tide, she remembers how a single dunk can cool an overheated body. And June is on fire.

The last time she hit the beach, she was with her parents. The scene that materializes before her now is as real as anything else she's seen tonight. In it, a younger version of herself rushes the surf, holding hands with her mother. A beautiful woman, still alive and healthy.

But the image fades out as quickly as it appeared, and June is left desperate to feel the icy sea on her arms and legs. Except the way into the water is a puzzle.

Start with your clothes, she tells herself. June undoes button after button, pausing only to loosen her coat's belt. She struggles with the mechanics of sleeves. When the thing is half off, she notices the rigidity of her leg muscles, the worsening tension in her thighs, her crampy calves. She wonders, *Will I be able to swim?*

June looks toward the man for help, but he's no longer atop the rock. Where did he go? And how long has she been standing there staring at her feet. Shit. Shoes. She goes to take off her flats, when someone says, "Leave them on. Lie down. Here."

The voice is familiar and also foreboding, muffled and muddled by night sounds and the swing of the sea.

Nothing makes sense now. The fringes of rocks and outer ledges light up until the entire landscape flashes red, white, and blue, in fireworks spectacular. Neon clouds obscure her vision and June is falling. Falling back, falling over, falling down, falling

2

Curious Vigil

THE PROVISIONAL STAGE is awash in candlelight. The night is long, the machinations for this vigil endless. Nell keeps telling herself that if her daughter is already gone, she would feel something more than numbness blanketing her skin. Where is the stitch in her side stifling the easy exchange of air? If Tali is dead, wouldn't this mother's heart already have experienced an electrical misfire so dramatic it would beat out an erratic rhythm or put a stop to her altogether? No, Nell would know.

Tali is alive. So where is she?

Nell stands between her husband, Zeke, and their oldest friend, Peter Danforth, on a platform that raises them above the crowd gathered on Boston Common. Their position declares them the unfortunate ones. Every time Nell looks to her left and sees Peter with his head bowed and his hands clasped in prayer, she's slammed with what's happening. Tali isn't the only one they're here to plead for. Peter's daughter, June, was last seen with Tali coming out of the

Performing Arts High School after an audition, a callback that went later than usual into the night. Grainy out-of-focus surveillance footage grabbed from the camera mounted above the entrance shows the girls walking side by side, unaware they are heading toward an unidentified male who will force them into a car and steal them away from their families. Tali and June have been missing two days.

When Nell isn't searching her body, trying to register some undeniable perception tethered to her daughter's well-being, her mind drifts. She visualizes a dank basement, a hidden bunker, a lightless place where Tali and June wait, desperate for someone to free them and bring them home. She won't allow herself to imagine the unspeakable things someone could be exacting upon her child against her will.

Nell understands how you miss a bus. Mislay an earring. Misplace your keys. How you mourn the loss of a loved one gone too soon. She knows there are a multitude of ways husbands go astray from good marriages and that, every day, people simply disappear, or mysteriously do, or pretend to, all without account. She is wise to it. What mother isn't keenly aware that children and teenagers have been known to vanish out of the blue—out of backyards and front yards, while on bikes or on foot, on their way to school or on their way home? Each of them last seen by someone who loves them or someone who knows them or someone merely passing by.

In the time it takes to tie a shoe or read a text message, a child can—*snap*—go out of sight. Nell knows this and still, despite the times she's worried about this very thing, she never thought it would happen to her child.

Reporters jockey for the best camera angles for capturing the unfolding drama. News vans send their satellite arms skyward above the rugged elms. The burnt orange and yellow leaves stun Nell, reminding her it is autumn and that she's no longer able to hold on to even the simplest of facts. It seems like seasons ago that she took a tentative step toward freedom from Zeke. Now standing here, overwhelmed by all these people raising their tiny flames at her, it's as if this is her punishment for even considering she might leave him and take Tali with her.

Nell recognizes many of the teenagers formed in clusters below the stage, not so much from having worked at PAHS for the past five years, but because these students sobbing for the girls wipe their eyes with the sleeves of logoed sweatshirts. Out of context here on the Common, they look like regular kids and not the stand-out prodigies they are. Dancers and actors and singers granted an excuse to be out, unexpectedly let loose from studios and theaters and music rooms where, like Tali and June, they dedicate countless hours to perfecting their craft.

Even though they're there to help, Nell wishes they'd all go home, taking their pinched looks and downturned smiles with them. It's her own mother she wishes were here. She'd know what to do next.

No one needs to tell Nell history is not on her side. If she could, she'd step up to the microphone and shout: "Tali and June will not be added to the dreaded list of names you're whispering, thinking I can't hear you: Levy, Bish, Holloway. No. Carrington and Danforth will join the ranks triumphant, linked with girls called Berry, Smart, Dugard."

But Nell does not take a step downstage. At least she won't until it's time to give her impassioned plea for their girls' safe return. Unlike her daughter, Nell doesn't crave the spotlight. She is a backstage mom.

In truth she needs every last one of these people to mobilize for Tali and June. And as far as she's concerned, the news networks willing to take part in this collective sensation are welcome to lash her to the stage for as long as it takes to get her daughter back.

It's a gentle pressure on Nell's spine that slows her racing brain. Zeke's touch, like it once had more power to do, momentarily stops her from spinning out. She turns to thank him for making the effort despite the fact that he knows she blames him. Instead, she finds it is Peter's hand giving off heat between her shoulder blades.

"It's almost time," he says, urging her closer to the podium. "Do you want to go first?"

Nell shakes her head. "You go. Where's Zeke?"

As Peter points beyond the makeshift stairs to the right of the dais, a look of disgust breaks through his otherwise morose demeanor.

The turnout is impressive and still Nell has no trouble finding her husband. In countless ways, Zeke has always been antithetical to anyone else. His hair, more salt than pepper, is unkempt, some say wild. He stands several inches taller than most men. Zeke is literally head and shoulders easy to find in a crowd. Stationed now on the backstage side of the platform steps, his head is down. His phone is out. Zeke is texting.

The woman responsible for directing the night's events, whose name keeps escaping Nell, speaks above the hum of the crowd. "I know the wait is hard. Another few minutes and you can address them."

She barely finishes showing Peter and Nell the signal she'll flash to indicate the networks are ready to go live, when in two giant steps, Zeke lands on stage and takes the podium.

"Thank you all for coming." His voice is shrill at first, the microphone kicking back the high notes of fear slurring his words. "Wow. Wherever she is, I hope Tali can see this. This is the biggest crowd the kid's ever drawn."

Nell yanks the back of Zeke's shirt. What is he doing? This isn't some opening for a play. Their girl isn't in the wings hoping the right critic or scout is in the house, ready to offer her a big break.

The woman in charge gestures frantically to the cameramen below, imploring anyone who's ready to start filming. Nell hears her say, "Don't miss this. He's one of the dads."

Zeke's head jerks in the direction of the organizer, then over to the cameraman, all while he ignores Nell. "Look, my friend Pete will tell you—my wife too—we're going through hell right now," he says, clearing his throat. "I hope you never find out how horrible it is not knowing what's happened to your kid."

Nell shouldn't care that Zeke is embarrassing himself— and her. This isn't about them. It's about Tali.

Hoping her contempt looks the same as her anguish, Nell steps forward and slides her body in front of her husband, replacing him at the podium.

"I'm Tali's mother," Nell says, her voice a whisper. "Our daughter is beautiful inside and out. She and June are both wonderful students and gifted artists. Everyone who knows them will tell you about the bright futures they have ahead of them." It takes forever for her to complete a sentence. Each pause she takes to control her breath is an effort to appear composed—and to hold back tears.

Instead of taking his rightful place beside her, Zeke is off, heavy feet down metal steps. As she speaks, he mills around inside the crowd, accepting hugs and claps on the back, leaving her and Peter alone on stage.

Nell grips the podium letting its sharp wood edges dig into her palms. "Tali and June haven't done anything to deserve this," she says. "None of it makes any sense. What kind of person does this?"

As Nell rambles, she feels the crowd draw back. Like Zeke, she's gone off script. She is breaking the rules set out for parents in this ugly little club. Members must not be loose cannons. Stoic works better to garner sympathy and searchers. A glimpse into the television monitor reveals a woman with dark eyes as expressive as her hands. The unrestrained physical energy and the desperation in her voice are unrecognizable to Nell. The overwrought mother staring back at her is painful to watch. But she can't help herself. She lifts her eyes from the prompter and stares straight into the camera, speaking boldly and directly to the miscreant who has her child.

"Let the girls go. We'll leave you alone. Drop them somewhere safe. Out in the open. Where help can find them."

Suddenly there's a familiar arm around her shoulder. With the grace of a dancer, Peter Danforth moves to her side. His is a compassionate takeover of the microphone. The terror of not knowing where his daughter is does not negatively affect his performance. On the contrary, Peter's narration is smooth. He's a man who can be counted on to put his daughter's well-being above his baser impulses.

"June and Tali are out there. Somewhere. And they need our help," he says. "I'm told that right now a hotline number is running at the bottom of your screen. Please put it in your cell phone contacts. Text it to your family and friends. Post it on Facebook. Be alert. No detail is too small to report. No one is above suspicion. Please help us bring our daughters home."

Despite the light breeze, the air is leaden. By the time Peter finishes, it suffocates. That's when Nell starts worrying about rain. With each degree the temperature falls, even a mist becomes a menace, turning core body heat down. What if they're being held outdoors, or hiding somewhere outside?

At least June had a coat, a pretty polka-dot thing with cuffed sleeves and a belt. The security footage Detective Jameson showed them—the same clip that's been replayed ad nauseum on cable news—establishes June donning the coat while her daughter wears only an inadequate sweater over a mini-skirt and leotard. Tali didn't always love the aqua cashmere Nell found in her size at the secondhand shop two blocks down on Newbury Street, the J. Crew tags dangling from one sleeve. But after several girls showed up at school in sunny yellow, azalea, and lime-green replicas wrapped tight around their slim frames, her girl was sold. Nell was deemed cool. All was right with the world.

Side-stepping her way to the edge of the stage, Nell calls down to Zeke. "Did Tali have a windbreaker or fleece in her backpack that morning—or maybe a sweatshirt?"

Zeke rakes his hand through his hair. "How would I know?" He looks at her the way he does when she's accused him of something he's inarguably done. Like she's the one in the wrong.

"Why would I go through my seventeen-year-old's backpack?"

"You didn't bother to check to see if your daughter came home from her audition either."

Nell will never forgive herself for not anticipating the dangers that hide in an ordinary night. For being away on an out-of-town job interview, leaving Tali at home. For trusting Zeke one time too many.

"How many times do I have to say it? I should've gone to her room," he says. "When she wasn't home by midnight, I should've called you. I should've called police."

The cameras pan and the crowd collectively pins stares on Zeke and Nell. The demise of their marriage playing out live on air is additional theater offered free of charge.

Nell doesn't know whether he's trying to put an end to the spectacle or if he has news, but Detective Fitz Jameson turns up out of nowhere, holding out one finger, the universal sign for wait a minute. Of the cadre of detectives assigned to what the media is calling The Boston Kidnapping, Fitz is hardest to read. Most of the police officers Nell has met are stereotypical rough and tumble, wouldn't recognize a feeling if one stole their cuffs or badge. In contrast, Fitz is attentive, almost sweet. His boyish looks and neat-as-a-pin suits provide a strange distraction. Throughout this nightmare, he's dedicated himself to keeping them informed about developments large and small. When he's talking to Peter and Nell, he's can-do, and she's reassured. More politician than cop, his impeccable speech belies his Southie roots, and his easy eye contact and kind words convince her: Fitz will find her girl. Other times Nell catches the way he commiserates with other detectives, the way he stares at Zeke, and it's as if he's drawn his weapon and has it pointed at her heart. Fitz, like the others, doesn't hide that he's suspicious of her husband.

The detective stands below Peter and Nell now, Zeke at his side. With his phone pressed to his ear, he nods like a bobble-head.

When the call ends, there's barely a beat before Fitz taps the screen of his cell. He's either about to place another call or he's using it to keep from facing them. Then Fitz lifts his head, looking first at Peter and then at her.

"One of their cellphones pinged south of Boston," he says. "And it looks like we have an ID on a girl."

3

Detective Story

"**F**OR THE RECORD, state your full name, date of birth, address, and occupation." Fitz Jameson straddles the metal chair in the dimly lit five-by-five room with the bravado he uses when playing interrogator. When that approach doesn't feel right this time, Fitz turns the chair around and sits, elbows off the table, like he would if he'd showed up at Ma's on M Street for Sunday supper. He tells himself to relax. He's on the right side of the table.

The faster Fitz interviews the old man who found the girls lying bruised, battered, and worse on the beach, the sooner he can get out of this sweat box.

If he hadn't drawn the short straw, he'd be on the South Shore right now, combing the coastal property, collecting evidence before the ocean does, not interviewing witnesses.

Back when Fitz joined the force, he knew full well it was only a matter of time before he got *the* case. The one with the power to absolve him of his sins. Five years later, he's ready.

"Name's Charles Turner Stockbridge. Everyone calls me Charlie. Born May 1941. I holed up in a couple rooms free-a-charge at the Glades property in Scituate, Mass. I'm the family's caretaker. Have been for fifty-odd years."

The way Charlie rests his hands on the table, twiddling his thumbs, reminds Fitz of his grandfather. The salty sea air must wreak havoc on skin because Charlie looks ten years older than Pops did when he was the same age. The yellowed fingernails and the gray glow the guy's face gives off are all the evidence Fitz needs to know Charlie is a smoker. Like Pops. If the interrogation wasn't being videotaped, and Detective Ross wasn't always on the lookout for something to justify calling Fitz, Care Bear, or some other demeaning nickname, he'd be tempted to scare Charlie off the butts, telling him how horrible those final hours can be when stiff lungs balk at the simple job of drawing air.

"Okay, Charlie, like I told you, this conversation is being taped. Understand? For the official record, I need you to tell me your account of what happened."

"Yeah. But first can you tell me where you took my Daisy?"

"Don't worry. She's across the street at the park." Fitz pats one of Charlie's nicotine-stained hands. When he remembers Dave Ross, he pulls his arm back. Christ, he's playing good cop/bad cop against himself. "Look, we've got an officer taking care of your dog. You said it yourself, the old girl looked like she needed to take a leak."

"All right then. Well, that reminds me. I was taking Daisy out for her constitutional. See, I let her do her duty by the water's edge, same time day and night, rain or shine—no need for them expensive plastic poo bags. I let the tide take her business out to sea."

"I got that part."

"Alls I'm saying is, if Daisy and me wasn't accustomed to our routines I coulda missed them girls on Watties Beach. At first, I couldn't make heads nor tails of what I was looking at. It was getting dark when I seen one rounded heap half in, half outta the water. But then the dang bundle moved, and she let out a helluva moan. Damn near dead, that one was. And Lord have mercy, the other one—not ten feet away—well, God rest her soul, I could tell she was no longer with us."

Charlie's story jabs at Fitz's own. A girl found dead on a shoreline, the same age as the Carrington and Danforth girls. But in the picture in his mind, his friend Maddie is fair-haired and athletic, bearing no resemblance to the lean dark physicality of June Danforth.

A scraping sound fills the room as Charlie pushes his chair away from the table like he's getting ready to bolt. "Where'd you say you put my Daisy?"

"She's fine, Charlie. Sit down. Your dog's at the park, remember? Now stay focused on the girls, okay? Then I'll bring Daisy to you, I promise."

Fitz wants to jump to his last question, but he stops himself. If he blows the case by rushing through a witness account in favor of getting into the field, he'll never hear the end of it.

"What happened next?"

Charlie settles back in the chair. "You know I feared it was a child I'd come upon, not no teenager. I knew before I looked at one of 'em that she was in rough shape. It was no joke the way that girl was carrying on. She wasn't acting like them kids do every other night come summer. Up to no good. Trying to pull one over on me when alls I'm doing is what they pay me for. Shooing trespassers off the property. No, this one was hurt, and bad."

"At any time did you touch either of the girls? Did you move them at all?"

Charlie puts a hand to his forehead, and shielding his eyes, he shakes his head. "No, but I'll never forget the one on her back, all tangled up in her raincoat. Her little dancing shoes covered in sand. Night or no night, it was clear that girl was dead."

As much for himself as for Charlie, Fitz places photos of Natalie Carrington and June Danforth in front of his witness. "Either of these young women look familiar to you? From the night you made rounds? Or from any other time?"

"Never seen either of them till right now. The girls on the beach didn't look nothing like that, no sir. You sure these here are the same ones? How's the hurt child doing anyways?"

"She's in the hospital. They say she's going to be okay. Tell me, you live out there in Scituate by yourself?"

"Yessir. Nice views of the lighthouse from my cottage. Minot Ledge Light. Like a sea monster floating on the waves, I always say."

"You're off track again, Charlie. You must be getting tired, so I'll ask you only a few more questions."

"Alrighty. You're a nice kid for a cop. You remind me a little of—"

"Charlie," Fitz says a little too loudly. "Focus."

The old man leans back in his chair as if Fitz were about to manhandle him. He's behaving the way innocent people do in the presence of cops.

Fitz's tough-guy demeanor is overplayed and poorly acted, plus he likes Charlie, so he course-corrects. "Last few questions, okay? Rough guess, how many people know you live alone out there at the Glades? That you're the caretaker?"

"I'm not bragging when I say, from Greenbush to Minot, all of Scituate knows Charlie Stockbridge. I'm what you call an institution." Charlie's laugh is genuine, the estimation of his popularity seemingly sincere.

"I've got to ask you—and Charlie, you need to tell me the truth—did you do anything to hurt those girls?"

The old man is understandably offended since there is zero evidence to suggest to Fitz or anyone else that the man's story is anything but legit. It's just a question that has to be asked. Charlie uses the table to heave himself out of the chair, eventually coming to a full stand. Fitz does nothing to stop him.

"No siree," Charlie says. "I never hurt nobody. And kid, now I need to ask you something. What did you do with my Daisy?"

4

I Bring You Flowers

THE LAST TIME Nell gave Tali a bath, she had to have been four, maybe five years old. Her daughter would've triumphed at three if she'd let her. Right from the start, without whining or asking permission, Tali would reach her tiny hand up to open the bathroom closet door and rummage the bin Nell kept inside, filled with water toys. On more than one occasion when Nell tried to help, she'd say, "I choose, Mommy. I do it myself."

Back then Tali's favorites were a host of plastic princesses, kings, and clowns. She'd make up fantastical stories and then act them out with her parade of characters. Nell would use the bathroom vanity as a make-shift desk to pay bills or check email, because once Tali's little body was submerged, it wasn't easy to get her out. She'd play in the cooling water till every last bubble burst, and her fingers and toes had shriveled to the size of tiny prunes.

Nell's vivid memories of Tali as a young girl are even more heartbreaking now that her teenage daughter sits in the same bathroom, wrapped in a plush towel, waiting for her mother to fill the tub with hot water and bath salts. Tali hasn't left Nell's side since she and Zeke brought her home from Brigham and Women's. She isn't talking much either.

Nell turns off the tap. "I'll be right outside the door."

Tali grabs her arm. "No. Stay with me."

"Okay, honey. Okay." Supporting her by the elbow, Nell guides her daughter to the side of the tub. Tali drops the towel and winces as she lowers her slim body into the suds. There aren't enough bubbles to hide the full outside picture of what has happened to her or the pain she's experiencing.

Like ugly bracelets, Tali's wrists are mottled purple, dark and light. According to police, the man who abducted her restrained her with duct tape wrapped so tight it had begun to cut off her circulation. That much of the story Nell knows. It's the sutured cuts, an array of cruel line drawings and jagged slits that run the length of her arms and legs that has Nell wondering what kind of tree branches raked her daughter's limbs and if night sand against her body soothed the pain or made it worse.

She wants to ask Tali how her knees became bruised and swollen, and about the person who did all of this to her, but what comes out is a whisper. "I'm so sorry."

Tali stares straight ahead, registering zero emotion. She isn't an overly modest girl, but if she were herself, she'd at least be covering her breasts with crossed arms. More likely she'd be yelling at Nell to get out of the bathroom. She'd be singing in the shower, not speechless in the bath. Tali would be rehearsing lines or calling to her through the closed door to tell her something thrilling or funny about school. Nell wouldn't be crouched here, focused on the swirls and pools she makes as she runs a sponge gingerly over her daughter's tender skin.

Hours ago, in her desperation to see Tali again, Nell pleaded with an otherwise unresponsive God to bring her daughter home to her. And here she is. Except looking at her now, she can see there's no way to undo the shattering or pretend something life altering hasn't happened. Tali is back and she isn't.

Despite the calming scent of lavender in the room, Nell can't breathe when it strikes her that they're washing away any remaining evidence that might help them catch the person who hurt Tali.

"You know you can tell me anything about what happened, right?" Nell asks. "I won't tell anyone—even police—if you don't want me to."

Tali turns her head toward Nell as if she's just noticing her there. Seconds go by before she responds. "No one hurt me. Not the way you think."

Every part of Nell wants to believe what Tali said back at the hospital when she'd refused the rape kit exam, when she told the nurse there was no need for it.

"You're not saying that because you think I can't handle it, are you?" Without going into her talent for coping with horrible things, all Nell says is, "Because I can."

"You need to believe me. It was awful—the whole thing. But *that* didn't happen."

It's the most she's shared with Nell since she reached the Emergency Room and found Tali lying on a stretcher turned to the wall. It's through this sliver opening she's given her that Nell is tempted to press her about what she remembers. Did she ever get a good look at the man who took her? Were they in Scituate the whole time? Was she with June when she died? Inside this one-way conversation, Nell hears a new voice: the psychiatrist's warning to take it slow. "Try not to push. Probing too much too soon can retraumatize," the woman had said back at the hospital.

Nell goes to hug her daughter but stops short when she sees remnants of a beach she once loved in Tali's hair. Specks of sand and the silky leather of kelp.

There's a knock on the bathroom door.

"It's Peter," Zeke says. "Should I tell him you'll call him back?"

Nell doesn't think she can handle talking to him right now, but how can she refuse Peter? His daughter suffered the same horror hers did, except June didn't survive it. She looks to Tali for permission. She'll say no to him if her daughter wants her to.

"Take it." Tali pulls her battered legs toward her chest, circling them with sudsy arms, rocking ever so slightly.

Nell opens the door to accept the phone.

"I'm so sorry." This time the same words she used moments ago with her daughter don't sail out on a whisper across a misty bathroom, they catch in her throat. Her family came within a hair's breadth of Peter's reality, and Nell can't imagine how his heart is still beating. Living all these years without Mei. And now, alone in the world without his daughter.

"She's okay," Nell says. "Right here. I'll tell her."

Tali stops moving. From the tilt of her head, it's clear she's listening and that she hears Peter ask Nell to come over. To help him pick out the clothes June will wear for eternity.

Again, she waits for Tali's cue for what to do. Tears make muddy rivers down her cheeks when she nods.

"I'll be there," Nell says. "Later. Only me."

With the phone down on the vanity, Nell eases Tali's head back to wash her hair. Loosening a barrette from matted curls, she lets the whole tangled business trail the length of her spine. "After this, you'll feel better. I'll give you one of the sedatives, and you can rest."

Two hours later, Tali's curled up on the couch. Her eyes closed, her breathing deep and regular. Nell can't stop taking long looks into the living room where the television is tuned to the notorious crime news network. Tali asked her not to shut it off. She said in a weird way it helped her to make sense of things. Zeke—no surprise—is sitting at his desk, glued to his computer.

It's been twenty-four hours since this family accepted a police escort from hospital to home, pushing past news crews, their only lifeline to the outside world a psychiatrist's business card tucked in the pocket of Nell's skirt.

Though Tali looks peaceful, Nell can't bring herself to go to Peter's yet. It's like those early days after her daughter was born when she couldn't imagine leaving her baby to go back to work. Throughout her pregnancy, the assumption was that she'd return as soon as she felt physically ready, foregoing any extra weeks of unpaid leave. Given that Zeke's sales commissions were unpredictable, they needed the money, and Nell's office job came with decent hours and great benefits. Then Tali arrived and Nell's world shifted. Everything she thought she wanted—a bigger house, a newer car—seemed superfluous. It wasn't long before that feeling extended to being married to Zeke, when, in the time before Tali, he'd been as essential as air.

He calls to her now from the other side of the den. "You're still here."

She shushes him and for once he gets the message the first time. Zeke comes to her, and when he reaches her side, he slips his hand in hers. They exchange a look of gratitude for their daughter's safe return. "Don't go," he says squeezing her hand. As conflicted as she is about what to do, Nell pulls him toward the kitchen.

"You know I have to. Peter's our friend and he's alone." Nell keeps her voice low when she says, "It could've been us."

They're still holding hands, and she can feel Zeke fingering her wedding ring. "She's okay," he says. "Tali's all right." It sounds like he's trying harder to convince himself than he is her. She pulls free.

"I'm sorry I didn't check on her," he says. "Can you ever forgive me?" Zeke's shoulders shake; he starts to cry.

"What were you doing that night? Were you even here?"

"I took your advice and went to a meeting, but I came right home. I watched some news, and then I went to look something up on the computer and got sucked into time tunnel vision. You know how I get."

"Tell me the truth. Were you gambling?"

"No, Nell. No. I've told you a hundred times, I'm done with all that. I was online and the next thing I know, Peter's knocking the door down, telling me June never came home."

Nell knows every terrible thing that happened after Peter showed up. How Zeke finally checked Tali's room. How together these men called police, and then her, waking her from a hotel night's sleep. The endless drive home from Connecticut. Two days of agony. The vigil. And then miraculously getting Tali back and hearing the news that June will never come home again.

"I want to believe you," she says.

"You can. I'm going to be better."

Recognizing the old ache in her chest, Nell doesn't have what it takes to replay this worn-out conversation. She starts up the back stairs to their bedroom; Zeke follows.

"I'll even go back on ADD meds if that's what you want."

"We'll talk later." Nell speaks calmly, though there's no guarantee that whatever she says won't set him off. "I have to go help with the arrangements."

She can't visit Peter without bringing tangible condolences. A casserole won't do. Stopping in front of her bureau, she pulls the priceless gift from her jewelry box and slips it into her pocket. Nell can only hope what she's come up with will soothe Peter more than hurt him.

When she turns back around, Zeke is still standing there as if he's waiting for instructions.

"I know you're sorry," she says. "Give me time, okay? And don't leave her alone for a single second. I don't care if you have to park yourself downstairs till I get back; do not leave this house."

Zeke nods vigorously. Fate has bestowed upon him one last chance. They both know he can't afford to fuck it up.

After checking on Tali to be sure she's still deep in a Klonopin sleep, Nell grabs her coat from the hall closet and heads downstairs. Bypassing reporters staked out in front of their home, she exits through a rarely used basement door. She counts on neighbors as careless as Zeke to have camouflaged it with hastily placed trash cans, forgotten bikes, skateboards, and strollers. Heading in the direction of the Danforth townhouse on Marlborough Street,

Nell pulls her scarf tight around her head and adjusts her coat's collar.

How many times over the years has she taken this route? At first to bring Tali to playdates with June and to have coffee with Mei. Then, later, to console Peter after she passed, and finally to lean on his friendship. Nell runs her hand over the wrought iron fences that separate private yards from public sidewalks. On her way to work, or other times she roams the city, Nell likes to clip a cluster of chokeberry or a stalk of butterfly weed, and sometimes when she is most in need of senseless beauty, she'll stop at the florist on Newbury Street to splurge on a single bloom to compliment the intricate paper vases Mei taught her how to make.

She begins to build a tiny arrangement for Peter, telling herself that she's doing the homeowners a favor since even the most well-tended gardens need deadheading to maintain their carefree vibe. Sprig of heather. Stem of laurel.

The closer she gets to Commonwealth Avenue, the more eerily reminiscent the landscape is of the days after the Boston Marathon bombing, when media burst on to the mall that runs from Kenmore Square to the Public Garden, like unwanted weeds. The strip's green space, every inch of it, covered by satellite vans and celebrity reporters.

Back then all the news was breaking. Suspects were identified; boys hunted down. Programming was interrupted again and again until coverage became continuous. Members of the National Guard were stationed on every corner, their assault weapons at the ready, all of it out of place in this lovely Boston neighborhood.

Before the city's order to shelter in place—an effort to protect them from the perpetrators at large—Nell was just another neighbor out walking, another woman tired of staying cooped up at home with fear and her husband.

Today, reporters mill around, marking time, or they sit in chairs positioned roadside, because nothing is new. No one has been found responsible for June's death. When evening news segments finally air, pretty people in fresh makeup will rehash what is already known about the case—which right now amounts to absolutely nothing. With no new leads and the public's waning attention span, the lot of them will likely pack up their toys and go back to their newsrooms. Or they'll move on to another town, inserting themselves into someone else's American horror story.

Nell's guess is that they won't go until they've successfully staged a takeover of June's funeral, sensationalizing the girl's death even more, making the act of saying goodbye harder on the ones who truly loved her. On Peter.

Nell snakes her way through the media caravan that overflows onto the sidewalk trying not to draw attention to herself. She tucks her less than perfect bouquet inside her breast pocket. What she does not do, as she moves toward his home, is waste a single wish or prayer on making it inside without being noticed. She'd prefer they don't recognize her, but she truly doesn't care if they do. Tali is back. Her daughter is home safe and sound. Nell has no right to hope for anything else ever again. And she vows right there on the flagstone path that leads to Peter's door to be content with this and only this.

Before she knocks, Nell digs one hand deep into her pocket, letting the sharp edges of her gift to Peter prick her skin, offering up the pain for him. This isn't going to be easy. Their positions could easily have been reversed, and they both know it.

As soon as the heavy oak door opens, the media swarms the entrance. Peter reaches for her and pulls her inside before reporters engulf them, but not before rapid-fire camera flashes blur her vision.

"You came." Peter hugs her tight. "Come in, come in."

As Nell registers his surprise that she kept her word, Peter looks over his shoulder toward the kitchen, where a chorus of voices can be heard clucking about food and how "the poor man cannot be made to eat." It's not at all shocking that the loudest of these belongs to Ana Wallace. Ana is Sam's mother and the chairperson of The Friends of the Performing Arts High School of Boston. She's as much a fixture in the school as any teacher or dramatist. Her contributions to the theater program, both on the clock and with cash, go unmatched. And hands down she is the most annoying woman Nell has ever met. Ana's demeanor is brusque, and she embodies the term *stage mother*. Her crowning achievement is that her son is a star. The shrillness of her voice often precedes her arrival on the scene, and Nell has been known to duck around corners to avoid her. Not the most becoming behavior for the assistant director of Human Resources.

Suddenly Nell wonders why Peter needs her when he already has a house full of characters willing to offer the feminine perspective he told her he needed.

Peter steers Nell away from the kitchen, past his room, toward June's. It's as if they're walking hand in hand through the years. The photograph-lined hallway holds a retrospective of his daughter's too-short life. There are photos of her in Christmas plays and Halloween costumes. One with her donning a first communion veil. Another of her and Peter at the Girl Scout father-daughter dance. There is June in her breakout role as Chloe in Naomi

Iizuka's *Good Kids*. Nell remembers opening night, watching this girl she'd known since she was a baby completely transform herself into a young woman so deep and compelling Nell forgot she was a teenager merely playing a part. June was in eighth grade back then, and that's when everyone started buzzing about her potential.

As the June gallery continues to go back in time, Nell notices empty spaces along the way, square and oval imprints where pictures used to be. Like a brain teaser game, she tries to remember which iconic ones have been removed. On the threshold to June's bedroom, she no longer needs to tax herself. Peter has covered his daughter's bed with pictures—some in frames, some loose—and it hits Nell that she will see all of these images again later, put together in a sharper presentation. Peter is collecting photos for the funeral home.

"This is my favorite," he says, picking up a black and white eight-by-ten of his wife holding June as a newborn.

"I remember. You chose that one for Mei's wake. It's beautiful," Nell says. *A real heartbreaker,* she doesn't say.

More artwork than photo album material, the image features a bare-shouldered Mei, her silky black hair off to one side, her eyes cast down at her swaddled infant. Mei Sheng Danforth, née Tan, was a fashion model in Singapore, where Peter met her on one of his business trips. Two years later Mei was expertly holding their baby, a girl with eyes so knowing it was as if June knew her destiny. That like her mother, and Nell's, she'd be prematurely committed to memory, thanks to film.

"Knowing they're together," Peter says, "it's the only thing that helps." His hands tremble, and the impression of Mei holding their baby girl quivers in midair.

"They won't tell me when I can have her," he says.

Peter is talking about police or a medical examiner, someone he is dealing with; someone Nell is not. He is delicate in the way he uses his fingers to brush his tears from the glass. Nell wants to hold him despite the likeness of his wife and daughter between them.

The last time they touched seems ages ago now, but it was only last Monday. Nell remembers sitting at Peter's dining room table and over a glass of wine, for the thousandth time, she'd spilled her guts to him about Zeke. Going on and on about her husband's latest infraction and how once again they were fighting about him not following through on what he'd promised to do.

"A half-dozen lottery receipts might not seem like a big deal, but it's the hiding and the lying," she'd said. "It's bad enough that he said he's taking his meds, and then I find a full bottle of Ritalin in his coat pocket. But now he's refusing to go to a Gamblers Anonymous meeting."

Before Nell started to cry, Peter slid a box of tissues across the table. "You're right—it's not the worst thing he's ever done. But you shouldn't have to act like his parent. He's the one who came up with the plan."

"I know addiction is an illness, and I've done my best to help him. But I can't keep doing this. He's not going to change. Is it wrong to want to focus on myself and Tali without feeling guilty?"

"It's been too much for too long." Peter sighed. "You have a right to be happy."

Nell, no longer used to a man giving her his full attention, sipped her wine.

"I've decided to go through with the interview at Hartford Academy. The open house is tomorrow, and after that I meet with the head of HR. If I get the job and they have a place for Tali, I think I'm doing this. I'm leaving him."

"Good. He doesn't deserve you." In an unpracticed attempt to take her hand, Peter caused her wine to sail up over the lip of her glass. They laughed. And that's when Peter first kissed her. Nell didn't resist. She didn't think of Mei or Zeke. Or either of their girls. Peter crossed the line between them, and she gave in easily because, in truth, for the longest time, this had been exactly what she'd wanted him to do.

Less than a week later, the murder of his child has changed everything. Nell and Peter stand in a room that belies June's absence. She is painfully present—and from Nell's experience, she always will be. What's left of her vivaciousness can be found amid colorful beads pooled atop her bureau. June's flowery scent wafts from the pretty pink clothes stacked on open shelves and hanging from closet doors. Nell had imagined a time when she'd be more than a family friend to June, to be there for the girl in ways no one had been for her after her own mother died.

Nell still wants Peter. But she got her daughter back. His envy of her must be immobilizing. If, inside, he's raging against her good fortune and his lack of it, that would be justifiable.

She produces the pin that belonged to her friend and his wife. The creamy pearls and brilliant diamonds cluster to form a collection of lotus flowers. "June gave this to me after Mei died. She wanted me to have it, but not to tell you or wear it around you. She thought it might make you sad. I tried to refuse her, but you know how persistent June can be." Nell offers a weak smile, suppressing the impulse to change the words *can be* to *could be*. Peter stares at the brooch, once pinned to the elegant sash of Mei's wedding dress.

"I kept it safe all these years," Nell says, offering it to him. "At the right time, I planned to give it back to June. I'd like to see her wear it now."

"You can't be at the funeral." Peter clutches the photo to his chest. He doesn't look at her when he makes it conditional. "Unless you come without Zeke."

"You know I can't leave him now. That would be cruel to him, and I won't do anything to upset Tali."

"I'm not talking about your marriage." Peter takes the brooch from her hand. "I think he's involved."

It's as if Peter has dragged the pin across her lifeline. She has shared with him in confidence every consequential act and petty sin Zeke has ever committed, and now he's twisting things, throwing it all back at her?

Nell steps away from him. "That's ridiculous. You're not thinking straight."

"You said it yourself last week. He's relapsed."

"I may not be happy in my marriage and at my wit's end with him, but how you go from Zeke's slip-up to this horrible crime is beyond me."

"He's not some small-time gambler. He's in deep trouble, and he owes some bad people a lot of money."

Despite the grandness of June's room, the space begins to suffocate. "Who told you that? How do you know?"

"I've overheard things, and police questioned me about him," Peter says. "The night of the vigil, they point-blank asked me if I thought he was involved."

"They have to do that. I'm sorry this happened to you. But you can't think Zeke would do anything to hurt our girls."

"I think someone planned to take Tali as a warning to him, and June was in the wrong place at the wrong time.

Zeke is under investigation, and I think they're about to find out some terrible things."

At the sound of Peter saying her husband's name, Nell freezes. Once again, she has left Tali home alone with him. "I need to go."

"I care for you, Nell. That's why I wanted you to hear it from me. Trust me, there's no one who wants all of this not to be happening more than me."

As Nell backs away from him, Peter keeps talking, saying something about not meaning to hurt her. On the threshold, she turns and runs down the hall, past the remaining images of June. Before she reaches the door to Marlborough Street, someone behind her shouts, "Stop!"

Ana Wallace's voice is neither shrill nor cloying when she warns Nell not to go out the way she came in. "My car's parked in the alley. I'll drive you."

Nell pulls her coat tight, inadvertently crushing the forgotten flowers against her chest, releasing bitter scents into the air.

5

Landscape of the Body

Fɪᴛᴢ Jᴀᴍᴇsᴏɴ ʟɪᴋᴇs to end his last set with an up-tempo tune. Despite its name, "Weary Blues" is a jazz standard more raggy than conventional, and it rings sweet throughout The Beehive. At ten till two, the place is nearly empty. Ray makes it clear it's closing time by clanking clean glasses back in their overhead racks and swishing and swiping his wet rag along the length of the bar. He reaches palm out toward reluctant tippers, tossing out "catch-you-laters" to the handful of regulars, who, with their asses half on, half off their stools, know they've got to go. Still they snap their heads back one last time, trying to squeeze every last drop from their glasses.

Fitz is well aware that no one is listening to him play. Disinterested patrons and preoccupied bar staff no longer get under his skin. His Monday night gig neither showcases a talent on the rise—a kid paying his dues—nor does it represent a has-been in free fall. It's merely the arrangement Fitz deserves. He needs a piano and The Beehive needs music. Simple as that.

When the final notes are played, and they are played expertly, Fitz pushes back the bench and stands, reaching his hand deep inside the oversized snifter that sits on the lid. Though it's hardly worth it, he pockets the crumpled bills and cast-off coins, then grabs his backpack from the chair next to him and moves toward the bar.

"If you can down it quick, I've got a Michael Collins with your name on it. On me." Ray comes out from behind the bar to lock the door after the last patron waves goodnight. "I've got a lady waiting on me," he says, winking.

"No whiskey for me tonight," Fitz says. "Gotta get back to HQ."

"After two AM? Must be some case. At least let me drive ya. I'm going down Tremont way."

"No thanks. I'll take a raincheck on the whiskey, though. Next Monday, okay, Ray?"

It's less than a mile from the bar to the station where Fitz left his car. Moving it around Boston is a pain in the ass. Plus, he does some of his best thinking when he's walking.

Tremont Street and West Dedham have enough nighttime traffic to upgrade the walk through this neighborhood from a stupid idea to only somewhat risky. When the Cathedral of the Holy Cross comes into view, Fitz hoists his backpack onto both shoulders, pats his holster, and clips his badge inside his jacket to the pocket of his dress shirt. Given he's white, on the short side, and (according to Dave Ross) a pretty boy, Fitz may well be a target, but he's got the brass to go with the gun, and he likes to think the balls to use both if he needs to.

Waved through security with a flash of his jacket and a nod to the guy on duty in the cage, Fitz takes the stairs two flights up. He likes the precinct this time of night.

Fewer cops, not as many perps, overall less commotion. And he doesn't have to deal with Ross breathing down his neck or Doyle taking up space. Mick Doyle, who rounds out the rest of the team working the Danforth case, is a cardboard cut-out of a cop who's counting the days till his pension kicks in. Doyle hasn't been lead on a case or asked a serious question in five years.

With an extra set of clothes in his backpack, Fitz plans to review the evidence they've got so far, catch an hour or two of sleep on the abandoned couch in the back hallway, and then change into clean pants and a fresh shirt before the morning briefing.

Fitz finds what he is looking for deep in the supply closet: a three-ring binder with a plastic slip front pocket. On the way back to his cubicle, with the notebook tucked under his arm, he wonders if he's got what it takes to focus now. All day long he's been crashing into waves of memory, all of them to do with Maddie.

Push on, he tells himself. It's redemption time. Fitz plans to use the connection his mind is making between the death of his friend twelve years ago and this case by immersing himself in the life and death of June Danforth. He'll get to know everything she liked, everyone she knew. And bring about an arrest—by himself if he can. In doing this, he'll pay homage to Maddie. At least that's the plan.

Fitz begins by honoring June. The first thing he does after signing out the box of evidence labeled "Carrington/ Danforth" and moving it to his desk is remove one of the photos given to police by the dead girl's father. He stares at her, allowing June's face to imprint on his mind. The professional head shot shows June in one of those contrived chin-in-hand poses. Despite the staging, the girl is commanding. Her dark eyes compel Fitz. It's as if she's speaking directly to him: *"Find the person who killed me."*

With June's photo slipped inside the plastic front of the binder and three-hole punched paper snapped in and at the ready, Fitz gets down to it. He sorts through the evidence box, starting with interviews obtained prior to finding the girls. Nothing much stands out until Fitz remembers the ping his intuition got when questioning Performing Arts High School sophomore Sam Wallace. The kid put on quite a show, crying and carrying on. Claiming he and June were sort of going out. Whatever that means. Fitz recalls the kid saying they planned to tell everyone after they landed the leads in the upcoming play; they'd celebrate by changing their statuses on Facebook.

Though Wallace is credited by nearly all the other students interviewed as being the star actor at the school—tears and all—Fitz hadn't found him terribly convincing. He scratches a note on a page in his binder: *Requestion Wallace.*

Fitz rifles through police reports and reads through each of the kids' interviews. Skimming parent statements and skipping the one he conducted with Charlie Stockbridge, Fitz comes to the only statement in evidence from Tali Carrington.

The initial incident narrative mostly tells Fitz what he already knows. June Danforth was pronounced dead at the scene while Natalie (Tali) Carrington was transported from Watties Beach in Scituate to the Boston hospital where she received treatment for multiple contusions and lacerations, severe dehydration, and emotional distress.

The attending psychiatrist, Dr. Cynthia Rawlins, advised limited questioning due to the victim's state of mind, claiming that to push the girl so soon after the ordeal could further traumatize her. Dave Ross was on duty that night. Surprise, surprise—he pushed anyway, encouraging Tali to tell as much of her story as she could. He guilted her into it, telling her she needed to do her part to protect public safety.

Tali's statement fits with what the surveillance footage captured. The girls leave the Performing Arts High School of Boston, heading in the direction of Commonwealth Avenue after an audition at 11:07 PM. They remain in view until they reach the intersection. Tali states that after they made the turn, a white male in his late thirties or early forties approached from the side. The man wore a faux fur jacket not unlike one owned by her father. At first, Tali thought it was her dad, there to pick them up.

Fitz makes a note in his binder to rewatch the footage, to hone in on anything he may have missed the first dozen times he's viewed it. He makes another note, this one involving Zeke Carrington: *Ask to see the look-alike jacket.*

According to the statement, the last thing Tali remembers is the man pointing to a silver vehicle she assumed belonged to him. He asks the girls for directions. Unable to hear him over the traffic, Tali and June step closer and that's when he opens the car door, grabs them, and throws them into the backseat.

At this point in the victim's account, Ross wrote that Tali became inconsolable, saying, "I can't believe June is dead." In response to the girl's meltdown, Dr. Rawlins halted questioning.

Fitz holds his pen inches above the paper, his mind a jumble of questions he can't write down fast enough: *Why doesn't Tali remember anything after being shoved in the vehicle? Did Ross ask her that? Did Tali refuse the rape kit exam because she hadn't been assaulted or because she's a kid and was afraid? Did Ross at least ask her that?*

Ross is an idiot and his report isn't worth the paper it's typed on. Fitz pulls the folder containing crime scene photos of June Danforth from the evidence box. As he slides the pics from their interoffice envelope, someone claps him on the back, causing him to drop the batch he'd been holding.

"Well look who's working overtime," Ross says.

The dead girl's body multiplies as scattered images of June Danforth slide across the cheap and dirty floor. Fitz gets that disoriented feeling that comes over you when you're surrounded by mirrors. Looking at her like this, the way the girl has been discarded, makes the whole thing more horrifying. Not to mention eerily familiar.

"How long have you been ransacking the evidence box, Care Bear?"

Fitz stands and still Dave Ross towers over him. The guy's six feet five if he's a foot. Ridiculously thin, with a huge head and receding hairline, suddenly Ross reminds Fitz of a giant lollipop.

Scrambling to pick up the photos, he can already hear Ross broadcasting tall tales to the rest of the squad about spooking him.

"What time is it?"

"Six forty-five. Briefing's at seven. Hurry the hell up. Doyle's already clocked in. I got something to show you guys."

When Ross speaks, his lips strangely disappear, curling inside his mouth with each phrase or sentence he utters. Sometimes Fitz is so distracted by the oddity of the quirk that he doesn't register what the guy is saying.

"What?"

"Go change. You reek." Ross waves a folder in front of Fitz, sending cool air and stale breath on to his face. "You got a spare set a clothes in there, am I right?" He points to Fitz's backpack parked on the windowsill.

"Show me now," Fitz demands.

"Listen to you. I forgot how cranky you get when you're tired." Ross drops the folder and, with a flick of the wrist, expertly lands the thing open in the center of Fitz's desk.

Once again pictures of June Danforth fan out in front of him. In these pre-autopsy shots taken by the medical examiner, the girl is lying naked in various positions on a steel table—front, back, and side.

Over the years, Fitz has seen his share of dead bodies. Victims trapped in cars or crushed by them. On streets and roads and highways. Heart attack sufferers lying dead in bed, sprawled on kitchen floors, lodged in bathtubs. All found too late, far too late. But none of them—not a single death due to accident, medical, or act of nature—has called up so completely seventeen-year-old Madeleine Townsend. Until today. Looking at June, Fitz is faced with what his brother's girlfriend must've looked like after police pulled her body from the waters off Castle Island.

Without warning, Fitz puts a hand to his mouth.

Ross grabs a nearby waste bin and with glee shoves it under Fitz's chin, expecting him to vomit.

Fitz swallows hard, pushing his hand away. He wipes his mouth on his shirtsleeve and reaches for the most disturbing of the photos. Like a penance, he commits every inch of this tragedy to memory. June's once beautiful face now wears the bluish mask of death. The absence of the same livor mortis on the back of her torso, arms, and legs tells Fitz she died facedown. Which contradicts how Charlie Stockbridge claimed he'd found her.

Notes made by the ME below the picture say, "Superficial abrasions, arms and legs, most notable on palms of victim's hands. No major trauma to head, neck, or chest. No evidence of sexual assault."

Fitz knows there is no precise core temperature at which the human body submits to the elements. He doesn't need to read the rest of the notes to know that June died from some combination of frigid wind and sea. The landscape of the body and his gut tell him this.

"Coroner's office is backed up yet again," Ross says. "Her toxicology isn't expected for another week or two."

Fitz puts the photos and notes back in the folder without reading the ME's conclusion. He hands it back to Ross. "Preliminary cause of death, hypothermia?"

"That's the theory for the time being," Ross says.

Lifting his backpack off the sill, Fitz takes a quick glance at June, alive, on the cover of the binder he's created to keep track of the case. "After briefing, I'm heading over to Carrington's to put eyes on Zeke's jacket," he says. "The one Tali mentioned in her statement looked like the one the kidnapper wore."

"We can head there together," Ross says. "I've got some questions of my own for the dad."

6

Next to Normal

THE PARK BENCH across the street from the row of brownstones is as good a place as any for Cyn Rawlins to stop and double-check the exact number of the Carrington's house. Pulling the discharge paperwork of her only remaining patient from her bag, she forces herself to focus. Tali's not to blame for being admitted to the ER on her last night on call.

The reporters who take up the sidewalk for a full block don't preoccupy her. Cyn's no stranger to reunification cases coming with cameras. Her racing thoughts and compulsive need to scan her surroundings for threats lead back to Noah. What can she do now but breathe in and out?

One and done, she tells herself. She'll feel better after this patient is seen and the intake assessment complete. Then she can go back to the office and concentrate on cleaning up the last of the mess her ex-partner, ex-lover has made. All ties to Noah Clarke officially severed.

As soon as it's appropriate, Cyn will tell the Carringtons she's closed her private practice. She'll do her best to assure them that she'll make a good match, referring them to a reputable colleague willing to oversee treatment of their daughter.

Her story, should they press her, on its face is true. She's traded patients for students and is off to teach forensic psychology at Boston College. What she won't say is that she's surrendered to compassion fatigue and will finally take a break from bearing witness to the horrific things men are capable of doing to women and girls. Those who no longer can, teach.

Shoulders back, chin high, gearing up to see her last client, Cyn crosses the street and enters the media bubble.

After pushing her way to the top of the brick steps and ringing the bell, Tali's father opens the door enough for her to slip inside. Cyn knows it's Zeke before she steps into the foyer. His mad scientist hair precedes him.

"I take it you didn't have trouble finding the place," he jokes. "In your experience, when can we expect the circus to pack up and move out of town?" He turns his clasped hands inside out, cracking his knuckles.

"It varies case to case," Cyn says. "A lot depends on the investigation and whether police name any suspects."

"Then all bets are off if there's an arrest or a trial." Zeke stares somewhere beyond her as if he's talking to himself. She steals a look around.

Across the hall into the main living space, the television blares, but no one is there to watch it. The place is more cramped on the inside than she'd expected, but it's as dark as every other home she's ever visited. Closed blinds block prying eyes, but sadly they keep out the healing light.

"After I spend time with Tali, I can go over a few things, including what to expect next." Cyn moves beyond the tight foyer, hoping Zeke will usher her all the way inside. "Is Tali here?"

Nell comes down the front hall stairs with one finger pressed to her lips. "She's asleep, and I hate to wake her. Do you mind if we meet with you first?"

"Not at all."

Zeke leads the way into their kitchen, an oddly shaped room overpowered by the sickly sweet smell of pastries. Countertops are cluttered with bakery boxes from Georgetown Cupcake and Honey, Honey Cafe. Dirty wine glasses form a line to the left of the sink, waiting to be washed and put away. The only bright spot is the clutch of buttercups poking their heads from a tiny vase made of intricately folded paper.

Nell clears the table of half-empty coffee mugs while Zeke brushes crumbs to the floor. After rolling her eyes at him and pulling out a chair for Cyn, Nell reaches for the miniature spray and places the flowers in the center of the table.

"Sorry," she says. "We're usually neater than this."

Nell's dark hair is loosely swept back, showcasing the softness of her face. According to Cyn's notes, she's in her early forties, though her slender figure and creamy skin make her look years younger. Her voice is subdued, as if her max volume is just above a whisper.

"You've had more important things on your mind," Cyn says. "Tell me, how's Tali doing?"

"I'm around kids her age all day at school, and my mother died when I was a little younger than she is now, but none of that compares to this," Nell says. "Tali's quiet and clingy. Once in a while she'll make a comment about

June, offer up a detail she remembers, but then as quickly she'll change the subject. I think it's going to be slow going."

"Exactly," Cyn says. "Teenagers typically can't sustain one feeling state for long, especially the intense ones. You can expect Tali to be sad one minute—even very down—and then seemingly happy the next. She may even appear giddy at times. As you probably know, it's all to be expected."

Nell and Zeke hang on Cyn's every word, though the string of them sounds oddly mechanical to her own ear.

"I'm sorry about your mother," Cyn says. "Grieving the loss of a parent is never easy, but it's especially difficult at that age."

When Nell pulls her sweater tight, Cyn realizes she isn't going to elaborate on her loss.

"I understand you work at Tali's school. In guidance?"

"Human Resources," Nell says. "I recruit staff and teachers. Handle payroll and benefits, that sort of thing. The job's a job. But Tali and her friends are in my office all the time, and there's always some kind of rehearsal or performance going on. I'm lucky I can be there."

"Doesn't hurt that we get a huge break on tuition," Zeke says.

Nell squeezes her eyes shut as if that alone can make her husband disappear.

"Do you work outside the home?" Cyn asks Zeke.

"I'm in sales. Office equipment mostly. I'm in between jobs right now. Back in the day, when she worked at Mass General and I was with Xerox, that's how Nell and I met. I walked into her office and sold her on me."

Nell taps a finger on the table, a not-so-subtle message for Zeke to rein in the storytelling.

Cyn reaches into her bag for Tali's medical record and a pen. "Do you mind if I take notes while we talk? A thorough family history helps someone like me get perspective on the work ahead."

"Whatever you need to do," Nell says. "I'll tell you anything if it helps Tali."

Taking her time, Cyn flips through her notes from the night this family arrived in her ER, not so much to refresh her memory on the details, but because it sounds like Nell's thrown down a challenge for Zeke. Cyn waits to see if he'll accept it.

"Yeah, well, I lost my job six months ago," he says. "It's not easy to find work after you've been fired."

"That can be hard." Cyn turns to him. "This may not be your priority right now given the events of the last few days, but if or when you're interested, I can put you in touch with a career counselor who specializes in that kind of search."

"We'd like that," Nell says. "I mean, *you* would, right?"

Zeke angles his body toward his wife and crosses his arms in front of his chest, as if he's both open to her opinion and closed to it at the same time. "Yeah, sure. Circle back to me."

"I'll make a note." Cyn has to be more careful with her language and stop inserting herself into a case she has no intention of managing long term. She jots down a reminder for the doctor taking over to follow up.

"Have there been any other recent life changes or any long-standing family issues you think I should know about?"

Zeke is out of his chair, moving away from Nell, toward the coffee pot. His hands shake as he reaches for a dirty mug and then fills it to the brim. "I'm an addict," he says in a practiced twelve-step way. "Gambling is my drug of choice, and I relapsed a week ago."

"Three," Nell says.

"Do you need to dig me when I'm in the middle of coming clean? Nineteen days. Happy now?"

Fifteen minutes. That's all the time it took for Cyn to break the ice and get sucked under the surface of this family, crashing right into their dysfunction.

"Are you willing to go into treatment?" Cyn asks.

"Yes. Without a doubt, yes."

The wine glasses. His jitteriness. "What about alcohol? Or any drug use?"

Zeke shakes his head and sits back down. "Just too much caffeine," he says, laughing, banging his mug on the table with enough force that coffee sloshes up over the lip. Nell stares at the spill like she's lost in another time, another place. Neither of the Carringtons moves to clean it up.

"Mind?" When Cyn points to the under-cabinet paper towel dispenser, Zeke and Nell nod their approval. It's the only thing they've done in unison since she stepped inside their home. Like every other family she's met, these people are desperate for someone to take care of them.

Before the coffee reaches the pretty vase, Cyn moves it toward Nell and blots the stained pages of their family history. After wiping the bottom of Zeke's mug, she places it back in front of him.

"It sounds like you've both been through a lot. How does Tali handle all of this? Does she open up to either of you?"

Nell touches the petals of the bright flowers. "It's no secret her father and I have issues. She's seventeen and things have been difficult off and on for a long time. That said, compared to what I hear from other mothers about their teenagers, Tali's a dream girl. I'd say she takes what's happening to Zeke and me in stride. She's incredibly focused on her own life, especially when it comes to school."

"Any difficulties socially? Any disturbances in thinking, panic attacks, periods of depressed mood?"

"Not with her. Nothing. No." Nell looks down, perhaps not wanting to out whoever does experience the hallmarks of anxiety and depression.

Cyn makes another note in the record for their new counselor to dig deeper on substance use issues and any other symptoms Zeke or Nell may want to lay claim to. And most especially those they do not.

"What I'm hearing you say is that while you've struggled together, Tali was emotionally healthy before all of this. Which means there's every reason to believe she'll draw on her good coping skills to work through what happened to her, making sense of it, with support, over time."

"I never thought I'd hear 'emotionally healthy' and 'Tali' in the same sentence." Zeke is wisecracking again, but Cyn doesn't need more inappropriate sarcasm to see that he's having trouble. From the moment he met her at the door, she's noticed his lack of eye contact, defensive posture, and how the timing of his gestures and the expressions and words he speaks are plain off.

Nell snaps her head in his direction, her voice now powered by a note of fury. "Nothing about this is funny, Zeke. Dr. Rawlins doesn't have time to deal with you."

"I only meant our daughter can be a drama queen. At least when it comes to me."

"She's an actress. So yes, Tali can be intense. Maybe she wouldn't run hot and cold with you if she didn't have to watch you wrecking your life. Not to mention, by association, hers and mine."

Cyn rests her pen on the table and closes Tali's record. Pushing her chair back a couple of inches, she makes a show of balancing her loyalties, looking from one parent to the other.

"I know it's unbelievably difficult to process what happened to Tali. What happened to the two of you too. Everything you're feeling is important, and for a while your emotions will be exaggerated, higher highs and lower lows. Can I ask you to commit to talking to each other more calmly?"

Sometimes silence is its own answer.

"I probably don't need to tell you that the challenges you had before Tali was abducted—and how you confront them now or don't—will impact how she recovers," Cyn says.

"I think it's sad that Tali and her father don't get along. Zeke and I were at an impasse before Tali went missing. He brings a lot of stress into our lives." Nell's voice is steady, noticeably flat, as if it's safer to recite her feelings as facts. It's an armor Cyn knows all too well how to wear.

Conversely, Zeke breaks down, wiping his eyes with the backs of his hands. He mumbles an apology. Something Cyn has never once seen Noah do.

"I'm not proud of the things I've done," Zeke says. "But I promised Nell I'd be better. And I think, deep down, she wants to give me this chance. We got our daughter back, and I'm going to be there for them both for once, instead of the other way around."

"I'm going to be better too." A drowsy voice comes from behind them. "I know our fights were stupid now, Daddy. I'm sorry."

The young woman standing in the entry way to the kitchen is taller than Cyn remembers her. Tali is more strikingly beautiful too. She has her mother's dark hair, though hers is shinier and falls beyond her shoulders. And the teal plaid shirt she wears like a tunic over a pair of gym shorts brings out the brighter blue-green of her eyes.

Zeke pops up from his chair, his movements jerky, unsteady. In comparison, Tali is slow moving. When they come together, she winces, either from the awkwardness of the contact or the tenderness of her bruises.

"Me too, honey," Zeke says. "You have no idea how sorry I am."

The hug is brief, and on both sides, the gesture half-hearted.

"Tali, do you remember Dr. Rawlins from the hospital?" Nell gets out of her chair.

Cyn watches Nell give her daughter a light kiss on the cheek and smooth wisps of hair from her face. Their contrasting and sweeter connection is most obvious when Tali lays her head on her mother's shoulder.

"Kind of," she says. "I met a lot of people that night."

"You certainly did," Cyn says.

"How about something to eat?" Nell asks. "I have chicken soup, and Sam's mom brought over those red velvet cupcakes you like."

"Maybe later. I'm not hungry."

"I came to check on you," Cyn says. "To see how you're doing. To talk a little, if that's all right."

"My mom and I talk."

"That's good to hear. I've worked with a lot of young women in your situation and I've found that moms should be allowed to be moms. And neither of you should have to get through this on your own."

Tali covers her mouth to yawn. The angry bruises on her wrists are hard to look at. "Okay. Can we go into the living room? It hurts to stand for too long. I need to lie down."

"Sure. Do you mind me asking when you took your last dose of Klonopin?"

Tali doesn't respond, but Nell moves toward the counter. Self-consciously, she pushes aside a half-empty bottle of wine and a stack of unopened mail.

"My mind is a mess," she says. "I need to write everything down."

After producing a spiral-bound notebook, Nell flips through it, and Cyn sees her land on a page with dates and times and tally marks. "I gave her two milligrams three hours ago."

"It's a good idea to keep track. These are powerful medicines. May I look?" Cyn puts a hand out for the record.

As Nell goes to give it to her, a "Missing" flyer slips out. All eyes watch as the pretty picture of Tali sails to the floor. Nell snatches it up and holds it close like it's a secret she's been keeping.

"Is it weird that I asked my mom to save one?" Tali asks Cyn.

"Not at all. Your life's been turned upside down. Reunifying is all about holding on to whatever tangible things help you to heal. Why don't you show me where you'd like us to talk?"

As they enter the living room, Cyn takes it as a good sign that Tali grabs her phone off the coffee table to check for messages. It's an even better one when she returns a text.

"Sorry, I won't keep doing this," she says, waving her cell. "I have this one friend who would freak if I didn't answer him."

"Go ahead." Cyn points to the remote. "But I'd like to turn off the TV."

"That's another thing I'm doing. Watching the news. Listening for stories about me and June. Is that normal?"

"I wouldn't worry too much about labeling things normal or not normal. It's better to ask yourself if what you're doing makes you feel better or worse."

"Talking to Sam makes me feel better. Reading all the posts on June's Facebook page makes me feel worse." Tali shuts off the TV and tucks her phone between the couch cushions, stifling the ping of an incoming message.

"For now," Cyn says, "maybe you could check it for shorter periods. See if that makes a difference."

Tali leans back against the arm of the couch, holding her breath as she arranges her body, slowly stretching out her contused legs on top of pillows.

"How does this work?" she asks. "Do I talk until I remember what happened?"

"You could—if remembering is the most important thing to you. I usually start by asking a few questions. But we can do this whatever way you want."

"Aren't you going to write stuff down?"

Cyn taps the side of her head. "Good memory. I can do that later."

"But you wrote stuff down when you were talking with my parents."

"I did. There isn't only one way that I help people. Sometimes, adults like it better when I act the way they expect a psychiatrist to. Most teenagers I work with like it better when we do things together or just talk. I'm up for whatever makes you comfortable."

Tali smiles coyly. "You can start with questions, but you don't need to write stuff down."

"Sounds good. I should say that almost everything I might ask could sound like I'm being nosy. You and I don't know each other. Will you tell me if you don't want to talk about something?"

"I'm fine. You can ask me anything."

"I know you overheard some of my conversation with your mom and dad. Can you tell me what you and your dad usually argue about?"

"Nothing, really. He's just irritating sometimes. I don't know how he stands not having a job. My mom's the one who mostly has to deal with him."

"It looks like you and your mom are close. Does she talk to you about what your father is going through? Or their relationship?"

"No. And I don't want her to. I hear enough." Tali traces her finger over the most rugged of the gashes that cover her legs. "I hate not knowing how I got these."

"In time, you might remember. It's also possible you won't."

"How come?"

"Sometimes during traumatic experiences, the brain stops recording events as a way of protecting you. And even if you did store what happened, memory is slippery. I tell my clients it's like a bar of wet soap. The more you try to grip it, the harder it is to hold on to. It's better to let things come when they come. How would you describe your memory before all of this?"

"Really good. You have to be sharp to act. To memorize lines and lyrics and all the blocking. June's better at monologues than me. She's like that kid with the photographic memory in that children's book. Cam Jansen." Tali's voice becomes high pitched. "They found her right next to me on the beach."

"That must be upsetting to think about," Cyn says.

"Is it weird that I keep talking like she's alive when I know she's dead?"

"It's pretty common. It even has a name. Beneficial irrationality. It's another example of your mind trying to make sense of things a little at a time."

"I think it's because they wouldn't let me see her. Even though I kinda do anyway. When I'm trying to fall asleep, I see flashes of her the way she must've looked."

"You're trying to process a terrible event."

"So that's normal?"

"Yes, Tali. As far as very unusual circumstances go, everything you're experiencing is normal."

"Sorry. I don't know why I'm stuck on that. I just don't feel like me. I'm jumpy and my legs are weak. My stomach feels empty, then full. One minute I'm hot, and the next I'm freezing."

"That's partially the Klonopin. It's pretty good at reducing nightmares and flashbacks, but it can make even a healthy girl like you feel ill. Like you have the flu. We could try cutting back on it if you want, but that might mean you have more intrusive thoughts. More of those flashes."

"I'll think about it." Another muffled message has Tali peeking at her phone. "Sam again."

"Do you want to text him back?" Cyn asks.

Before Tali can answer, a car door slams beyond the window, and the abruptness of it sends a jolt through her body, proving that she's telling the truth about her symptoms of hyper-vigilance.

Tali lifts a corner of the window blinds to reveal the press descending on two men dressed in similar navy jackets, their shiny badges affixed to breast pockets. As they make their way up the brick path toward the house, Cyn recognizes the taller one.

Bastard.

The night Tali was brought into the hospital, it didn't take long for Detective Ross to set Cyn off. She was already in a horrible mood, having spent the morning with her accountant, learning that without Noah she can't afford the Back Bay office, and her afternoon watching his sister empty the apartment of his things.

Ross's mistake was pushing Tali for a statement within minutes of her ER admission, underestimating the fierceness of Cyn's advocacy for her patients. He was completely out of line when he tried to intimidate the girl into rehashing the abduction after she had expressly told him not to.

How many times has Cyn seen police pressure witnesses to talk before memories are clear? It's one of many things she won't miss about trauma work. Cops—mostly the men—who should know better. Insensitive professionals she has personally trained who don't have a clue what it feels like to be misled and mistreated. No matter how many times she tells law enforcement that coerced victim statements backfire, detectives rise another day to do it again.

"Why are they here?" Tali asks in a childlike voice. "Oh my God, did something else bad happen?" Trembling like a frightened cat, she inches closer to Cyn.

"There could be news. But look at me," Cyn says. "You're okay. You're safe now. I'll be right here."

The girl's full body response—one she has seen countless times before— triggers something deeply protective in her. And that's when Cyn decides she's keeping the case.

7

A Doll's House

FOR A LONG time after Tali was born, Nell left the small spare room at the top of the stairs completely empty. Her thinking at the time was that if she refused to assign it an interim purpose, her heart would remain open to having another child with Zeke.

Slowly but surely it became crammed with boxes of old toys and baby clothes and assorted broken things that neither she nor Zeke were willing to part with, until it served as nothing more than a glorified storage closet.

Today, before Cyn arrived for Tali's first session, Nell sought refuge in this forgotten space to get away from Zeke. With the press out front, her regular walk is out of the question. And Zeke's having trouble being alone even for short periods of time; he follows her room to room, overwhelming her with small talk. Ironically, as messy as it is in here, it's the only place in the house where she can feel the lightness of the air.

She's back now with a purpose because of something Cyn said. When the "Missing" flyer slipped out of Nell's notebook and Cyn talked about how tangible things can help people heal, she immediately thought of Tali's childhood memory box. It's in here somewhere. She'll find it, look through it, and decide if the collection of keepsakes will help Tali remember happier times. Maybe it will calm Nell too.

Her foot kicks the bin nearest the door to move it out of the way. When it doesn't budge, she unsnaps the plastic lid. Inside, there are odd fusers, printer drums, and maintenance kits from Zeke's time at Xerox. A similar bin holds several years of his college textbooks. Useless stuff taking up space.

Yet there's a moment when Nell is so lost in taking stock of what fills shopping bags and cardboard boxes that she almost forgets the reason she's in here. It is grounding and freeing all at once to be preoccupied. Until she spies the ghost of Tali's dollhouse, its shape unmistakable, even covered by a bed sheet.

The night it came to be here, Nell had been stretched out on the couch, flipping through the latest *People* magazine. It was Zeke's turn to read and tuck Tali in, but he was back downstairs in no time. *That was quick,* she thought. Tali never dropped off that fast when she put her to bed.

The racket Zeke was making maneuvering something heavy through the front entrance could be heard through the glass doors that separated living room from hallway. Nell wanted to shout, "What are you doing?" But she couldn't risk waking her daughter.

Not wanting to deal with Zeke, but knowing she should before Tali ended up back downstairs too, she tossed aside the magazine and went to see what he was doing.

"Wait—don't look," Zeke said. "I want to give you the full effect."

The dollhouse was a monstrosity. Almost as tall as their five-year-old, and from the way Zeke was struggling to lower it onto the coffee table, nearly as heavy.

"So, what do you think?" he asks. "It's got inside and outside lighting. Pine floors and porcelain bath fixtures. It needs a little work but nothing a little paint and patience can't conquer. Once I fix it up, Tali's gonna love it."

Funny that Zeke mentioned patience, because the person who'd likely have to have it by the boatload would be her. Nell envisioned Tali getting super excited and begging unceasingly to play with it, while Zeke would start off with good intentions, only to leave it undone, hammers and glue guns and wood pieces scattered all over the living room. Just what they needed, more unfinished business to fight about.

"We can't keep it," she said. "It's bigger than she is, and it's meant for adult collectors, not little kids."

Staring at Zeke, Nell felt her stomach drop. There was no way this was going back from whence it came. "Where did you get it? Or should I ask, how did you end up with it?"

"Look, Nell, please don't be mad. I slipped up. But I'm trying to make it right with you."

There was a story. There was always a story.

"You remember that night last month when I went out with a few buddies from work? I didn't tell you we went to Twin River."

"Come on, Zeke. We agreed you wouldn't go there, or any other casino. You never know when to quit."

"I know, I know. And I won't ever go again. You're right. I get sucked in. It didn't help that the guys egged me on."

"How much? How much did you lose?"

"Not that much."

"I'm confused. Why would you confess to doing something we agreed you wouldn't do unless you're in the hole? And what does any of that have to do with this?" Nell waved her arm at the dollhouse, barely missing the tip of the turret. Then, before he got the words out, it dawned on her.

"I sold my ring," he said. "Blame capitalism. They put up a pawnshop next to the casino, knowing sick people like me would be tempted."

"Your ring? You pawned your wedding ring?"

"I'm not the first person to do something stupid after a few drinks. But then I missed the grace period by two days. Forty-eight damn hours, and when I go back to get it, it's gone."

"Let me get this straight. You thought you could use our daughter to get me to go easier on you."

"Yes. I mean no, not exactly. The dollhouse is a peace offering. I think I have a problem. I mean, I know I do. I need help."

Had they become so distant of late that for over a month Nell hadn't registered his missing wedding ring? Whose fault was that?

She had worked hard for years to control her emotional reactions to him, yet all of a sudden, she had an intense desire to be heard.

"This is huge, Zeke. You broke your promise." How many times had he assured her that he had this under control? That now that they had a child, they literally couldn't afford his selfish version of fun. "The worst of it is you kept this a secret from me for over a month. It's almost unforgivable."

"Are you kidding? Unforgivable? I'm apologizing! I said I need help."

"Lower your voice," Nell says. "You'll wake Tali."

"Don't *shh* me. What's the big deal? Couples fight. She can't hear us. She's asleep. I put her to bed myself. I'm the one who read to her."

"You think that makes you father of the year? Because you spend some time with your daughter in between gambling?"

In that moment she was acting as badly as he was.

"I'm trying to make it right." His hands were fists now; his face bright red, and eyes tear filled. "You have to help me."

It was a chilling display of frustration, directed at her and also meant for himself. His vulnerability touched her and made her want to make things right for him—for their family.

And for more than a decade since that night, she had tried mightily, hadn't she?

After the incident surrounding the dollhouse, Nell went back to putting on a happy face, smoothing things out between them. And Zeke didn't wait to hit bottom; he entered treatment for a gambling addiction.

He did well for a while, and during that period, their drama-laced interactions were few and far between. Then, every time Nell had relaxed and stopped micromanaging his every move, he would relapse. *Here we go again*, she'd think.

During the first several downward spirals, she tried to be giving and kind, to forgive him when he made mistakes. Still, it became chancy to count on him. It was easier for Nell to create a disturbing lie for herself—and for everyone else in her life: He is ill and I'm the caretaker. It's unfair, but that's the way it is and always will be.

Nell lost all sense of what was normal, entering a state of non-movement, letting his relapses and remissions take center stage in their lives. Zeke's existence, and Tali's too, became more important than her own. And because of this she never took in the overwhelming totality of how bad things were. Uncanny as it was, she had been forced out of her familiar state of denial less than a week ago by a handful of lottery tickets in Zeke's coat pocket and a kiss with Peter.

Then her daughter was taken from her, and none of what Nell had been through—or wanted—mattered. Not one bit of it.

Nell rearranges the sheet over the doll's house as a way to declare it past history. Tali is home safe. She and Zeke will have to find a way to coexist. Peter is wrong. It's been days since he warned her that Zeke is in trouble. As flawed a person as he is, Nell is an expert at seeing through clouds of doubt, and she's certain Zeke had nothing to do with what happened to Tali and June.

At the moment Nell spies the corner of Tali's memory box, the doorbell rings. It's possible she'll come back for it after she answers the door. She'll have to see.

8

Relative Strangers

F ITZ ISN'T SEARCHING for random things to compare the two cases; they keep surfacing. He doesn't confuse the Carrington's South End with his and Maddie's South Boston, but there's no denying that Tali's bow-front row house looks nearly identical to Maddie's parents' brick place. At least the way it did the last time he drove by it.

When she died, Maddie was the same age Tali Carrington is now. For one long month before she drowned, Fitz endured her dating his younger brother. He wasn't the only one who thought Madeleine Townsend and Connor Jameson were an unlikely pair. It couldn't have been more obvious. She got all A's in advanced placement classes like calculus, history, and French; she doubled on clarinet and soprano sax in the school's jazz band, and captained the field hockey team. Maddie was great at everything—except choosing boyfriends. Con, on the other hand, was only good at one thing. Being a class-A fuck-up. He's still an expert in his field, or so Fitz is told by his sister Keira, the only family member besides Ma who talks to him.

Back when Maddie was alive, Connor's appeal was his male-model good looks and quick wit. In spite of his assets, with little effort, he got into more trouble than Ma could stay ahead of, and that was saying something since she'd cut her teeth on Da.

As Fitz and Ross head toward the Carringtons' front door, reporters start barking out questions.

"Do you have a suspect?"

"What's taking so long?"

"Can you confirm that Tali's father is a person of interest?"

Fitz and Ross say nothing. They don't have a warrant, so they'll need to be careful not to spook the Carringtons. Fitz will have to find a way to ask about the jacket without appearing overeager. Though it's a long shot, it could be a game changer if it points him toward the brand of the real thing. He'll leave Zeke to Ross while he makes headway getting to know Tali. Then, if it works out, he'll ask to see it.

They're not standing there long before Nell hurries them inside, like every other time they've shown up at her door unannounced. Except today she looks different. Gone are the red eyes and ashen face. She's put on a little makeup—less than Keira wears, but more than Ma.

Nell may no longer be terrified they've come to speak the unspeakable words they were forced to deliver to Peter Danforth, but she's not happy to see them.

She stands with her back against a closet door. Her arms are wrapped around her body as if she's trying to stay warm, except the visible pulse in the ropey vein of her neck tells him she's panicked about something.

Fitz takes another step into the foyer and spies Tali through glass doors. She sits on the couch with her back to him. There's a benefit to having taken the time to sit with her parents and let them rifle through hundreds of photos of their kid at every age, memorizing the way she tilts her head and angles her shoulders. Even from behind, Fitz would know Tali anywhere.

She's sitting next to a woman he hasn't met yet. An aunt or maybe an older cousin. Could be a neighbor on her lunch break from an office job. The outfit she wears, dark jacket over white blouse, hair pulled tight and pinned high, is too dressy for a teacher from the high school.

"Tali's with Dr. Rawlins," Nell says.

Fitz is pleased with himself. A few more seconds and he would've figured out on his own that the woman is Tali's psychiatrist. The hard edges of her face and the way she glowers at Ross is the only other clue he would've needed. It's been a few hours since Fitz read the part of Tali's statement about how Rawlins put an end to the questioning when the girl became upset. Ross must've pissed her off good.

If the doctor has no use for his partner, Fitz likes her already. But as he smiles at her through the glass, she shoots him the same daggers. Ten-four; Rawlins doesn't like cops.

The way Nell blocks the entrance to the living room makes it clear that her daughter is off limits. Maybe now, maybe forever. "Are you here with news?" she asks.

"Nothing yet," Ross says. "But we would like to talk to your husband."

Her eyes flick toward the kitchen before she drops her head as if this is the bad news she'd been expecting. Pointing down the hall, she says, "In there."

Zeke's on his cell, pacing the circular space. "Have him call me. Now." When he notices them, he ends it, though Fitz can hear someone in mid-sentence when he does. It's strange how he doesn't ask what the detectives are doing there; he doesn't stop pacing at first either.

"Mind if we ask you a few questions?" Ross asks.

"It depends."

"I'm trying to save you a trip to the station." Ross starts the slow volley for who will be in charge of this conversation. "Tell me, which gives you a better kick, the ponies or blackjack?"

Zeke halts behind a chair. His knuckles go white as he clutches the top rail. His abrupt lack of movement tells Fitz Dad is about to lawyer up. If he hasn't already.

Black looks fly all around. Wife at husband. Zeke at Ross. When his partner lobs one to him, it's his cue to get Nell into another room. If there's any chance Zeke will cooperate, it'll only happen if she's out of earshot.

"Would I be able to meet Tali?" he asks Nell. "No questions, promise. I'd just like to say hello."

At the sounds of movement coming from the living room, Nell barely hesitates. There's no question where she'd rather be when she leads Fitz toward her daughter through the kind of back hall maze old homes like this are prized for.

Tali's psychiatrist is no longer next to her patient. She's parked at a nearby desk, recording what must be session notes in a folder. Tali is stretched out on the couch. Her fingers fly across her phone, texting the way only a teenager can.

Fitz is struck by how much more arresting Tali is in real life than in pictures. When Nell sits beside her, it's the first time he realizes that the daughter is a sharper, brighter image of the mother. It's as if everything about Nell is beginning to fade.

Tali clutches her phone to her chest, and Fitz could swear she's holding her breath.

"Honey, this is one of the detectives who helped us find you," she says. "He's checking in and wanted to say hi."

Standing there, his mind drifts, and Fitz is seeing a completely different girl. The kind of little wave Tali gives him is something Maddie used to do.

"I'm glad you're okay," he says. "Must be good to be home."

"Thanks," she says shyly. "It is."

Like a mama bear, the doctor stands and steps forward. Message received: no one gets between her and her patient.

He puts his hand out. "We haven't worked a case together. I'm Fitz."

"Oh, sorry," Nell says. "I don't know why I assumed you two already knew each other."

"Cyn," she says shaking his hand. Polite smile through clenched jaw, the woman is brushed steel.

"It's good work you do. Counseling the returned," he says.

"Wasn't that a TV show?" Nell asks.

Tali simulates a voice-over. "The Returned."

"She's back," Nell says, laughing. The look on her face says she's desperate to make whatever this moment is something normal.

But thanks to him they've landed in awkward territory—unless he's the only one who knows that show's central premise: that the deceased hang around indefinitely, waiting till the right time to come back to haunt you.

"Have you ever done any TV or film, or are you all about the stage?" he asks Tali.

The question sounds lame, even to him. No wonder Tali goes back to texting.

Cyn gathers her things—file, coat, and bag. "We'll show ourselves out." She's speaking to Nell, but she's talking to him.

"When do I get to see you again?" Tali asks the doctor.

"How about Friday morning?"

Tali looks to her mother for approval.

"We'll be here," Nell says.

"Good," Cyn says. "Tali, will you think of something we can do together, here at home? Like prepare a meal or play a game? Something you'd enjoy doing with me."

"Okay," Tali says as she rubs both her arms.

"Oh honey, you're shivering again," Nell says. "Let me get you a blanket."

As Nell gets up, Tali reaches for her in a don't-leave-me gesture typical of younger kids, but she's looking at Cyn. "See? I'm freezing out of the blue for no reason."

While Tali and her doctor start talking about symptoms and the side effects of medicine, Fitz steps toward the hall. "I can grab it for her." he says.

"Thanks," Nell says. "There's a stack in the cedar chest next to the front hall closet."

As he moves into the entryway, he realizes this is his chance to play dumb and get a look inside the closet without breaking the rules of search and seizure. If a similar jacket to the one Tali mentioned in her statement is in there, this will be the kind of God wink Ma works the beads for.

Fitz whips out his phone. He needs to snap a picture of the label if there's time.

Closet open, Fitz scans the clothing. Behind him he hears the scraping sound of chairs across the kitchen floor.

Whatever Ross is saying, Fitz can't quite make it out, but he's pretty sure Carrington just asked if they have a warrant.

Hanger after hanger. Sweaters, hoodies, rain gear. There it is. Tucked in back. A bomber jacket made entirely of faux fur.

There's no mistaking it. Rust-colored flecks mark a pattern on both sleeves. Fitz knows enough to use his own sleeve to lift the hanger from the rod. To remove the coyote-ugly thing from the closet without contaminating it.

Above the thrum of his pulse, Tali is talking. "Sam texted, the cast list is up. They gave me the lead." Now she and Cyn go back and forth about whether it's okay to feel happy.

Zeke and Ross converge in the hallway at the same time Nell comes from the living room to see what's taking him so long.

Again, Fitz hasn't heard what Ross has said, but clear as day he hears Zeke say, "I haven't seen that thing in ages."

Fitz holds the jacket away from his body so everyone can see it. "Are you talking about this?" he asks Zeke, scanning his face for a reaction. It doesn't take a detective to figure out that what's dotting the fake fur is blood.

When no one moves or speaks, Fitz gives the hanger a little shake, and as if he'd planned it for effect, sand rains down. "When was the last time you wore this fur jacket to the beach?"

9

A Sea of White Horses

NELL FEELS ZEKE watching her and Tali from the window as they walk toward the limousine Peter has sent for them. It's too big for two people, and once inside, the fracture in their family is more glaringly obvious. Zeke's absence hurts Nell more than she imagined it would the countless times she has imagined it.

She's asked him to be gone before they get back from June's wake. The fact that he has no credible explanation for his jacket, bloodstained and sandy, found shoved in the back of their front hall closet, is reason enough for the ultimatum: move out or they will.

Yet, there's so much more to it. Nell is exhausted by the rush and surge that is life with Zeke. His rise and fall that becomes her rise and fall. The delicate hopefulness she's been known to cling to, famously whisked off on a breeze when she opens a bank statement to find missing money or when the phone rings late at night and there is silence on the line. His endless promises to change. And those blessed few days—weeks, even months—when it looks as if he has.

Except it's past time to face reality: Zeke will always be unpredictable to her vulnerable. Her little boat of a heart is no match for his sea of white horses.

It would be one thing if this were yet another test of her loyalty that functions like glue—if all she needed to learn was to settle for even less in her marriage. But after what's happened to Tali, she can no longer afford to be a devoted wife.

Inside the limo, Tali behaves like a child, pressing buttons, opening and closing cabinets. Before all of this, Tali was her own person, mature for her age. She walked early. Talked early. Tali started reading at four and acting at ten. Watching her grow, Nell believed that, like sand in an oyster shell works to form a uniquely beautiful pearl, having this father at home was better than having no father at all.

When Tali tires of flashing the neon lights along the floor and around the ceiling, and raising and lowering the partition that separates passengers from driver, she pulls a split of champagne from the mini-fridge and says, "Mom, you need a drink."

"No, put it back. I can hardly show up for the wake with a buzz on."

"Why, because people are going to talk about us?"

Seven days. Tali has been home one week and, as her psychiatrist predicted, some of the time she is sullen, the next minute skittish and blue. Then, during moments like this, when Nell catches a glimpse of her funny girl shining through—her sense of humor, her irreverence—it's as if none of this has happened. June is not gone. Peter is not lost to her. Zeke is being Zeke, and they are merely doing what they always do, putting up with him.

"What the hell," Nell says. "Let them talk, right?"

Because who would begrudge her a drink when police are circling her husband?

Tali smiles, and with a satisfying pop, the cork is free and she sips the escaping foam.

"Hey, none for you," Nell says. "I don't want them talking that much."

"You know I *could* make you feel guilty for everything I've been through." Tali makes an exaggerated sad face. "Mommy, please let me have a little?" Her daughter hands her the flute. "But Dr. Rawlins says Klonopin and alcohol are a deadly combination, and I don't think it's a good idea to push my luck."

"Smart girl," Nell says, savoring a sip. The glass feels a little too good in her hand. She can't believe they are talking casually about the situation they're in. "I like her, don't you?"

"Dr. Rawlins? She's okay. Seems kinda sad to me."

"Maybe she feels bad for you—for us. It can't be easy doing the work she does."

"I don't need anyone feeling sorry for me." Tali turns toward the window, hiding her face from her mother. Even as a little girl, she hated to let other people see her upset.

Nell parks the glass at her feet. Reaching across the aisle, she places both hands on her daughter's knees. Tali winces and Nell pulls her hands back. How could she forget that would hurt her?

"This isn't going to be easy," Nell says. "Seeing June. And Mr. Danforth. All of your friends from school."

"I have to face them sometime. And no way was I staying home with Dad, watching him pack up his stuff."

"Are you mad at me for telling him to move out? It's okay if you are."

"I don't know. Kinda. Even though I see why you did."

"The jacket's not the only reason I asked him to leave.

"He's losing money again, isn't he?"

Nell doesn't answer. How can she possibly reassure her daughter when she has no idea what other lies sleep inside that man?

"Why won't you say it? He's gambling again."

"Because I don't know. He says he isn't. Two months ago, I took permanent steps to wall off our finances from him. If he is, I don't know where he's getting the money. He's always told me the truth before—once I've confronted him. For all his problems, what I know for sure is that your father would never hurt you or June. I believe that."

"How can you trust anything he says? And if that's not why you kicked him out, why did you?"

"The reasons keep adding up, but honestly, if I thought I could handle it, I'd probably let him stay—for you," Nell says. "No matter what, he's your father."

"Don't put that on me. You never asked me what I want. You still haven't."

There aren't words to explain how responsible Nell feels for Zeke. Has there ever been a time when it wasn't her job to save him from himself? It isn't easy to give up on someone you love.

"My intentions were good. I didn't want to lay any of this on you. I never knew my father, and after I lost my mother, I felt so different from my friends. So alone. I didn't want you to grow up feeling that way."

One minute, Tali is smoothing out the stiff fabric of her skirt, and the next she lifts it above the knee, and with the prongs of her ring, claws a four-inch run in her tights.

Nell covers her daughter's hand, putting pressure on it. "Honey, stop. I did everything I could to help him get better. I wanted things to go back to the way they were in the beginning. I wanted us to be a family. But we don't have control over other people. Almost losing you made me see that."

Tali pushes Nell's hands away. "I'm not a kid. You should've told me all of this before."

"I thought I was protecting you from the awful details. But I'm telling you now. You can talk to me too. About anything, okay?"

Tali nods, turning her face toward the window again. She smooths out the fabric of her skirt, the tear in her tights effectively concealed.

When the limo comes to a stop, the champagne flute tips and spills. Tali locks eyes with her mother and kicks the glass under her seat. "We're here," she says. "Let's get this over with."

Detective Jameson opens the door to the limo. Warned that her daughter's first outing might bring out the nut jobs, Nell asked if he'd be their escort.

Tali gets out first. The anger she wore inside the car rolls off her body the minute she steps onto the strip of carpet that leads from the sidewalk to the funeral home. Nell accepts the detective's hand as she exits the vehicle. Leaning her shoulder into his, she whispers her watchwords: "Don't take your eyes off her. Not for one second."

Fitz nods.

Inside the funeral home, white noise is punctuated by random sobs and high-pitched cackles—the unmistakable sound of teenagers. A hush falls over the crowd as one by one the prodigies from PAHS realize Tali has arrived. None of her friends know what to do; they stand in silent groups. The funeral director, a man obviously primed for the arrival of the Carringtons, ushers Nell and Tali to the front of the receiving line. Nell doesn't trust herself to meet Peter's gaze. Knowing she'll lose it if she looks at him, she keeps her focus on his mother. Violet Danforth is an elegant woman, bone-thin, with a blunt haircut. She's wearing a black shift that emits the bitter smell of mothballs. It's the same dress she wore seven years ago to Mei's wake and funeral.

"I'm sorry." Nell takes Violet into a tight hug.

"It isn't right. I'm an old woman. Peter should be standing here for me. Not our Junie."

"None of this makes sense," Nell says.

Then Peter reaches for her, stealing Nell from his mother's arms. As he holds her, she closes her eyes and drinks him in. It feels good to be held. The pressure of his chest against hers, the warmth of his cheek next to hers. His scent, sandalwood, rich and pleasing.

To this room full of people, Peter and Nell are grieving friends. They shared the unique horror of sitting vigil for two days when the whereabouts of their children was unknown. Mei is gone. Now June is gone. And since their future together is uncertain and unlikely, Nell is in no hurry to let Peter go. Then she hears him say, "Come here, kiddo. I'm over the moon you're okay."

Nell steps back to let Peter bring Tali into his arms. Her daughter's body goes slack as she sobs loudly into his shoulder, a flood of tears released into the seams of his suit. It hits Nell then that Zeke has never held Tali so protectively, so tenderly. This is the first time since the whole nightmare started that Tali has completely let her guard down.

With his head lowered, Peter gestures toward the casket. "Do you want me to go up with you?" he asks, his voice kind but shaky.

Tali stands there, staring at her friend lying in the open casket.

"I'll go with you," Nell says, a hand on her daughter's back.

"I can do it myself."

All eyes go to Tali as she folds her hands in prayer. Without ever looking away from June, Tali begins to sing softly. "I just came to say goodbye, love. Goodbye. Just came to say goodbye."

It's surreal to see these girls together in this way. Cheerful Tali, a mourner. And June—a girl who danced her way to everywhere she went—lying still. The white georgette dress with puffed sleeves is the costume she wore in a *Midsummer Night's Dream*. Nell's tears come when she sees Mei's lotus flower brooch pinned carefully to the dress's pale pink neckline. She's overwhelmed by shame-filled relief because it is June laid out in that casket and not her daughter.

When Tali finishes singing, Sam Wallace is the first to rally around her. The dark circles under his eyes and his nearly constant sniffling confirm the rumor that he'd been more than friends with June. Taking their cue from Sam, the other kids begin to shower Tali with attention and affection, though not one of them asks how she is.

When the buzz in the room verges on loud, a priest steps forward and asks the group to observe a moment of silence.

In less than a minute, he looks up and announces that he will recite the final prayer of the evening, and they are all invited to attend June's funeral, which will take place the following morning at St. Cecilia Church.

"Bow your heads and pray for God's blessing. Lord, the loss of our beloved June is a weight and burden to those who mourn her. In this time of sorrow—"

As if the mourners are a gospel choir and have rehearsed it a thousand times, they raise their heads and look to the sound of a stir coming from the lobby.

Nell has a finely tuned sensor when it comes to Zeke—she knows he's there before she sees or hears him.

"Let me in," he shouts. "I need to see them."

Like a wave through the crowd, Nell watches the growing awareness register on all of their faces that it is Tali's father making this scene.

Detective Jameson, who until now has been invisible, moves toward the disturbance. As does Nell.

Not in a million years did she think Zeke would show up, disregarding Peter's wishes. And hers. But there he is on the threshold to the parlor, punch drunk and pushing against the chest of a police officer.

That's when Ana Wallace steps in, corralling teenagers out the side exit. "Let's give Mr. Danforth some privacy, okay, kids? Anyone who wants can come back to our house."

In short order the main room is cleared except for poor Violet sitting in a chair with her head in her hands. Peter stands above her, rubbing her back. Tali hasn't moved from in front of June's casket. Flower hearts and wreathes with massive sashes are her backdrop.

Nell watches Detective Jameson cup Zeke's elbow, forcibly moving him toward the entrance of the building. Funeral home staff—half a dozen men in identical black suits—slide into the room. Keeping their backs to the wall, their appearance is more a show of support than it is any kind of threat. But it does more to infuriate Nell than it does to register with Zeke.

"What is wrong with you?" Nell's voice is a growl, low and mean. Her body is rigid and there's a heaviness in her limbs. "You're hurting Tali. Can't you see that?"

Typically, when Nell confronts Zeke with an array of his wrongdoings, her rage is in check because he is remorseful.

As the detective tightens his grip on his arm, Zeke starts shouting. "Where is she? I need to talk to Tali. She has to know I had nothing to do with this."

"Don't make this any worse for yourself," the detective says. "Think of your family."

Instead of responding to Fitz by calming down, Zeke escalates. In a clumsy move, he tries to twist the detective's arm behind his back, but finds himself, in seconds, pinned to the carpet. The cuffs are on, and Fitz is hauling Zeke out the door as he reads him his rights.

All along Nell's been afraid that if she left Zeke, he'd fail disastrously, and people would blame her for not having tried harder to help him. Who leaves a man who was once good, and who is now struggling, to suffer? Over the years of sleepless nights, she's played out many scenarios in her head. But never this one. Never this.

As hard as it is to put one foot in front of the other, Nell walks back into the parlor. Peter can't possibly want them here now.

Poor Tali. She's standing perfectly still in front of the casket, staring above June at a gaudy urn of mums. All at once, Nell's overcome by another tidal wave of anger toward Zeke. Tali is different enough in the eyes of her friends after the events of the last two weeks. She didn't need the whole school to have a front-row seat to her father's bad behavior.

The funeral director and the priest are encouraging Peter to take a weary Violet home.

Nell tries to get Tali's attention so they can leave them in peace, but Peter gestures for her to join them.

"Come here," he says.

The priest steps forward and begins again to recite his litany. Peter has one arm around Violet, and he reaches over to take Tali's hand. In Nell's direction, he mouths the words, "Not your fault."

Standing there, they are a collection of parts from two broken families.

After reciting "Amen," they take turns bending to one knee, making the sign of the cross—Violet, Nell, Tali, and finally Peter. After he stands, he presses his lips to June's forehead and strokes her silky jet hair woven into a single braid, trailing down the length of one shoulder. Nell hears him whisper, "Give your mother a kiss for me."

The funeral director gestures toward the lobby. Peter stops on the threshold.

"Wait," he says. "I'd like for you to close the casket now. This is all too much. I don't have the strength to see her again like this tomorrow."

Without a sound, the funeral director moves in front of the casket and gently lowers the lid. And like that, June is gone forever.

Peter, Violet, and Nell walk in slow motion toward the place where moments ago Zeke's hidden self was on full display.

When Nell realizes Tali isn't behind her, she stops. Peter and Violet do too.

"Let's go home, honey," Nell says.

"I need another minute." Tali's voice cracks, and she lowers her head to mask that she's crying.

"Take all the time you need," Peter says. "We'll be outside."

The funeral director helps Violet down the stone steps and into the waiting limousine. Nell and Peter stand together on the landing. "I told him not to come," she says. "I can't believe he did this."

"No one knows better than you do, Zeke does whatever Zeke wants to do. I'm not upset. At least not now. There's no worse feeling in the world than losing your wife and then your daughter. It's impossible for me to muster a single ounce of animosity toward him."

"Trust me, you will be angry later." Nell brushes Peter's hair away from his face, leaving her hand to linger. "You'll be very angry. And when you are, I hope you'll call me."

Peter doesn't say that he will. Instead, he places his lips on her forehead. It's such a tender gesture, Nell wishes she could sink into his kindness, but all she can visualize is the last time he did this. Only moments ago, when he'd been saying goodbye to his child.

10

Story Theater

CYN ISN'T A crier, but here she is, fighting back tears as she descends the stairs to the lobby of her stately office building. It's the last time she'll ever be inside the renovated brownstone that sits on the corners of Beacon and Berkeley Streets.

She hesitates in front of the bank of mail slots, then slips her ring of keys—and Noah's—into the one labeled "Property Manager."

The movers stream past her like a colony of soldier ants; it's her things they carry. In the years she and Noah ran the practice together, Cyn had perfected the look and feel of the place, adding touches in both suites, aimed at calming the disorganized thinking and dark moods of the patients who came to them for help.

Mahogany desks, leather chairs, lowboys and book-shelves and standing lamps—taken separately, each item is unremarkable, and Cyn finds it easy to detach from what this mass exodus means. When six months into their relationship as a couple Noah and Cyn decided to open an office together, they agreed that work would be work, and home, home. Standing there, watching each piece make its way onto the moving van, Cyn can see this is what got her into trouble. Her finely honed art of compartmentalizing is exactly the reason she missed what Noah was doing.

For most people, painful breakups have a way of coloring an entire relationship. Cyn thinks she might be better off if his betrayal had tainted her memory of falling for him.

They met at McLean Hospital in a building called Appleton. More than a historic mansion, the in-patient residence catered to the compassionate care of women with severe mental illness. Cyn's patient was a young woman with bipolar disorder who'd been victimized by a man she'd met through an online dating app. Noah's patient, a forty-year-old woman with crippling depression, had been hospitalized for a complete overhaul of her medications.

When Cyn told friends and family she'd met a guy at, of all places, the nurse's station in a locked ward at a psychiatric hospital as the pair commiserated over the havoc early morning rounds and late-night emergencies have on a doctor's sleep, it sounded antiseptic, so clinical and unsexy.

But the way Noah recounted it, their meeting ranked high on the list of most romantic where-did-you-meet stories.

The first time he'd told it, they'd been at a cocktail party hosted by friends of Keira Jameson's from Boston College. Handsomely dressed in black slacks and wool jacket, Noah drew an audience; a circle of women gathered around him in front of a roaring fireplace. Cyn knew all eyes were on him because Noah was officially her new boyfriend, but also because he was lively, intelligent, and self-assured. Noah was seductive.

"I couldn't take my eyes off Cyn," he said. "There she was, on call for forty hours straight, and she was sharp, funny, and—look at her . . . she's gorgeous."

Noah commanded the room at that party, going on and on about his devotion to her—the same way he tried to make her feel after he got caught having an affair with a patient.

The members of the Board of Registration in Medicine were not susceptible to his charms either. After the young woman pressed charges and the authorities reported his ethics violation, the Board's vote to suspend Noah's license was unanimous.

Everything they'd worked for, all the plans they'd made for a future together, all of it built on lies. Cyn didn't blame the victim. The woman came to Noah for help, and instead of honoring his oath to do no harm, he took advantage of her vulnerability.

Two portly men exit the brownstone, walking past Cyn, carrying her favorite couch, an upholstered mid-century modern in cheerful shades of yellow and blue. Decorating that office, she'd paid attention to every last detail, right down to the fabric choices. For their patients, Cyn put herself in their shoes, trying to imagine which aesthetics might comfort and soothe. She'd gone with subtle patterns over exaggerated florals—nothing too busy, no stripes, no plaid. Without giving any thought to what it would do to her, Noah ripped it all up with his deception.

Her tears run free now. It's ridiculous that after everything she's handled in the last month—his confession, her financial ruin, his sister ravaging the apartment—Cyn is coming undone over a couch. That's it. She can't do this. She can't watch the final dismantling.

Hooking her bag over her shoulder, she gives a thumbs-up to one of the movers, then gestures for him to call her if he needs to. She crosses the street to walk the Commonwealth Avenue Mall to get to the Carringtons. Hopefully Nell won't mind her showing up early for Tali's appointment. Cyn's heart might be jagged slivers of glass, but before she can walk away from this life, she has to finish it by taking care of one more girl.

Ten minutes later, Cyn is sitting across from Nell in her living room, getting an earful about another man's transgressions.

"Zeke's been arrested—for disorderly conduct," she says. "He made a horrible scene at June's wake. I thought you should know before meeting with Tali."

"Did she witness it?"

"Yes and no. She was there and knows what happened. But she was so consumed by seeing June that I don't know how much of it got through to her."

"And she's not talking to you about it?"

"I tried not to push. You told me to go slow. All I said to her was that I'm here anytime she wants to talk, and she practically bit my head off."

"It makes perfect sense that Tali's overwhelmed, and she probably can't put it into words. That's where I come in. No one expects you to weather this by yourself. Why don't you tell her I'm here?"

A backpack with Tali's initials is parked near Cyn on the floor. Every zippered compartment is open and bursting with books and folders and the kind of ratty paper that's torn from spiral notebooks. The coffee table looks like a craft store exploded onto it. Fabric swatches, ribbons, and buttons, along with scissors, glue, and a stack of magazines, are spread all over a large piece of poster board.

"Hey," Tali says entering the room. She's wearing black leggings, a pale pink off-the-shoulder sweater, and flip-flops. Her curly dark hair is gathered in a messy bun, and it shakes a little when she drops onto the couch.

"I'll be in the kitchen," Nell says, backing out of the room.

"I'm glad you agreed to see me again," Cyn says. "I heard yesterday was difficult."

"I don't want to talk about it. Especially not the part about my dad."

"Fair enough. Did you think of something we can do together this morning? It's okay if you didn't."

Tali pulls books from her backpack and stacks them on the coffee table, on the edge of the chaos. She waves a full-page note in the air before handing it to Cyn. From anatomy to world history, someone's gone to great lengths to compile a long list of assignments Tali owes teachers.

"I thought you could do my homework while I watch."

Like lots of girls her age, Tali has already learned to bury a request for help in either politeness or sarcasm or in this case a combination of the two.

"It's been a while, but I remember loving this." Cyn puts down the list and picks up the script: *The Seagull.* "Do you want me to read lines with you?"

"I feel ashamed and terrified to act before you."

"It's just a suggestion," Cyn says.

Tali laughs at her. "That's one of Nina's lines from Act I."

For a moment Cyn enjoys a flicker of Tali's cleverness, but as quickly as the lightness comes, it goes.

"I'm not kidding about my schoolwork, though," Tali says. "I don't have the energy to do any of this."

"It looks like a lot. I'm pretty sure anyone would feel swamped. If you want, we could choose one easy thing to do together. It might feel good to cross something off the list."

"Before yesterday I was excited to finish this vision board for my character in *Spring Awakening*." Tali taps the poster. "Now I don't even want to be in the play."

"The other day you were glad you got the lead. What's changed?"

"I saw June."

In one of the tamer ways girls try to wake up from the numbness that follows trauma, Tali starts picking at the skin around her nails, though she hasn't yet drawn blood.

"Up till then, I had to keep reminding myself June is gone," Tali says. "Seeing her made the whole thing real. When her father hugged me, I completely lost it. I couldn't believe, with everything he's going through, that he could be that nice to me. I cried so hard I thought I was going to throw up."

"Did you get sick?"

"No, but I hated every single second of being there."

"Are you feeling that bad right now, while we're talking about it?"

Tali shakes her head. "But I think I might if you make me talk about my dad."

"I'm not going to do that. You get to decide when you're ready to do things or talk about things. I want you to know that even the most intense emotions are fleeting. How you felt at the wake is different from how you feel now. Feelings change."

"I know all about it. Before the night of the callback, I was happy. But how can I ever be happy again? Going back to school without June is going to be awful. And I never wanted to get the lead because the director pities me."

"Going back isn't your only option. There are other schools. Or you could go back, but not be in the play."

"You don't understand. I could never refuse a role like this."

"What would happen if you did?"

"As it is, my window for making it professionally is starting to close." Tali leans forward and taps a handful of printed pictures pasted to her vision board. "She was eighteen when she played Kim in *Miss Saigon*. And this actress was twenty when she played my part on Broadway. This girl was considered old for the lead when she joined the national touring cast at twenty-two."

"That sounds like a lot of pressure."

"That's not the half of it. School's not going to be patient with me. My teachers—especially in my drama classes—are going to expect me to suck it up. *"Use the pain, Tali."* And I'll probably be kicked out of school altogether if I flunk any academics."

Tali leans back against the couch as if she's suddenly dizzy. "I'm not trying to be negative; it's just the way it is."

"It could be too much right now. Or, maybe when you do feel ready, your mom and I could help you work out some compromises with your teachers."

"What if I go back and it turns out I don't care about school or theater or my friends the way I used to?"

"That's a pretty significant question. I like to think the answers to big things come to us when we focus on something much smaller. Like working on a vision board."

Cyn opens a magazine and begins to leaf through it. Tali doesn't move or speak for a few seconds. Then she leans forward and slaps her hand down on a page to stop Cyn. She picks up the scissors and hands it to her. "I like that hairstyle."

"I do too," Cyn says as she carefully cuts around the outline of a girl.

11

Six Degrees of Separation

I T ISN'T UNTIL Fitz sees his name on the marquee outside The Beehive that he realizes he's been duped. Ray didn't call an hour ago, begging him to make an exception, to fill in for some lame-ass Berklee kid who blew off his Saturday gig. He's booked Fitz to play the busiest night of the week, intentionally and without his permission, knowing damn well Fitz would've said no if he'd been asked ahead of time. The deceit is out of the blue and surprising given Ray is one of the few people who doesn't press Fitz about his self-imposed exile to Monday nights.

One week to the day after Maddie's funeral twelve years ago, Ray agreed to the permanent gig, no questions asked. When weeks later Ray wondered out loud when he was leaving for Juilliard, Fitz merely shrugged and started playing Parker's "Blues for Alice," never telling his friend that he'd passed up the chance to go by failing to show. Back in 2003, the odds of a musician auditioning and being accepted to the most prestigious performing arts school in the country were eight percent. Making the grade came down to luck in single digits. There is no equivalent percentage of likelihood that a good Catholic kid from Southie would cover up his brother's crime, keeping critical information from law enforcement and a dead girl's devastated parents.

It's the least Fitz can do to keep punishing himself with his music. To give up playing altogether would be taking the easy way out. It hurts more to play for people who don't appreciate him, boozers who don't listen. To be reminded, every time he comps an upper structure triad or improvises a blues progression, how good he is. Disallowing recognition—this is his penance. If Fitz plays piano every Monday night for the rest of his life, it won't be enough to make up for what he didn't do for Maddie.

Never before has he caved under the weight of his guilt. Not when he broke Ma's heart for washing his hands of his brother without explanation. Not when Fitz joined the force and had to recite the officer's oath of honor in a room full of dignitaries and family. Inconsequential as his vow may be in comparison, he will not be double-crossed into playing piano in prime time. Not tonight. And not by Ray, a man who up till now has been complicit in Fitz's weekly retribution.

Perfectly okay with being labeled a no-show, Fitz backs away from the entrance to The Beehive. Two nights from now, he'll let Ray have it, telling him never to pull a fast one like that on him again. If he does, Fitz will walk for good. There are other joints and club owners willing to let a talent like Fitz flog himself for a nearly empty jar of ones and pocket change.

"Oh no you don't." The hand on his back is bony, the damn fingernails birdlike and beaky. Fitz should've known this stunt bore the mark of his sister.

"Where do you think you're going," Keira says. "You have to play. It's my birthday."

"You can't make me. I'm not doing it." Jesus, even to himself Fitz sounds petty and pouty. His bossy big sister has a way of bringing out the brat in him. Older by ten months and taller by two inches, Keira is a woman of out-and-out presence.

"Come on—I've got friends inside I want you to meet. You won't owe me a gift," she says, throwing her arms around him.

"No wonder you didn't give a shit I couldn't make it over to Ma's for cake. Did you wait out here so you could nab me? You had to know I wouldn't do this voluntarily."

"It's stupid, what you're doing, Fitz. Maddie wouldn't want you squandering your talent."

"Don't, Keira. I'm warning you. Don't."

"I'm worried about you. Ma told me you're working that case."

Fitz has the childish urge to put his hands over his ears, to block out his sister's line of questioning. Instead, he keeps his eyes trained on the light spilling from The Beehive, and tries to ignore his personal banshee. Like an Irish folk fairy, whenever his sister senses impending doom—or, more to the point, worries that Fitz is becoming weak willed enough to come clean about Connor—she shows up wailing and moaning. Right there to be sure Fitz isn't about to do something that would incriminate their brother and devastate their mother.

The door to the bar opens, and a ginger beauty leans out, stopping short of the threshold.

All the hairs on the back of Fitz's neck stand up. His attraction to this woman is immediate. Her magnetic pull is like something you read about. Fitz takes in the fine curves of her shoulders, the plunging neckline that draws his attention to her breasts, as if he needed an arrow.

"I'm going to call it a night," the woman says to Keira.

The minute Fitz hears the break and lift of her voice, he recognizes her. All at once, she places Fitz too.

"Didn't expect to see you here," he says.

Cyn Rawlins is a knockout with that hair falling down, her off-duty style all loose and breezy. She looks completely different without her psychiatrist's uniform and her prim and proper posturing.

"How do you two know each other?" Keira asks.

"We don't," Cyn says.

"Met once," Fitz says. "Work."

"Oh, now I get it," Keira says, looking at Cyn. "It's not that jackass that has you in a funk. You're on the case too. Am I right?"

Cyn gives Keira the kind of look a friend gives another, telling her to zip it.

"Fitz is the brother I told you about," Keira says. "Cyn and I know each other from BC. She's joining the department full time next week. Isn't Boston such a small town?"

Now Ray pokes his head out the door. In a jumpy sort of move, all antsy and tense, Cyn makes room for him, inadvertently edging closer to Fitz.

"It's like a goddamn wake in here," Ray says. "You're killing me, man. Will ya get ya butt inside and play?"

Kill. Killing. Killed. Fitz wishes people wouldn't be indifferent to that word and all its incarnations.

Keira takes the opportunity to get behind Fitz and Cyn, placing a hand on each of their backs. With those devilish nails, she prods them through the entrance. "I won't let either of you ruin my birthday. If you don't play, I'll make a scene. Come on. Ray's been good to you. You can't let him down. And Cyn—you promised to buy me a drink."

Fitz smiles for the first time all day. "Keira—the travel agent who books deluxe guilt trips."

Standing next to Cyn, his arm touching her arm, Fitz wants to believe he is executing a choice rather than knuckling under to his sister's grand plan. He tells himself he'll make this one exception. He'll do it on behalf of the case. Play piano tonight and then later, over drinks, get to know Dr. Rawlins. More than a beautiful woman, she's a fast pass to the Carringtons. And Tali is Fitz's ticket to Sam Wallace and the school. Reinterviewing the dubious kid is next on his to-do list.

"Ma taught me well," Keira says, exaggerating a grin. "Now get going, Fitzy. Time to tickle the ivories."

"Fitzy?" Now Cyn is the one cracking a smile. It's like the lights inside the place came on. For all his efforts to resist the keys, suddenly Fitz wants to impress her. To see Cyn melt as he plays "Stella by Starlight," "Autumn Leaves," his rendition of "The Nearness of You." It's as if his set list is composing itself.

Fitz isn't even parked on the bench, and already he's full of himself. He knows damn well this is a mistake. He's about to beg out and tell Keira off, when she leans in. "You can go to confession next week for breaking your asinine vow. Now get over there and play the hell out of it. For Maddie."

12

Dirty Little Secrets

O N THE OTHER side of the city, her husband is behind bars, inside a holding cell awaiting arraignment while she tosses and turns in a bed too big for one person.

Nell's experience with detainees is negligible, though in counterpoint it spans nearly a decade. Before taking the job at PAHS, day in and day out, she walked by the old Charles Street jail on her way to the Phillips House clinic at Mass General, where she managed the practice of two renowned physicians. At least weekly, she'd pass a hand-cuffed prisoner, dragging and scuffling shackled feet, his elbow gripped by a guard. She'd look, but not for long. Eyes ahead. It's not polite to stare.

In the early nineties, Charles Street was converted into The Liberty Hotel, with a bar cavalierly called The Clink. Not once when Nell went there to meet Zeke for drinks did she think about real injustice. Or the stories those walls could tell. Or the families those prisoners ruined. The place was merely a colorful set piece.

Back then, she had every reason to be fully vested in their relationship. Zeke was easy and fun. Talkative and adventurous, he liked to surprise her with trips to exotic restaurants or inventive gallery openings. His energy and spontaneity were antidotes to the carefully planned quiet life she'd built for one.

The first time they went away together, he'd splurged on a place she'd never been to on the Cape. The waterfront inn sat on West Dennis Beach, and their room had expansive views of the Atlantic. The trunk of his car was packed with newly purchased folding chairs and an umbrella he'd bought so Nell wouldn't get a sunburn. Once they staked out an ideal spot, near the shore, to spend the afternoon, he opened a cooler brimming with chilled wines, select cheeses, and an array of artfully decorated chocolate-covered strawberries. Zeke lured Nell into feeling so cared for that she finally told him about her mother.

"Her name was Lucy. She grew up with my grandmother in a beach town on the South Shore. Parker's Cottage sits on this little hill with views of the harbor. Everywhere you look you can see wild beach roses."

In a sweet but clumsy way, Zeke lifted his beach chair, body and all, to turn from the ocean to face her.

"My mother was irresponsible exactly two nights in her life. The first, when she slept with a married man and ended up pregnant with me. And the last, when she agreed to go on a blind date with a guy careless enough to drink too much and then blow through a red light at two in the morning, getting broadsided by an oncoming van. My mother died. He walked away without a scratch."

As chatty as Zeke usually was, Nell liked that he knew not to interrupt her. All he did was lift her hand to his lips and then hold it to his chest while she continued.

"I was fifteen, but I wasn't used to her going out. I knew something was wrong when she didn't come home. She would have called. I freaked out when I saw my mother's best friend at the back door. I remember screaming because I couldn't think of a single good reason for Darcy to be standing there at six o'clock in the morning on a Saturday."

"I don't remember much about the weeks that followed except that Darcy wanted me to come live with her and her husband and their two girls and three boys. Her life was happy chaos. But like a rich dessert, I couldn't imagine making a habit of exposing my heart and body to it."

At the mention of sweets, Zeke lifted the lid to the cooler to offer her a pretty strawberry before taking one for himself. She shook her head.

"I changed schools and went to live at Parker's Cottage. Nana made space for me in an upstairs room under the eaves. It had been my mother's room when she was a girl, and it looked almost exactly the way she'd left it except for the unlit candle on the bedside table and a bright new quilt at the end of the bed. I could feel my mother everywhere, both inside and outside the cottage. Whenever I smell ocean air, I'm right back there. Sitting outside that first night by the sea, I was overwhelmed by how many stars there are in a midnight sky. I've never felt so small in my life."

"Is Nana your only family?" Zeke asked.

"Eighty-eight and going strong." As Nell said this, she was struck by two things: that she hadn't been to see Nana in over a month, and that Zeke had yet to tell her about his family.

"We'll make our own happy chaos," he said. "You and me and as many kids as you're willing to put up with."

Whether he was trying to lift her mood or float a proposal, Nell didn't press him. Instead, she clinked his plastic wine glass with hers and sealed the toast with a kiss. "To family," she said.

On that Sunday, before heading back to Boston, they took one last walk on the nearly empty beach. Unselfconsciously they ran like children—toward and away from the ocean—holding hands and playing games with the surf.

"From beginning to end, this weekend was perfect," Nell said.

"It doesn't have to be over." Zeke pulled her toward the parking lot, stopping at the towering swing set that faced the water. He chose one for her and then positioned himself like the wind at her back, gently pushing her until she was flying. "I'll show you how to stay young without ever feeling small," he said.

In that moment, Nell's heart filled with joyful anticipation of a life with Zeke, one that promised to be as colorful as the dusky sky above them.

It wasn't until after they were married that Nell could see that his big personality had a darker side. As she became intimate with Zeke's pattern of falling in and out of trouble, the more that swing became the perfect trope for their relationship. Every time he said *this* was the last time he would steal from her, lie to her, betray her, she had believed him. Or at least she tried to believe him. But never did she see him on the wrong side of things permanently. And never legally.

Now, in their bed, her overwrought brain pictures Zeke sitting on the edge of a metal bunk, his head in his hands, wondering why in three days she hasn't come to see him. Bone-tired—as if she were the one pacing the six-by-eight space, porcelain toilet to solid door, to stainless steel sink, and back again—Nell gets up.

She walks by Tali's door and peeks inside. Her girl is buried beneath a mound of patchwork comforters and soft blankets. The room is dark. Nell is careful to go down the stairs quietly so she won't wake her.

When Tali is up and willing to talk, it's getting harder to reassure her Zeke isn't involved.

The charges he's being held on are minor in comparison to what Nell fears will come next. Days ago, police searched the house, and much of what they got their hands on was seized. Now everyone, including the media, knows about the blood-stained jacket Zeke insists he hasn't seen in months. He has no explanation for how it came to be in their closet looking the way that it did.

There's more the police know but aren't telling her; even Fitz won't fill her in. Because Zeke is under lock and key, they don't need to show their hand to her yet.

Downstairs, early morning light creeps in through the slits in the blinds, casting shadows on Zeke's desk. How many times has shame rooted Nell to this exact spot, paralyzed in the face of her husband's deceit? Yet the gravity of this situation demands action. Courage. She's already complicit in keeping certain things from police; Nell has nothing to lose. Running her hand under the smooth mahogany surface, she finds the hidden release lever and pulls. There it is. Zeke's laptop, resting right where he left it.

Somewhere on the hard drive, there could be information that might make things better for him—or, obviously, much worse. When police need more to ensnare her husband, beyond the charges of reckless behavior at June's wake, detectives will come looking for more of his things. It's only a matter of time before the knock. The only way to know what she's up against is to open it and look. She lifts the lid and the screen comes to life.

Nell goes through the motions, starting with the obvious, a novice's approach. As expected, the history is blank. The trash is empty. She uses one of her old tricks, typing a single letter, A to Z, into the browser, letting Zeke's Internet searches drop down before her eyes. But her husband is a master now; the cache has been cleared. A damning find on its face.

She types into Google, "how to search a hard drive." Hundreds of computer nerds, and countless wives and girlfriends, offer advice on where to dig to find evidence of deception. Nell is drawn to a website dedicated to helping searchers confirm their suspicions. *Are you sure you want to know?*

She does and she doesn't.

Technical jargon slows her down. Mentions of index.dat files and keyloggers confound her. Scanning to the end of the post, she lands on *"Hope everything turns out for the best."*

The next post is less baffling but equally compassionate; it reads, *"Really need to know his dirty little secrets? Try this,"* the blogger writes. *"Make friends with a geek."*

"What are you smiling at?"

Tali is over Nell's shoulder before she hears her there. She's wearing her loose-fitting pajama bottoms and a camisole top.

Nell slaps the laptop shut and pushes off the chair. "Nothing. What are you doing up this early?"

"I keep having this dream—I'm lying on a beach in winter and I'm wondering why I'm the only one there."

"If your thoughts are racing, I can ask Dr. Rawlins to go up on the medication or change it to something else," Nell says. "She says you're not taking that much."

Nell grabs the throw from the back of the sectional and wraps it around her daughter, hugging her. "You're cold. I'm going to buy you a warm bathrobe, or do you want a new school sweatshirt?"

Nell holds on to Tali for as long as she'll let her. Moments like these are infrequent, a rarity really. As a little girl, Tali was never the snuggly type. Always busy playing, running, dancing, she never settled for long. The more Nell corralled her into an embrace, the more her daughter resisted. Zeke said Nell tried too hard. Then Tali found acting, and Nell could get away with big clumsy displays after every play because it was acceptable for parents to ooh and ahh over their child's performance.

"That would be okay, I guess." Tali breaks away from her mother and eases her body down on the couch. "Do the police know you have Dad's laptop?"

Nell takes the chair across from her daughter. "I didn't lie. But I didn't tell them they missed it either. If they find out it's here and come back for it, I'll plead ignorance."

"Why would you risk getting in trouble for him?"

"It's hard to stop being the responsible one. I thought I'd try to find something that could help him."

"After what he did at June's wake? It's pretty obvious you were right to kick him out. Dad's a fuck-up."

"Don't talk that way. God knows I'm furious with him too, but we can't walk away and leave him to deal with this alone."

"Sam says people think some guy took me and June because of Dad's debts." Tali pulls at a stray piece of yarn on the throw, unraveling it and twirling it around one finger.

"By people you mean his mother? Ana's a gossip. She doesn't know what she's talking about."

"Then why are you snooping?" Tali asks.

"I guess I need the rumors not to be true. Desperate, huh?" Nell smiles weakly.

"Not really. He *said* he didn't have anything to do with it. And Dad *is* a pretty bad actor."

There is a split-second pause before mother and daughter are laughing.

"Look at you," Nell says. "I can't believe how you're handling all of this. You're amazing."

"It's not like the stuff with him is new. You think you shielded me from his stealing and lying, but you couldn't. I live here and I'm not stupid."

"No, you aren't. I guess I thought it was better to let you think I had it all under control."

"But you didn't."

"No, Tali, I didn't. Sometimes I took a break from staring too long at my life."

"And Dad's good at roping you back in."

Tali's right about that too. Beyond his promises to get help and do better, Zeke would make amends with gifts. He wouldn't buy her flowers or jewelry, since even modest presents afforded her the right to accuse him of using her money to pay for his pardon. Instead, he'd offer her small treasures of apology, perfect leaves or heart-shaped stones she could add to her miniature arrangements. Nothing that could be traced to any gambling. Except even precious things when given with increased frequency lose their value.

"Not this time," Nell says. "I'm not saying I won't ever help him again, but it's all about us now. We'll put ourselves first, okay?"

Tali sits up, pulling the throw tight around her chest. "Then you won't make me go see him?"

"In jail? Oh, honey, I would never do that. I'm not going today either. I'm staying here with you. We should do something fun."

"How about I help you?"

"With what?"

"Finding out stuff about Dad. I might not want him living here, but I don't want him to be guilty either."

"No way. Leave that to the police. You've been through enough, young lady."

"Dr. Rawlins said I know best when I'm ready to do stuff." Tali pauses for effect. "I want to go back to the beach."

"In Scituate? Absolutely not."

"I need to remember. I think if I can see the real place again, I'll dream about it less. You don't understand how hard it is not knowing."

Nell knows exactly how hard it is not to know.

"Come on. It's a sunny day," Tali says. "We can drive there and walk around a little. That's all. What harm could it do?"

Despite Nell's objections and her insistence that they at least wait for her psychiatrist to call back to run this all by her, Tali is convincing. By noon they're dressed and in the car driving south on 93, heading for the seaside town her grandmother called the Irish Riviera.

Nell hasn't traveled these roads in over ten years. The tiny cottage she inherited when her grandmother passed away has long been sold to cover one of Zeke's more substantial gambling debts. Even before Nana Parker died, Nell had difficulty going back to visit. She'd always bring flowers—she is better able to meet people when she's carrying flowers—but after the blooms were arranged in a mason jar, and she and Nana had tea and went for a beach walk, they'd run out of things to say that didn't involve her mother.

This time, the closer Nell gets to town, the tighter she grips the steering wheel. As she and Tali drive past one familiar landmark after another, it's harder for Nell to call up those memories. All she can think of is that some monster took the girls here, and June died.

"We could hit The Silent Chef for takeout if it's still there," Nell says. "I used to like to bring lunch to the lighthouse. Or we could get a window table at the Mill Wharf. Whatever you want."

Tali's silence cuts Nell. Maybe she's having second thoughts too. For the entirety of the trip, she's done nothing more than stare out the window. Nell would give anything to be arguing about the volume of the music or which radio station to listen to.

"Do you remember that time Nana took you to the Farmer's Market in the harbor?" Nell asks. "You named every single zucchini and all of the tomatoes. By the time I picked you up, you were inconsolable. You were only four and didn't get that Nana planned to sell everything."

Her daughter doesn't answer. When Tali finally speaks, it's not about Nana Parker and the fruit of her harvest.

"The last thing I remember is being pushed in the car," Tali says. "It was old and the backseat was cracked plastic. It smelled like pot and something sour."

Whenever Tali recounts the details of the abduction, however small they may be, Nell pretends to be calm, when inside she's jangled like ice cubes being dropped in an empty glass.

"I want to go to the Glades," Tali says.

"That's not a good idea. I should try Dr. Rawlins again."

"I *need* to go to the Glades."

Against her better judgment, Nell stops resisting. They've come this far, and Tali will get her way eventually. Instead of heading toward the harbor shops and restaurants, Nell takes a left on Gannett Road. In minutes the sea comes into view. It's high tide and the waves lap the sea wall, erasing any evidence of a beach. Left turn again, they're on Glades Road.

Tali taps the window. "I can do this. Go faster."

Nell drives past the area known to locals as The Hazards, an area of surf harboring rocks of every shape and size, some submerged, some visible. Every townie has a tall tale involving Bar Rock or Smith Rocks. All of them pale in comparison to the story Tali might someday be able to tell about Scituate Neck.

For a split second, Nell is pulled back to the night of the vigil. That horrible moment when Fitz told them that a teenage girl had been found dead on the beach at the site of the old Glades Hotel, the other girl alive but in rough shape. As if Tali has read her mother's mind, she reaches over to pat Nell's arm.

"Through there," she says.

The isolated peninsula of rocky ledges and salt marsh is a gated community that occupies the entire promontory and is cut off from the rest of the town. Access to the Glades is restricted. You're either invited in, or you're trespassing. Undeterred, Nell gets out to lift the gate and then drives through the center of the point along a dirt road. The further in they go, the more heavily wooded the area becomes. Trees rise over thick tangles of brush and vine until they come to the break in the woods that offers glimpses of the sea. This is where her daughter begs to get out.

"We walked this way," Tali says. "I had to go slow because my hands were tied and it was dark."

Nell hurries to catch up so she can hear Tali above the surf.

"Somehow June got away. He chased her but I waited. Here. I don't know if I was afraid to make a run for it or if I froze." Tali sits down on a boulder and her feet disappear into a mound of red-orange leaves. She scans the ground, and with her hands she disturbs the vegetation, breathing deep through her nose.

"What are you looking for?" Nell asks.

Tali snaps to, as if only now realizing that her mother is near. "I'm putting myself back here. The way I get into character."

Seconds later she's up again, moving toward the sound of the sea. "This way."

It takes Nell a second to register that what Tali is doing cannot be good. She should've waited until the doctor called her back. Nell never should've agreed to bring her here. Dread moves her forward. But Tali is a dancer, fit and fast. She disappears behind Pulpit's Rock, and when Nell finally catches up, rounding the boulder, she nearly crashes into her. Tali's face is drained of color. Her eyes are glassy with tears and fixed on a bit of cloth; she doesn't conceal that she is shaken. The scrap of stark white fabric covered in multicolored polka dots clings to a branch; it's a piece of June's pretty coat.

13

After

IT'S PAST NOON when Fitz comes to. He is immediately leveled by shame and the after effects of too many shots. It's been years since he's played piano that well or drunk that much. Wherever Da is, he'd be proud. Not for Fitz's talent—no, not for that—but for getting right shite-faced and not making a fool a hisself.

The longer he focuses on last night, the more Fitz can't be too sure he didn't do anything to embarrass himself in front of Cyn. Still he resists the urge to call Keira. He can hear himself now, interrogating his sister for the details. Pitiful. He won't do it.

Instead, he digs deep for the ability to stand. Getting out of bed too quickly, he's forced to lean on a chair to get the dizziness under control. Water. Fitz needs at least a gallon of the stuff to course-correct this monumental hangover. For a millisecond he contemplates downing one of the Harpoons sitting lonely in the fridge. It would put him out of his misery, except Fitz deserves every ounce of the wretchedness he is feeling.

What the hell made him cave after all these years? It's Keira's fault. Somehow she heard he was working the Danforth case and got it in her head that his conscience would have him going back on his word to protect Connor.

Maybe Keira has good reason to worry. After all, Fitz did go soft and play the keys in prime time, breaking his self-imposed penance.

He grabs the jug of water from the fridge, takes a swig, and carries the thing into the living room, halting in front of the floor-to-ceiling bookcase as if he doesn't know exactly where the photos of Maddie are hidden.

Fitz believes she will only be gone if he stops remembering her. Twelve years in, it takes all he's got to call up the details.

If Connor were here, he'd say Fitz hasn't earned the right to torture himself with Maddie's story. He wasn't there. Fitz doesn't know. Still he goes over and over his contrived account—the only version he has—for this is the primary way Fitzhugh Jameson pummels himself. By living in the space between what Maddie's parents and his brother have told him and what he suspects happened. All Fitz has is what he imagines.

*   *   *

Madeleine Townsend sits at her desk, working hard to finish an essay for AP English on who benefits from the lottery and the ways in which it exploits the poor. The phone on her bedside table rings, interrupting her. The last sentence she will ever write ("The biological risk for addiction remains undetermined") has no punctuation, no period, no end.

Connor is on the line. He sweet-talks her into meeting him on a school night. To watch the sunset. He is minutes from her house and will wait for her on the corner where Gate of Heaven Church intersects East Broadway. He assumes her parents will disapprove of him showing up at her door. Maddie knows Connor is right.

"You can finish the essay later," he tells her. "Even turn it in late, if you want. Nothing bad is going to happen to you."

Maddie is every teacher's pet.

"Tell your mom you're studying with Fitz," Con says, laughing.

Fitz is every mother's pet.

Against the niggling doubt that Connor might not be good for her, she combs her pretty hair and pulls on a sweatshirt to minimize her curves. Connor is beautiful—he makes her heart race and her skin tingle. Of all the girls he could be with, he has chosen her. Without telling her mother where she is going, she asks to borrow the car.

Maddie is a good girl. Her parents have no reason to mistrust her. To quiz her or to curfew her. She is given the keys and a kiss.

She picks up Connor and they drive for the time it takes to get to their romantic destination. Out of the car, hand in hand, the couple walks the three-mile stretch to Castle Island, down to Pleasure Bay, past M Street and Carson beaches. The sun sits behind a bundle of clouds, casting shadows, putting buildings and people in silhouette against the sea. In spite of this being their neighborhood, they don't bump into anyone they know.

Connor's memory is good for only a few things, like the best places to make out inside Fort Independence, the pentagonal structure that dominates Castle Island. And the tactics that work on reluctant girls. He has yet to learn Maddie is different. She has a mind of her own.

The kissing is fine, nice really. It's when Connor slips his hand up her sweatshirt in search of her breasts, that she begins to feel this isn't right. Not for her. Connor, sensing her hesitancy, switches gears before Maddie becomes adamant. He knows his way around such obstacles.

"Let's go swimming," he says. "It's warm and it might be our last chance till spring."

"I'm not wearing my suit," she says.

"Keep your underwear on. I will too. Let's do it. It'll be fun."

He takes his pants and shirt off before Maddie can object. Counting on her naiveté, he uses it to his advantage. "Tell me when you're ready," he says, turning away from her to face the water.

Connor reaches one hand back until Maddie slips hers in his, and together they run to the shoreline. One look at each other and they dive into the cold but not yet frigid ocean. It's New England after all, and Maddie and Connor are not strangers to icy dips and the shock they impose upon the system.

Once in the water, after a few playful attempts to jump their way to getting used to it, Connor swims to Maddie. He kisses her, and like magic, she opens her arms to him.

"I want to make love to you," he whispers, kissing her neck, flicking his tongue around her ear.

"I can't. I'm not ready. I don't—"

"I won't come inside you. We're in the water. You can't get pregnant doing it this way. I promise."

Maddie hears his persuasion as lines from a play, rehearsed and used on simpler girls. Needier girls.

"I have to go," she says.

But Connor grabs the back of her bra before she has a chance to swim away. He is rough, trying to pull aside her panties, to penetrate her against her will. Maddie screams once, but the next time she opens her mouth, Connor pushes her under. To stop her from drawing attention to them. To silence her.

His hand is on her head, holding her down. He is strong. Maddie is too. She struggles mightily, but in minutes without air, the violent movement under the water stops. Abruptly. That's when Connor lets go. He treads water, moving away from her body as it floats to the surface. Her hair fans out as if she's making one final attempt to reach out to him for mercy.

Fitz is the person Connor calls. He claims there's been an accident. Brother begs brother to come to the Fort. Quickly. With a car. Don't tell anyone anything.

Fitz is a good boy. The Jameson family crest has been impressed upon him from an early age: Freastal creideamh agus teaghlaigh gan eagla—*serve faith and family without fear. But then Fitz does not yet know what he is getting himself into.*

At first he doesn't see Connor cowering in a far corner of the Fort, wearing only his boxers. His brother stares down at Maddie's clothes—her jeans, her sweatshirt, her tee-shirt—in a heap.

"We were fooling around," Connor says. "I was teasing. I pushed her down, but when I tried to pull her up, she started fighting me. It was like she wanted this to happen. She broke away from me, swam further out. I couldn't keep up. Then all of a sudden, she stopped moving. I knew something was wrong. But by the time I got to her, she was gone."

"What the fuck, Connor? Where is she? Where's Maddie?"

"She's dead, Fitz. Jesus Christ, she goddamned drowned."

"Don't tell me you left her out there." Fitz is shaking Connor now. "Did you leave her out there?"

"You have to help me. I didn't mean to. It was an accident. You have to get me home without anyone seeing me. I wasn't here. Understand?"

"We need to find her. If you didn't do anything, it'll be okay."

"No. No one can know I was here. Do you understand? You need to cover for me."

"Why would I do that?"

* * *

Why had Fitz protected his brother? How long did it take for Connor to convince him to drive the car home with his brother hunkered down in the front seat? To this day, Fitz is unable to answer that most fundamental of questions. Why had he done that?

After Maddie's parents reported her missing and the abandoned family car was found down by the causeway, authorities began a massive search of Southie, from M Street to Dorchester Avenue. Police dogs picked up a scent during the search and led investigators to the east side of the Fort, where Maddie's clothes were recovered.

When one of the Finnegan girls hinted that Maddie might have had a thing with Connor Jameson, he was questioned. Connor led investigators to believe Maddie was contemplating suicide when she disappeared. *"She couldn't take the pressure to be perfect anymore,"* he'd said.

Fitz's asshole of a brother didn't just kill Maddie; he drowned her reputation right along with her body and soul.

Three days later, Maddie's body was pulled from the waters off Castle Island. According to a statement released by the medical examiner, the final autopsy determination, pending the results of toxicology tests, would take several weeks. The unofficial word from the Suffolk County prosecutor was that there were no signs of trauma to her body and no indication that foul play had contributed to her death. And like that, the ordeal was over.

Except it never was. It will never be over.

There's a banging on his apartment door, and it startles Fitz. "Police. Open up."

Disoriented, he exits Maddie's story, coming back to the present awash in fresh guilt. He opens the door to a beat cop, secretly hoping he's about to be arrested for keeping his suspicions of Connor's role in Maddie's death from everyone except Keira.

"You look scared shitless," the cop says. "You got somebody's wife holed up in there or something?" When the cop chuckles, there's a gurgle of phlegm in his throat.

"What do you want?" Fitz asks, suddenly aware that he's clad only in tattered boxers.

"You're not answering ya phone. Ross sent me. Said to get your ass outta bed and give him a call."

"What's going on?"

"I know nothing. Alls I do is what I'm told. Call Ross."

Pissed he has to shift his focus to someone else entirely, especially Ross, Fitz takes his time to pull on jeans and brush his teeth. He plugs in his phone. In his drunken stupor last night, he must've shut the thing off to save the last of the charge.

When he's good and ready, he dials Ross. "It's Sunday. I'm off."

"Sorry, did I interrupt church with Ma, or were you praying to the porcelain god?"

Fitz wracks his brain trying to think of something worth throwing back at Ross but comes up empty.

"Tali Carrington and her mother took a little trip to the beach this afternoon," Ross says. "The kid's trying her damnedest to remember what happened to her out there at The Glades. Looks like she and her mother bumped smack into possible evidence."

"What the hell?"

"Before we go blaming the first cops on the scene, let's find out what or if anything's relevant. It's a big area. Shit could've been dropped there after the fact."

"Does anything look promising?"

"Yes and no. An empty prescription pill bottle for high-dose benzos. Could be completely unrelated to the case, but Doyle's got a man on the street who says Carrington sells the stuff for cash to play the ponies."

"I'll be down there in little over an hour to pitch in," Fitz says, reaching for a sweatshirt.

"No need. You took too damn long to get back to me. We're already done here. Forensics just bagged the last thing. A scrap of fabric that looks like it was ripped from the coat the Danforth kid was wearing that night. Meet me at the precinct first thing tomorrow. There's a lot to do."

"June," Fitz says. "The Danforth kid's name is June."

Act Two

"This is one of the cruelties of the theater of life;
we all think of ourselves as stars . . ."
—Robertson Davies,
The Fifth Business

14

Dreams

T HAT THE NEWS media has lessened its scrutiny of the Carringtons at this point in the investigation is predictable, and still Cyn is surprised to see only a few second-stringers camped out in front of their brownstone.

Unless no one's inside.

Before putting herself through a barrage of questions she has no intention of answering, Cyn sits on the park bench across the street and pulls out her phone to dial Nell. No answer at home; she tries her cell.

"Hold on. Let me step out of my meeting," Nell says.

"Oh, I didn't realize you were back at work."

Cyn hears a door closing, and Nell's voice is once again audible. "I hadn't planned on it, but when Tali wanted to come to school, there was no way I was letting her come alone."

"Tali's in school?"

"She says she wants things to go back to normal. We thought maybe you wouldn't mind pushing her session off until later today? I probably should've waited to hear what you thought, but I've already bothered you enough. You must be busy."

Nell's tone is biting. She isn't the first family member to let Cyn know she's jealous over the time she spends with other patients. What she doesn't know is that right now Cyn doesn't have any other patients.

"You haven't bothered me. I told you to call me anytime."

"I did. Twice yesterday. And then again this morning."

Noah is the gift that keeps on giving. Cyn didn't get a single message, never mind three. "I'm in the process of changing my answering service," she says. "There must be a mix-up. I could meet you now, if that works. I could come to you. You and I haven't had much time to connect, and I'd love to see Tali's school."

The Performing Arts High School of Boston takes up two Newbury Street blocks, Fairfield to Dartmouth, and its showpiece—the Exeter Street Theatre—is situated smack in the middle. Living and working in Back Bay, Cyn's walked by the main building countless times, but never has she been more tuned in to the flurry of activity that surrounds it. A parade of musicians forms around the entrance. Two teenagers holding scripts lean against the Romanesque facade, animatedly running lines. Cyn looks for Tali.

And there is the pool of reporters transplanted from a few streets over, milling around the school, looking camera ready, though bored.

The inside of the theater is more impressive than she'd imagined. Cyn doesn't need to be an architect to appreciate how the classical and decorative elements merge throughout the space in a balance of old and new. Nell stands by the reception desk, waving her over. "I take it you've never been here before. Isn't it something?"

Looking around, Cyn wonders why she's never been to a concert or play here, until she remembers that's not something Noah ever wanted to do.

"I haven't," she says. "You can bet I'll come to one now."

"We can talk in my office. Second floor."

As they travel the stairways and hallways, passing rooms filled with singers and small ensembles rehearsing, Cyn is jarred by the contrast to the noise and movement that defined the entrance to the lobby.

"Quiet, isn't it? All of the practice rooms and studios are soundproof," Nell says. "I don't have to tell you teenagers can be pretty distractible."

Nell opens the door to her office, an unremarkable space with a desk, a mesh chair, and seats for two guests. The only extraordinary thing about the place is the wall covered in cast photos labeled with show titles: *The Miracle Worker, You Can't Take It with You, The Crucible, Rent.*

"Since I've been here we've done all the classic theater pieces—several times. If they stage one more production of *Our Town*, I'll need to get a new job."

Again, Cyn finds that she's looking for Tali, this time among the rows and rows of actors in costume.

Nell wastes no time getting to what's on her mind. "I'm worried about Tali being back here."

"How so?"

"The expectations are over the top in this place. Not only the academics. The artistic director chooses plays that are intense even for adult actors. Last season they put on *Finish Line*, a documentary theater piece about the Boston

Marathon bombing. A lot of these kids have personal experiences because it happened right outside our doors. I wasn't the only one worried they couldn't handle it; lots of parents were up in arms."

"Was Tali cast in that?" Cyn asks.

"She had a doubling role. It's when a handful of actors play more than one part. Turns out the director was right. I know I'm her mother and definitely biased, but you should've seen her. Tali nailed it. But that was before."

Cyn scans the cast photo labeled *Finish Line*.

Nell taps the glass. "That's her director, Greg Normand."

"He looks like one of the kids," Cyn says. "Is this Tali?" She points to a young woman who exudes the kind of confidence she's only seen glimmers of. The Tali Cyn knows is mostly on edge, her movements dulled, and her energy diminished. In this context, the light in her eyes is unmistakable.

"She looks happy," Cyn says.

Nell gestures to the guest chairs, inviting her to sit. "What I'd give to have that girl back. It's like walking on eggshells, being around her. One minute we'll be contentedly watching a movie, and the next thing I know she's closed up in her bedroom and won't talk to me. I need you to tell me, will she ever be herself again?"

"I'd be lying if I told you the trauma won't impact her life going forward. But from what you've told me and what I've seen for myself, Tali strikes me as a resilient young woman. Lots of strong people do amazing things after adversity."

Nell swallows hard, like she's getting ready to unload about something. Cyn braces herself for more ranting about Zeke.

"Tali told me she's dedicating her performance to June," Nell says. "I know my daughter. She's going to drive herself hard. It's another mature piece, and trust me, Greg will not be cutting anybody any slack."

"Tali told me what it is but tell me again."

"*Spring Awakening*. Another one of Greg's edgy choices. A lot of people see it as a play about sexual coming of age. Don't get me wrong; I'm not condoning teenagers having sex, but that's not what's bothering me. It's the other themes. Abuse, rape, suicide."

"You're worried Tali is too fragile for all of this?"

"I am. The play raises lots of questions that don't have easy answers."

"You and Zeke and Tali have all said acting is what makes her tick. In the beginning, a little avoidance can be a helpful coping mechanism. If she's focused on the play, that means she's not focused on everything else."

"I'm not convinced. She still has all her academic work to make up. The rehearsal schedule is ridiculous. And she's going to be spending even more time with Sam. Given how he's doing, I'm not sure Tali's avoiding anything."

"Tell me about Sam. He's the friend she's always texting?"

"They've known each other since day one freshman year. He's a great kid and he's always been a good friend to Tali—though his mother is an entirely different story. Ana says he's taking June's death hard, because June and Sam were going out. Which is news to me. But now he and Tali are cast in this intense play with all these intimate scenes. Do you ever work with the other kids affected by abductions?"

"Sometimes I do. It depends on how my primary patient feels about it. It would be up to Tali."

"I know she's only one of your responsibilities," Nell says, "but if you can find a way to help these kids get through this production, I'd be grateful. Somedays I wish I could take Tali and go into hiding. Move somewhere. Start over."

Zeke is the subtext of Nell's escape fantasy. Hearing her talk about running away reminds Cyn of her lost office, her nearly empty apartment, the new job. Given everything she knows about the way heartache works, her own plans seem silly now. You can't hide from anguish; it finds you no matter where you go.

"How are you holding up?" Cyn asks. "What's going on with your husband?"

"Talk about avoidance. It's unbelievable. He's in jail, and all I want to do right now is focus on my daughter."

"Maybe it's not an either-or situation. Is Tali talking to you about Zeke? She said she's not ready to talk about him with me."

"A little. I'm honest but not effusive when it comes to him. Partly because I don't know what to say and also because I don't want to dump things on her. He's her dad."

"It's good you're not out to demonize him, but the reality is, his legal trouble is going to get worse before it gets better. And then there's his emotional health. Maybe I can help you and Tali talk about it in a session together."

In a wistful way, Nell glances beyond Cyn's shoulder to the wall of photos. "I'd like that. I'm doing my best not to push Tali to tell me everything, when that's all I want to do."

Cyn reaches across the desk for a Post-It and a pen. "I'm sorry about not getting back to you yesterday. For now, this is a better way to get in touch."

In the awkward silence, Nell accepts the slip of paper, and the two women stand.

"You never asked me why I don't put my foot down and say, 'No, Tali, you can't be in a play right now.'"

"Tell me."

"I'd rather show you."

Nell leads Cyn out of her office, in the opposite direction of the lobby entrance. Whenever Cyn notices a ping of worry that she's spending too much time here, she lets it go. Until classes start, she's got all the time in the world.

Within minutes, the warren of formal hallways opens to a more contemporary space. Large double doors, dark wood and carved with the twin masks of tragedy and comedy, take up most of one wall. A sign above the doors reads "Sock and Buskin Theater."

Nell puts a finger to her lips and opens the door.

The theater is small, as theaters go, and while the teenagers on stage don't miss a beat at Nell and Cyn's arrival, the man standing to the left of the stage briefly turns and glares in their direction.

"That's Greg," Nell whispers as they drop into two seats on the aisle. "He hates that I have permission to tour people during rehearsals."

Cyn is spellbound. Not by the innovative theater with its dark walls and bare appearance, or its black chairs squaring off all sides of the stage, but by Tali.

The girl stands center stage, singing a ballad. The weight of her voice is powerful, rich with dark notes. Cyn doesn't know what she expected. But definitely a voice less developed, maybe something light and bright and breathy.

"See what I mean?" Nell asks.

When Cyn doesn't respond, Nell's irritation rises above a whisper. "That song. *I'm going to be wounded. You're going to be my bruise.*' How can she move on if she has to sing this all day?"

Preoccupied by Tali's hypnotic talent and command-ing presence on stage, Cyn missed the lyrics coming out of her mouth.

When another thick beam of light pours into the dark-ened theater, the director turns again in their direction. At first the silhouette is indistinguishable, but the closer the man gets, the more familiar he is.

Making his way down the aisle, it's like he owns the place.

The teenage boy on stage stops moving and swats Tali's arm to get her attention. She stops singing, but the music continues to play.

"Mrs. Carrington," the director bellows above the pia-nist, "anyone else you're expecting to interrupt rehearsal?"

Before Nell can say anything, the man makes it to the front of the stage and flashes his badge at the director. "I need to talk to Sam Wallace."

15

The Secret School

Fitz has been inside the Performing Arts High School of Boston all of six minutes, and already the place is on his last nerve. Everywhere he goes there's a piano.

He tells the director he's there to talk to Sam, though he's careful not to use the words *question* or *interview*. Normand takes one look at his badge and doesn't refuse him.

With an exasperated wave of his notebook, the director tells the pianist to cut the sound. "People, listen up. Mr. Wallace—you're dismissed, but take your script. I want you off-book on that scene by tonight. Everybody else take five—but only five. We've got a lot to get through."

All the kids plus piano man disappear through the wings, leaving only Sam and Tali in the spotlight. Seconds ago, the girl was belting out a show tune, and now she cowers in front of this guy like a puppy about to get whacked.

"I have to go too," she says, pointing to the back of the theater.

Normand throws the notebook on the stage, making a loud thwack, sending the pencil flying. "This isn't *High School Musical*," he says. "I told you the schedule was grueling. You said you could handle it."

In the world of places like this, the director is god. And this guy plays his part Old Testament. There's a whiff of desperation about him. A bitterness, like this school and these kids are beneath him.

Fitz has been in pissing matches with scarier guys, so he's about to call him out. It's only been two weeks since the kid was abducted. Nell beats him to it. She storms the apron of the stage, followed by Cyn Rawlins. Like Fitz needs to see her right now.

"Sam, Tali—get your things. Meet Detective Jameson and Dr. Rawlins at the front of house," Nell says.

The pair backs upstage, suddenly looking like the kids they are, and then they turn and run, talking to each other the whole way.

"Greg, this is Tali's psychiatrist," Nell says. "She's too nice to tell you off, so I will. If you talk to my daughter like that again—or in any way intimidate her—lead or no lead, I will pull her from this production faster than you can say *curtain*."

Unfazed, the director collects a stack of scripts and his notebook from the front of the stage while Nell keeps going at him.

Normand has missed the pencil, which is covered in bite marks. It's almost too easy. Fitz discreetly slips a small evidence bag from his coat pocket, covers his fingertips with plastic, and slides the pencil toward him without contaminating it.

"It's not my forte," Normand says. "But I can try to be more sensitive. What I won't do is coddle her. Tali has potential to be great in this part, and I *will* be pushing her."

"Well then, you can expect to have more visitors during rehearsals," Nell says. "I'll see you this afternoon."

Normand exits the theater by a side door.

"Go, Mom," Fitz says, clapping. "Couldn't have done better myself."

"This is exactly what I'm worried about," she says to Cyn. "Should Tali be doing this? One minute she's finding evidence at the beach, and the next she's singing about bruises and wounds to the body, with that jerk yelling at her."

The baffled look on Cyn's face tells Fitz she doesn't know about Nell and Tali day-tripping it to Scituate yesterday.

"Is that why you called me?" Cyn asks.

"I wanted your opinion about whether or not we should go. If you thought Tali could handle it. Later, after she convinced me to take her, I tried you again to see if you could talk to her. She was upset. We both were."

Nell turns her attention to Fitz now. She'd called him last night too: the first time to be sure Ross filled him in on what they'd found at the beach; the second to press him for details about what he planned to do next. Both times to let him know she was royally pissed that evidence had been missed on the first pass at the crime scene.

"What about what we found?" Nell asks.

"The fabric snagged on the shrub is likely a piece of June's coat, but it'll have to be analyzed to be sure."

"That's it? All you're going to do is test it?"

"No, no. We ordered a second sweep of the area. Investigators finished up last night, and we're analyzing other potential evidence as we speak."

Nell's fire is directed at him. He's used to it. It's part of the job to take heat for things that aren't your fault. She's probably more ticked at herself for being talked into taking her daughter back there.

Cyn puts a hand on Nell's shoulder. "I'll talk to Tali and help her sort this out."

Fitz's initial attraction to Cyn still holds, even though she's back to wearing her therapy clothes. There's a twist in his gut when he remembers the way she looked Saturday night at The Beehive. How a few drinks in, Cyn sat next to him on the piano bench, their sides touching as he played.

Fitz zeroes back in on Nell when she asks about her husband.

"When do you think they'll let Zeke out?"

"You should talk to his lawyer," he says. "For now, his case is classified no bond, and I'm not the one to go over specifics."

Nell shushes him when Tali and Sam materialize back on stage. "There you are," she says.

"You told us to meet you at front of house." With Tali's arms crossed tight and one hip cocked, she's acting out the all-American teenager. Normal looks good on her.

"That's right, I did," Nell says. "Are there dressing rooms free out back? That might work better."

Tali says, "Uh-huh." Sam looks at his feet.

"Follow me."

Even though Nell gave the directive, she tags along behind Tali and Sam, leaving Cyn and Fitz to bring up the rear.

"Should you be questioning him without an adult present, a parent or a lawyer maybe?" Cyn whispers.

"I'm here to go over a couple of details, that's all."

Cyn might be morally right, but she's not technically right. Fitz isn't required to contact Sam's mother or obtain any kind of permission before approaching and questioning him. That doesn't mean he likes the way she's staring at him.

To get backstage, they ignore the roped-off passageway and climb five flights up to a landing with no exit. Sam pushes the wall in a seemingly random space, and a secret door opens, leading to a hallway lined with dressing rooms.

Greg Normand strides in their direction. He's shouting again. "People. It's been a lot longer than five minutes. If you're not in places before I get to that stage, you will be replaced. There are plenty of students who would kill to be in your shoes."

Cast members spill from dressing rooms like it's a raid on a rave.

Tali stops momentarily and whispers something to her mother.

"It's fine. I'll take care of him," Nell says. "Go ahead."

Acting like she owns the place, Nell parks Cyn and Tali in a dressing room with bright light coming in from the balcony fire escape. She sticks Fitz and Sam across the hall in a space the size of a closet. Fitz is tempted to say, "I get it. You're mad," but then she closes the door, and he's alone with the boy.

They both sit. Sam leans back in his chair a little too hard, tipping it, then righting it. He doesn't know what to do with his hands.

"Thanks for taking the time," Fitz says, keeping it light, starting off slow. As cut off as they are from the other dressing room, he can't shake the look Cyn gave him about what he's doing.

"Congrats, man," Fitz says.

"Huh?"

"On the part. You got the lead. I don't think you knew that the last time we talked."

"No. Yeah. It's good."

Sam is tall and lean, with broad shoulders. A dark, slick kind of good-looking, the lucky bastard is every casting director's dream. All he needs is to be marginally talented, and he'll make out fine in the business.

"You're a sophomore. It's a big deal, am I right?"

"I guess."

"I get it. It's hard to be happy when you've lost your girlfriend."

"Who told you June was my girlfriend?" It's the first time the kid's looked directly at Fitz. The dark circles under his bloodshot eyes weren't visible from the audience. Neither was the sweat beading up on his brow.

"You did. Remember?"

"Oh yeah. My memory's a mess. And Normand's all over me for not remembering lines from a play we only started rehearsing."

"You've got to get it together. I know his type. He'll be all over you until you leave it on that stage." Fitz drums the arm of his chair.

"You did plays?" Sam drops his shoulders, and for a second he stops licking his lips.

"Accompanist, *Chicago*. And I played for a show called *Thrill Me*. Wow, now that I think about it, those shows are pretty dark—both about murder."

Sam shakes his head. "Never heard of it. The last one—not *Chicago*. I've heard of *Chicago*."

"Enough about me." Fitz reaches inside his coat pocket to pull out his notebook. "I'd like to follow up on some things we talked about last time. You said you don't know much, so this shouldn't be too painful."

Pretending to read from the notebook, Fitz watches Sam. A better detective would focus on facts and logic. Instead, Fitz compares Sam to Connor, unable to stop himself from sizing up his body language, looking for the same tells that forecasted his brother's guilt.

"The night of the audition, you left before the girls. You got picked up by your mother. Is that right?"

"Yeah. Tali and June and Robin had the last callback auditions for the part of Wendla. It was late and I was tired, so I left." Sam settles back in his chair, then leans forward again. He can't seem to figure out which position makes him look less uptight.

"Who else was here with the girls?"

"Just Mr. Normand. He sent Mr. Garber home too. I left with him."

"Garber—he's the accompanist? He'd be able to back up your story that you got picked up by your mother?"

"I guess. But it's not a story."

"Aside from being a dick about rehearsals, anything else bother you about Mr. Normand? Any rumors about him? Is he ever inappropriate with the girls? Or the guys?"

Sam doesn't have Connor's poker face. Fitz has hit on something. "He didn't have a thing for June, did he?" Fitz asks.

"Not June."

"Okay, but he likes the girls? What about Tali?"

"No." Sam is sweating like crazy, wiping his hands on his pants.

"My partner—Detective Ross—you met him? He thinks Tali's father is involved somehow. He's shady, to be sure. But my gut says something's not right at this school."

"I don't know. Mr. Carrington's always been nice to me. And Mr. Normand is tough on us, but that's his job."

"Are there any serious cliques, hush-hush clubs, secret societies? Any hazing that you know of?"

"I wouldn't know. I'm always studying or rehearsing."

"Sure, sure. But you hear things. I'll bet kids trust you and tell you stuff."

"Not really."

"Competition in a place like this has to be brutal. Makes people do crazy things."

"It's not that bad."

"Because you're like the big star, right? The one with the most potential to make it professionally. No need for you to get into the gossip or join in on any backstabbing."

Sam doesn't take the compliment about being top dog; he doesn't reject it either. What he does do is keep pulling at the front of his shirt.

"Let me ask your opinion on something. Anybody at the school who you *could* see getting carried away? Who might do something to take June and Tali out of the picture?" Fitz hesitates long enough to flip through his notebook. "Like this other contender—what's her name? Robin?"

"Chandler. No, Robin wouldn't do anything like that. She doesn't care enough."

"What about her parents? Mothers are the worst."

Sam drops his head, and as if the kid's panic alarm went off, the door flies open and in walks Ana Wallace. Or maybe Fitz conjured her with his talk of stage mothers.

The first time he'd met Ana, Tali and June were still missing, and Fitz was holed up in Nell's office on the second floor of the Exeter Street Theatre conducting interviews. In comes this mother–son act. Mom was clearly shaken, exuding genuine concern for the girls, and Sam was unresponsive with fear. When Fitz started asking about the night the girls went missing, it pained him to watch the kid knuckle under to his mother. The way she pressed him and hushed him, the way she pulled his strings. And how he marched to her beat. If her pride and pressure, the grinding ambition that has his name on it, wasn't so obvious, Fitz would've thought Ana was a lawyer. But her Hollywood hair and the jolt of pink lips clued him in: she'd been an actress. Her last chance at celebrity would need to come through her kid.

Now here she is again, coming out of nowhere. Fitz offers her his chair. "Sam and I were going over a few things."

"I'm glad he was helpful to you. He needs to get back to rehearsal," she says, more like an order than a fact. Ana opens the door wider and motions for Sam to leave.

Fitz claps the kid on the shoulder, his firm grip effectively pinning him to his seat. "We'll catch up another time. I'm taken with this place. You know what I mean?"

"Sam. Go."

For someone so small and girly, Ana is a force of nature. She doesn't have to speak twice before her son hightails it out of the room.

"I'd appreciate it if you didn't speak to my son again without contacting me first. He and June cared deeply for each other, and this whole thing has been difficult for him. I can't let you add to his grief."

"No, ma'am. Wouldn't want to do that."

Out in the hallway, Ana falls in line with Nell, Cyn, and Tali as they come out of the dressing room. The three women look at him, their message clear. No more talking to kids without parents. Tali runs ahead to catch up with Sam on the stairs.

"Dr. Rawlins, got a minute?" Fitz asks.

The women stop as a pack; Nell and Ana look at Cyn. "Go ahead," she says. "I know my way out."

After they're gone, Fitz says, "Thanks for the endorsement."

"You can't bully these kids."

"Who said anything about bullying?"

Fitz moves toward the bigger of the two dressing rooms, the one Cyn had been in with Tali. He's tempted to put his hand on her back, to guide her inside, but he's pretty sure she wouldn't want him to touch her here.

"How can you be a detective and not know anything about trauma?" she asks, closing the door behind her.

"What, you think I'm purposely trying to upset Sam? I'm looking for answers to who might be involved in June's murder. I am not the bad guy here."

As Cyn softens, he catches a glimmer of the woman he met at the entrance to his home-sweet-jazz club.

"You need to be careful," she says. "Imagine what it's like for them. Every time you make them talk about that night, it's like it's happening all over again. June was their friend."

Fitz can't tell if she's knowingly digging him or she just picked up his kryptonite, thinking it's ordinary rock. There's no way Keira would've told Cyn about Maddie.

Her phone rings, and after fishing it out of her bag, she glances at it. "I need to take this." Cyn moves to the other side of the room, where there's another goddamn piano.

He moves to the threshold of the fire escape, scoping out the iconic Boston buildings that surround the alley.

"Yes. That's everything," she says. "I'll swing by later to sign." Short and sweet, Cyn ends the call and then looks over at Fitz as if she's annoyed he's still there.

"I wanted to ask if you could spare some time to meet with me," he says.

She drops her phone into her bag.

"I thought maybe I could pick your brain. I've got a few general questions about teenagers and parents. And I'm worried about Sam in particular."

"You can't trick me into talking about my patient."

Fitz lowers his voice. "Asking you out for coffee shouldn't be this difficult."

Cyn props her bag on the top of the piano, then runs her hand along the key slip. "It's Monday," she says. "Are you playing tonight?"

Jesus, Keira. Before Fitz can stop himself, he says, "I am. We could talk between sets. Or if you're a night owl, we could meet for last call."

"I don't think that's a good idea."

"Which one? Between sets or last call?"

"Neither. I have patients first thing in the morning."

The doctor is lying. Fitz doesn't need Cyn to tell him how spectacularly her ex took down her practice. Keira talks to him too.

"If you change your mind," he says, "you know where to find me."

CHAPTER

16

Mirror, Mirror

THE BELL RINGS, signaling time to change classes. If Nell moves quickly enough from behind her desk to in front of the file cabinet, she can catch a glimpse of Tali before her daughter ducks into pre-calc. Mornings at the high school are dedicated to traditional academics, and with all the classrooms located in the area near Nell's office, it's pretty easy to keep tabs on Tali's whereabouts.

Up until two weeks ago, the only time Nell was aware of Tali in school was if she happened to pass a music studio and heard her distinctive voice ring out during a lesson, or if, on a mission to deliver a message to a teacher, she found her mid-rehearsal. A delightful surprise, Tali is the hyacinth you come upon on a walk, not realizing how desperate you've become to see bright colors bursting through winter.

Now Nell can't go one full class period without angling for a way to make sure her daughter is safe inside the building.

No sign of her. Nell pockets her phone and grabs a random file to take with her on what should look to others like a purposeful walk around the school. She doesn't make it to the center of the atrium when Ana breaks through the hallway traffic, charging straight for her.

"There's the woman I came to see."

"You'll have to make an appointment. I'm off to—" Nell can't think of where she might be going fast enough. She's a terrible liar and Ana knows it.

"I'm not here on school business," she says, lowering her voice. "I came to see how you are."

Ana looks different today. She wears less makeup, no jewelry. Her hair is flat, and her clothes, a combination of softer than usual fabrics, are all light blues and blush. Almost muted, it's easier to look past this woman who's been known to drive Nell crazy.

"If you're looking for Tali, she's with Sam," Ana says. "She's helping him run lines so that prick Normand will get off his case about being off-book."

Before Nell can deny she's been looking for her daughter, she gives Ana a "watch-your- language" look.

"Oh, please. These kids call him much worse behind his back. And it's not like I haven't told him as much to his face. Imagine tearing into our kids after everything they've been through."

Suddenly Nell feels capable of strangling Ana. How dare she compare what Sam's experiencing to what Tali is dealing with?

"I mean it's been less than two weeks since the table-read and only a few days since June's services," Ana says. "It's bordering on vicious."

"You can't be worried Greg will replace Sam."

"Well, no. He didn't even cast an understudy for his role," she says with pride. "Look, I'm all for pushing Sam to do his best, but bullying him shuts him down. And I won't have that."

"I feel the same way about Tali. I'm keeping an eye on Greg. I told him if he crosses the line into intimidating her, I'll pull her from the production, and he can give the part to Robin."

"Well, you can't do that. Robin's dreadful. No one but June could hold a candle to Tali. Go ahead and put Greg in his place, but whatever you do, don't take this away from Tali. This is everything to her."

"Did she tell you that?"

"She doesn't have to, honey. Have you seen her in rehearsal? She was born to play Wendla. Mark my words, talent scouts and casting agents who see her in this will be fighting over who gets to sign her."

At the second bell, Ana scans the atrium, and it strikes Nell that Sam's mother is about to divulge the real reason she came to see her.

"To be honest, I'm worried about Sam," Ana says. "As talented as he is, his heart isn't in it. He can't sleep. Can't eat. We had a knock-down, drag-out last night over memorizing his lines. It was my idea that he rehearse with Tali. She's handling things so well."

Nell wants to refute Ana, to say her daughter is still terribly affected and taking this hard, but the truth is, with Klonopin at night and play rehearsal during the day, Tali is doing better. She's waking up for school on her own, eating a little breakfast, and talking about her ordeal less and less.

"She's got a wonderful therapist." Nell hears the defensiveness in her own voice, though she isn't sure where it's coming from. Is she really competing with another mother over whose child is more depressed? "Maybe Sam should talk to someone. It's not a silver bullet, certainly, but it helps."

"So Tali talks about it? Did she ever tell you what happened? I think if I knew more about June's final moments I might be able to help Sam myself. Reassure him she didn't suffer, you know?"

As Ana's questioning wears on, the hallway becomes less crowded, until only the students looking to skip remain milling about, their acting less credible without scripts.

"They should be in class," Nell says.

"That's not your job, is it? To police these kids."

"I'm talking about Tali and Sam. Missing a math lesson at their level is a setup for failing the course," Nell says. "Where did you say they are?"

"Carnegie Mellon and Juilliard don't care about grades and test scores. It's all about the audition. My money's on Sam and Tali getting whisked off to New York or LA before we even have to go that route."

Ana's appearance may be toned down and off-kilter, but nothing else about her has changed.

"I should go find the kids," Nell says.

Before she can disengage from Ana, Tali and Sam appear at the top of the atrium stairs.

"You have to tell him to stop," Tali says, shaking her new phone at her mother. "Please."

"Slow down," Nell says. "What's going on?"

"I didn't recognize the number, so I answered and it was Dad." Tali throws herself at her mother, and like a reflex, Nell envelops her and starts rubbing her back.

"It's my fault. I should have taken his calls," Nell says.

Despite pressure coming from all sides, she hasn't visited Zeke in jail. Thanks to his public defender and newly acquired phone privileges, he keeps calling her too. He needs to explain things. At least that's what he says in the messages he leaves for her.

"You haven't been talking to Zeke?" Ana asks.

Of all the people Nell would not want participating in this conversation, Ana tops the list.

Tali steps back from Nell. "Can you go now? And tell him to leave me alone?"

"I've already taken too much time off," Nell says. "I planned to work late while you're at rehearsal tonight to get caught up." This is the excuse she has practiced, her cover story for not leaving Tali alone at school.

"You have to face him sooner or later," Ana says. "I'll be here all afternoon dealing with costumes."

"Beverly's not in today," Nell says.

"You don't think a minor detail like our costume designer being out sick can stop me from crashing a closed rehearsal, do you?" Ana links one arm with Tali's as if they're part of a cliquey group of school girls. "Don't worry. I won't let her out of my sight," Ana says, motioning for Sam to come closer. He's kept his distance the whole time his mother's been talking.

Nell can't tell if Ana's offer to stick around is mostly to reassure her or to browbeat Sam. One thing is certain, though. Ana knows her son. Sam isn't his usual charming self. He looks like he's having an out-of-body experience. His face, though intensely calm, is vacant.

"Are you okay, honey?" Nell asks.

Sam shakes his head as if to rouse himself. "Yeah, fine. Just tired. And worried about the play."

Ana drops Tali's arm and guides Nell a few steps away from their children. "This is how we help them get through this," she says. "We let them immerse themselves in the only thing that makes them feel alive. Go. See your husband. I'll be here the whole time."

No longer willing to be backed into a corner by Zeke or anyone else, Nell takes charge.

"Excuse me. Tali, can you come into my office for a minute please?"

Ana's facial expression is everything when Nell and her daughter leave her and Sam standing in the middle of the atrium. Tali shuts her office door. "I'm fine," she says. "You can go."

"You didn't look okay a few minutes ago. Do you want me to call Dr. Rawlins?"

"I overreacted. I didn't expect Dad to call me. That's all. Really."

"I don't feel comfortable leaving you here alone."

In a sweet gesture, Tali places both hands on her mother's shoulders. "I'm definitely not alone here. Come on—it's our chance to finally put Mrs. Wallace's overprotectiveness to use."

Once again, Tali impresses Nell with her ability to roll with what's being thrown at her. "Don't leave this building for anything. Promise?"

"I won't even leave this office—until rehearsal. If it's okay with you, Sam and I can run lines in here. He can't bump into Mr. Normand until he's off-book for at least two more scenes. Can you give us a pass to miss math and Russian lit?"

Nell is about to protest, to push back on Tali skipping academics and falling further behind. Except it's nice to see her daughter relaxed. Instead of cracking down, Nell relishes the normalcy of their mother–daughter moment and gets permission to leave work early.

It takes twenty minutes to get from the high school to Nashua Street, which only accentuates the guilt Nell feels for having delayed the visit. In this part of the city known for its eclectic hospital buildings and the Museum of Science, the correctional facility is just another building on the edge of the Charles River, with the Zakim Bridge connecting the West End of Boston to East Cambridge. Looking up, taking in the tower of windows, Nell foolishly hopes Zeke was lucky enough to get a cell with a view.

She's never been inside a jail. None of the television shows and movies she's suffered through watching because Zeke likes a good crime drama have prepared her for this. The visitors' waiting room has a split personality. As much as she tries to calm herself by focusing on the ordinary chairs and white walls, it's jarring when police officers appear out of nowhere, their guns and handcuffs and night-sticks strapped to their waists at her eye level.

Of the dozen or so women in the room, most are checked out, glued to phones or feigning sleep. But more than a few give Nell the once-over without pretense. She doesn't want them figuring out how they might know her, but unlike a doctor's waiting room, there aren't any magazines or newspapers, and people watching here feels dangerous.

Across from Nell, a woman in her thirties leans forward, tattooed elbows on her knees. "You the mother of that kid that got found?" The smell of hard liquor on the woman's breath chokes Nell, making it hard for her to find words. All she can do is nod and wonder when she might be able to have a drink of her own.

The whole room wakes up. Suddenly everyone is staring at her.

"You think your man kidnapped 'em?" The woman annunciates each word like she's singing a country song, packing a punch on the words *your man*.

"I wouldn't be here if I did," Nell says.

Several of the women crack smiles; three of them laugh outright.

"Yeah, none of our guys did what they're in here for either, right, ladies?"

Nell looks toward the glass partition, willing the officer to call her name.

"She all right, your lucky girl?" the woman asks.

"I think so," Nell says. "She's a strong person."

The words *"I am not"* pound out a rhythm in Nell's head. She wants to shout it out to the circle of women. Instead, she mutters, "I have to go."

Nell is halfway to the door when her name is called. Now the police officers raise their heads and stare. The visitation room is closer than the door to the street. Nell chooses Zeke.

After she is wanded and her bag confiscated, a female officer runs gloved hands up her legs and under her breasts, and she is led into a small room with no windows. It's hard to breathe when she sees him.

Zeke sits in a chair on one side of a steel table bolted to the floor. He's wearing a jumpsuit the color of cement, his hands and feet tethered by shackles. Nell has the urge to reach out and smooth down his wild hair.

An emotionless guard stands sharp-eyed in one corner of the room. "No touching," he says.

Nell takes her seat.

"You're growing a beard," she says.

"I thought it went well with the suit."

Appalled that these are the first words they've exchanged in a week, she whispers. "I should've come sooner."

Until now she's always believed that if she could only be more patient and generous, less sensitive to his slights, Zeke would finally be able to give her what she wanted: love without deception. As many times as she's chosen forgiveness, each betrayal left a stain. Sitting across from him, fully and totally soiled by all his bad choices, Nell realizes the only person she cares about now is Tali.

"How is she?" Zeke asks.

"Up and down. Like Dr. Rawlins said she would be." Nell doesn't say that most of the downs have to do with him.

The trouble with Zeke happened over time and began with imperceptible things. Like water cuts a path over ground, the divide between them went from a stream to a river, until it forced each of them to opposite banks. She never wanted Tali to have to pick a side, but now that she has, it's Nell's job to help her live with it.

"Tali doesn't want to talk to you. You need to stop calling her."

"I know. She hung up on me the minute she heard my voice."

"Can you blame her? This whole thing with you being here—it's surreal." Nells uses a harsh tone. She wants to come out with things she's learned to keep to herself.

Zeke unclasps his hands and moves them flat on the table; the clink of his cuffs, metal against metal, accentuate Nell's point.

"All publicity is good publicity, right?"

"What's wrong with you? Tali wants to be known because she's good. Because she's great. This isn't anything close to what she wants. It isn't what I want." Nell clenches her jaw, afraid if she unloads on him she'll never be able to stop.

"Nell, come on. I'm not trying to piss you off. This isn't easy for me. I'm glad you came," Zeke says.

This is hard for him? Here we go.

"I've done terrible things." Zeke pauses as if the next words are trapped in his throat.

"What?"

"Criminal things."

"Shh, don't say that." Nell lowers her own voice, as if the guard nearby isn't trained to hear confessions from wherever he stands.

She waits for the tears. Or for the dam that holds back her rage to finally let go. There's no explanation for the absence of feeling.

"After you kept me from getting at our money. Your money. I got involved with some bad people—so I could gamble."

"Oh, Zeke, what did you do?" Now the floodgates open. Nell is crying, wiping her eyes with the back of her hand.

"When I couldn't pay them back what I owed, they threatened me. My only way out now is to tell police what I know."

There it is, confirmation she should've severed things with him a long time ago.

"I need you to tell me you weren't at the beach with the girls."

"Of course not. No. But these guys know where we live. They know where Tali goes to school."

"You brought them into our house? Near our child?"

"Never when she was home. I swear."

"What about the jacket?" Nell asks.

Zeke drops his head.

Nell bangs her fists on the table. "What about the jacket? How did it get into our closet looking like that?"

"I was as surprised as you were to see it. I haven't laid eyes on that thing in forever. The person Tali described to police, the guy she says threw them in the car, I think I know who that is. My best guess is that he took it from the house at some point, and then put it back to implicate me. Or to give me a warning. I was never at the beach, Nell. I didn't hurt Tali or June. But there's no question about it. This is all my fault."

"You're a horrible liar. You're making this up. This is an outrageous story even coming from you."

"I am horrible and I am a liar. Except it's the truth. We'll all be better off with me in here, or wherever else I land. I'm being interviewed this afternoon."

"If you implicate these men, you won't be safe even here. Have you talked to your lawyer?"

"No, have you?"

"Don't you dare put this on me. This is not my mess. It's never my mess."

"I know. But I need help. It's why I'm coming clean. To police. And to you."

Zeke straightens his fingers out toward her and she can feel the heat from his hands across the table. He's trying to hold her without touch.

"I love you," he says. "I have always loved you. I screwed up big this time, but I never meant to hurt you or Tali. I didn't set out to do any of this damage to our family. We can get through this. I know we can. I'm going to ask to be somewhere near you and Tali as part of my plea deal."

"This is not happening."

It's a relief for Nell to suddenly realize that just because she can stand by him, doesn't mean she should.

"I could say I'm cutting you off for Tali's sake. Because that's true—I am. She's been through enough because of you. But I won't pretend I'm not also doing it for me. I won't say I'm all right or that I forgive you—you're on your own."

The guard steps forward and says "Time's up. Say goodbye to the wife."

Nell doesn't wait to hear another word from Zeke. She uses the last sturdy thing about her to get up and walk out.

17

An Impossible Cure

MOMENTS AFTER CYN ends the phone call with Fitz, agreeing to meet him for coffee, his sister materializes in her new Boston College office. Keira Jameson holds a colorful ceramic bowl filled with an elegant orchid.

"I'd say welcome to Campion Hall," Keira says, "but your guilty face is throwing me. Please tell me you weren't talking to Noah."

Keira's concern is touching, and her kindness the only constant in Cyn's life right now.

"Don't worry. I want nothing to do with him." Cyn steps around a stack of boxes to accept the gift.

"If you promise to keep it that way," Keira says, "I could fix you up with someone much nicer."

"And who would that be? Like I don't already know."

Keira throws her shoulders back in mock indignation. "You forget I am Southie born and raised. Fitz isn't the only fine Irishman I can think of for you. Although I will say he's the most talented. And you have to admit my brother is cute."

"In all seriousness, you didn't tell Fitz about Noah, did you?"

"I might have." Keira pushes a pile of interoffice envelopes off to one side of a table, to make room for the plant.

"How in the world did that come up?"

"I thought you two looked kinda cozy the other night, and after you left, I might've told him that you weren't seeing anybody right now. Blame it on the bourbon—the story slipped out."

Cyn doesn't need to ask Keira which part. Anybody telling it would cut right to the sensational climax.

The night everything fell apart, Cyn had finished work before seven. Noah stayed behind to see one more patient. As he ushered an anxious twenty-something into his office, he told Cyn that if she could wait to eat, he'd grab some Thai takeout on his way home. Using his body to block his client's view, he'd kissed her and whispered, "Love you."

At first, walking to their apartment ten blocks east of the office brownstone, Cyn looked forward to having a little time to herself. A comfy nightgown, curled up with a good book sounded good to her. Except the later it got without Noah at home, the more bent out of shape she became. When he didn't answer his phone, irritation turned to panic. Quickly dressing in jeans and a sweater, Cyn retraced the route Noah would've taken to get home. The Thai place they frequented had closed already, and without anyone inside, there was no way to find out if he'd even made it that far. Cyn started to run.

At the office brownstone, she took the elevator to their suite. The simplest explanation was that a dog-tired Noah had lost track of time, writing session notes. That had happened before. Except those times he'd always answered his phone.

The waiting room was empty, and though her office was dark, his was dimly lit. Now that she knew he was okay, Cyn wasn't about to hold back. She'd lay into to him for scaring her, for being so thoughtless.

At first it was impossible to make sense of what she was seeing. And then it wasn't. Noah and his seven o'clock patient were wrapped in each other's arms, sound asleep on the floor. Her dress wrongly buttoned. The snap on his pants undone and the zip of his fly at half-mast.

"I'm sorry," Keira says, breaking into Cyn's trance. "My ma always said this mouth of mine would be the death of me. Say something. Please."

"It's okay." She couldn't blame Keira for gossiping. She might be tempted to do it too if the whole thing weren't so tawdry, and if it wasn't her life.

Cyn shifts the piles of papers from one corner of the desk to the other, inadvertently uncovering the receipt from Castle Storage. The place in South Boston where all her office treasures sit in a heap, getting dusty in the dark.

"It doesn't matter. I'm not with Noah now. And I'm not interested in your brother either. I'm going to concentrate on myself for a while."

"Will you forgive me for squealing to Fitz if I help you get this place shipshape?" Keira asks. "My next class doesn't start for an hour."

"There's nothing to forgive. Plus, I have a client coming. We're going to work on the office together."

Cyn's tack with her reunification clients is to put them to work. To see how each girl copes with doing ordinary things, bumping up against everyday demands and inevitable frustrations.

"Tali Carrington's coming here?"

"You know I can't talk about my clients."

"I get it," Keira says, tidying papers on the desk, scanning the list of items Cyn has placed in storage. "Even though we're friends *and* colleagues, you can't trust me now because I blabbed to my brother."

"That's not it at all."

"Yes, it is. You already told me you handed off all your other clients to different doctors. You're pissed at me. Go ahead. Let me have it."

"I'm not angry. You're the only person who's been there for me. As far as friends go, beggars can't be choosers."

Keira's joyful laugh rings out in the office. "You can be quite funny when you want to be."

Cyn shakes her head and exaggerates a smile. "Yeah, I'm a laugh riot."

"I'll miss you squatting in my office before classes," Keira says. "Now that you've gone from adjunct to full professor and have this snazzy office all to yourself, I'll probably never see you."

"Yes, very snazzy." Cyn's been trying not to obsess over the reality of her space. The room with its cinder block walls and low ceiling is nothing more than an oversized shoe box. "You have my permission to come in here to annoy me anytime you like."

"Are you sure you don't want any of your things from the Beacon Street office? Your bookcase would look great over there." Keira points to a narrow space next to the window. "Or maybe replace that shabby table with one of your own."

In the years they've been friends, Keira's always been easy for Cyn to talk to. That doesn't mean she tells her everything. Like how much she misses their things. Noah's leather chair. Her Tiffany lamp. How foolish would she sound if she admitted to aching for their couch?

Cyn takes the storage unit receipt from the top of the pile Keira made and places it inside a desk drawer. "I'll make this work for now."

"Can I say one more thing, and then I'll shut up?" The Keira she knows isn't asking for permission as much as preparing Cyn to hear something out of bounds.

"Should I sit for this?"

"In all seriousness, I know you're starting a new chapter here. But what you've done for so many girls over the years is remarkable."

The catch in Keira's voice, the change in her otherwise cheery demeanor, moves Cyn.

"What's the matter?"

"Nothing. I just wish I had someone like you to talk to when I was in high school, that's all," Keira says.

"Did something bad happen?"

"We lost a family friend when I was eighteen. She was the same age as June Danforth."

"I'm sorry. That's awful."

"Back then, no one thought kids like me needed someone to lean on. I had to figure things out on my own. I want you to know, I think Tali's lucky to have you."

Keira's friendship is exuberant and honest and exactly what Cyn needs. "I'm here to listen whenever you want. It's the least I can do."

"It's a story for another day. Get me drunk and I'll probably spill the whole scandalous thing. Well, anyway, welcome to Campion Hall," Keira says, trying to be cheerful.

At the sound of a knock, both women turn to find Tali and Nell standing in the doorway, acting awkward, as if they've overheard some part of the conversation.

Despite her penchant for inserting herself in Cyn's social life, Keira is a consummate professional. Without introducing herself—potentially generating questions about a last name that matches a certain detective's—she says something innocuous and polite and she's off, making room for Nell and Tali in the crowded space.

"You weren't kidding. You really do need help." Nell takes in the disarray of the office. Tali lifts the lid on a box and sighs like she's wondering what she's gotten herself into.

"When the movers came, I wasn't here to orchestrate where to put things." Cyn says. "I appreciate Tali helping me begin to sort it out."

"As long as I'm back at school by three thirty." The girl's rosy cheeks and bright eyes have her looking healthier and more relaxed than she did during Monday's session. A good sign given, as far as Cyn knows, taking the T to the Chestnut Hill campus is the first time Tali's been anywhere but home and school, and that one trip to the beach, since they met.

"You have my word," Cyn says.

Nell clears her throat and turns to her daughter. "Want me to wait? I could walk around a little, then grab us coffees. We could go back downtown together."

"Dr. Rawlins doesn't want you to." Tali drops her backpack on top of a box. "I mean, this is part of what I'm supposed to do. On my own. Right?"

"Tali will be fine," Cyn says. "I'll be sure she makes her rehearsal. Isn't that what you have to get back for?"

"I always have rehearsal." There's a lift in Tali's voice, a high note of pride she takes in stating this as fact.

Nell waves goodbye like she's leaving her child at a playdate, willing Tali to have a good time.

With little direction, Tali is efficient shelving books and arranging chairs. Cyn is quiet, giving her space, waiting for her to bring up what's on her mind.

"Why don't you have any personal things to put around your office?" Tali asks.

"I have a few. They're here somewhere." Cyn opens and closes one box after another until she finds the one that holds the gifts she's been given by former patients. "Here we go. Want to see?"

Tali walks toward her and peers inside. Cyn encourages her to dig around, to take things out if she wants. She removes a framed piece of artwork. In the foreground, painted on a piece of old newsprint is an open black umbrella. Colorful raindrops in the form of the words *responsible*, *enraged*, and *hopeful* take up the rest of the page.

"I like this. It's sad and it's not."

"The artist who gave it to me said she was inspired by a word association we did once."

"She was your patient? What happened to her?"

"I can't go into it. You wouldn't want me to talk to other people about your ordeal, right?"

"I don't think I'd care." Tali props the painting between some books in a prominent place on the bookshelf. "Is she doing okay now?"

"She is. You seem better too, since the last time I saw you."

"I'm all right. Are you going to do that word thing with me?"

"If you're interested, sure. It's simple. You come up with three words to describe yourself, and together we figure out why you chose them."

"Does self-sufficient count as one or two?" Tali steps into the light from the window, making it hard for Cyn to read her face, to know if she's teasing or serious.

"Let's call it one," Cyn says. "Tell me what that means to you."

"I'm independent. I don't mind being on my own. Good thing."

"Why's that?"

"Have you met my parents? Even when my dad's not gambling, I can't count on him. I act more like an adult than he does."

It's the most pointed thing Tali has said about her father so far. If she's ready to talk about the innumerable ways he's let her down, she'll steer the conversation back to him.

"What about your mother?" Cyn asks. "Is she there for you?"

"Mom and I don't fight, but it's not like we're best friends. She thinks she's protecting me when she won't tell me things about my dad. But I'm not a little kid. And I hate the way she checks out after she's had a couple glasses of wine. It's not like she gets drunk or anything. It's more like she stops listening."

"When we met that first time at your house, you said you and your mom talk."

Tali drops into Cyn's desk chair and spins one full rotation. "I wasn't sure I wanted to meet with you."

"I'm glad you decided to give me a chance. It sounds like your parents can be unpredictable."

"That's a good way to put it."

"What would it look like if your mom was honest with you?"

No answer, Tali pushes off the desk chair. "We should move this table next to the window. Your mail and keys can go in the drawer. And the plant needs sun."

Cyn lets Tali direct the session, and together they move furniture. After the table is in place, they shift the desk and chair with an eye toward perfect symmetry.

Tali stands back to take in the changes. "That's better."

"Have you thought of your second word?" Cyn asks.

"Disciplined."

"I remember you telling me about the dedication it takes to act and sing. To memorize your lines and all the staging."

"That, and you have to constantly work to be better, to stand out. Before I started Arts High, not everyone got how much you have to give up to be good. Most of my friends get it now because they feel the same way. It's worth it." Tali looks right at Cyn. "I shouldn't have worried before, when I thought I might not want to still do it. Because when I'm acting, nothing else matters."

"Does Sam feel like you do?"

"He used to." Tali pauses as though she's waiting to see if Cyn will probe further. But she doesn't speak or move, leaving room for stillness to do its magic.

"He's worse lately. Mostly because of June."

"Was Sam having a hard time before June died?"

Tali goes quiet again, and this time, Cyn does nudge her. "You can tell me. I don't share what we talk about with anyone. The only exception would be if Sam is planning to hurt himself. Is he?"

"Not on purpose. No."

"But he's doing risky things?" Cyn steadies her voice. She is practiced at not shutting girls down by pressing too hard.

"Party drugs mostly."

"Does anyone else know what he's doing? Someone who could help him?"

"Our director knows. You should see the way he tortures him."

"That's probably not the best way to help him. How about you?"

"I've tried to get him to stop. I help him constantly with the play. Learning his lines and trying to find his character."

"I didn't mean you should try to make him stop. As much as you might want to, you're not responsible for his choices."

"Oh, you're asking me if I use? Don't worry. The only thing I'm addicted to is acting." Tali offers a weak smile. "I'm not like them. Sam and my dad. I can't even stand how numb I feel on that stupid Klonopin you gave me."

"How much are you taking now?"

"I let my mom think I take them at night, but I'm not. I'm lucky to be in this play. And I won't let anything screw up this one good thing. Is that awful to say?"

There is the inner strength Cyn recognized running beneath the surface. "Not at all," she says. "But what's the harm in telling your mom the truth?"

"She'd make it into a big deal. I mean how many times can I say I don't know what happened that night, or the next day on the beach? I told her what you said, that remembering isn't always the most important thing. I'll be fine if people let me power through."

"Sounds like you're angry."

"I don't feel rage like she did." Tali walks toward the bookshelf and the painting she'd only moments ago positioned there.

"Maybe not," Cyn says. "But maybe you could allow for the possibility that deep down you do. Or that someday you will be very angry about everything you've been through. And I'm not talking about the abduction and losing June."

"You want me to say how pissed I am at my dad for absolutely everything? Or at my mom because she didn't tell me she protected our money from him? She could've saved me from all the times I worried we were about to go broke because of his crappy choices. Or maybe you want me to say how embarrassed I am that everyone knows my father's in fucking jail."

"I'm not here to make you say anything. Unless you want to."

"Well, I don't." She reaches into a box and pulls out a handful of books, loudly clacking their spines against wood as she shelves them.

"This is a place for you to take charge, Tali. Even if all it involves is where to put a table and some books. That especially goes for what you want to talk about."

"This thing you do—having girls do stuff with you so you can figure out how they are—it's kind of weird. Wouldn't meeting me at school to see me rehearse the play accomplish the same thing?"

"Given the words you've chosen, I'll bet you can see the value in getting out of your comfort zone. I want to give you a safe space to do that, some place away from home and school."

"Do you like the words I picked?"

"I'm surprised you didn't say *talented*."

"I haven't told you my third one yet." Tali lowers her head and shoots Cyn a sidelong glance. She is definitely playing coy now.

"That's it, then? You pick *talented*?"

"I think I like *bold* better. Not all talented people are successful. I know what I've chosen to do with my life isn't going to be easy. You have to take risks to be noticed and get cast in high-profile shows. Whether it's the roles I go after or the way I tackle a character, I need to be confident and daring."

"You certainly are that. I was mesmerized by your performance the other day. I hope you know I'm not just saying that."

Tali lights up as if she could live for two months on the compliment.

"I think that's enough unpacking for today," Cyn says. "Let's get you back to school."

"You don't have to come with me."

"I promised your mother. And I have a meeting downtown anyway."

Tali reaches into the bottom front pocket of her backpack. "Do you have a T pass? I have an extra CharlieCard if you need it."

"I'm all set," Cyn says, producing one of her own from her purse.

Side by side, they walk across campus, down the hill to the inbound stop where they'll hop a trolley train to Back Bay.

Within minutes of standing on the platform, one arrives, mostly filled with students jostling backpacks, like Tali. The green line is known for being fairly clean and mostly safe, but with never enough seats for its riders, it isn't easy to move into the car. Some people are notorious for exercising what little control they have in their lives by being non-budgers. Making an effort to stay together, Cyn and Tali find a pole with space enough for two.

"If my mom were here and you did that word thing with her, I'm pretty sure one of hers would be *uptight*. She hates the T."

Before Cyn can lightheartedly ask Tali not to weaponize the exercise against unwitting family members, they're interrupted.

"Hey, you're that kid who got kidnapped. Natalie something?"

"Tali Carrington."

A group of teenagers, a boy and three girls, both younger and older than Tali, crowd around her.

Protectively, Cyn steps closer too, worried Tali will be overwhelmed by the attention. She waits and watches, gauging whether to ask them to give her some space.

But Tali accommodates them. The vibe she gives off is friendly.

A young woman too old to be wearing a headband bedecked with daisies and bows hangs on Tali's every word. "It must've been the worst."

"Seriously." The boy in the group accentuates his disgust by repeatedly hoisting his messenger bag onto his hip.

"I miss June," Tali says. "But I think she'd want me to keep acting, you know?"

Passengers in the seats around them begin to whisper. A woman standing next to Cyn, patting the round ball of an infant kangarooed to her chest, leans in. "Who is she?"

Right before entering the underground tunnel, the train comes to an abrupt stop, throwing Cyn against the pole she's been gripping. Tali never loses her footing.

As the girls in the group move closer to Tali to hear her talk about school and her play, a gap opens in the crowd. That's when Cyn sees Noah. He's in a rear-facing seat with his head down, reading a book.

Between the bumpy ride and the act of whipping her head—to the left to make sure Tali's okay, and to the right to get a closer look at Noah—Cyn is dizzy.

Noah is less commanding somehow, sitting there. His shoulders less broad; his posture less confident; his hair too long, with tiny black curls covering his ears. When Noah was with her, he preferred a clean cut and close shave.

Cyn wills him to turn around so she can see how he is, but when he does, she steps in front of Tali to avoid being seen. The longer Cyn debates what she wants, the more her uneasiness progresses from cold sweat to tight chest.

Meanwhile, Tali, in a gesture neither showy nor shy, digs into her backpack, pulling from it a handful of colorful flyers announcing *Spring Awakening*. She hands one out to each of the kids gathered around. "We're totally going to sell out. My director had to move the play from our school theater to Holden Hall next door."

The girl with the headband pulls out a pen. "Can you sign mine?"

"Mine too," says the boy with the recalcitrant bag.

Cyn has an urgent need to get off the train right as it pulls into their stop, Copley Station. In slow motion, she watches Noah stand and turn and move toward the door closest to her.

It isn't him.

Stepping from the train, Cyn is unsteady and sorrowful. Her mind is a trickster. All that talk about Noah with Keira must have evoked him. She's more out of sorts than the patient she's treating.

Crisp fall air hits her face when she reaches the top of the escalator, and she's grateful for it. Out of the tunnel, up above ground, she can finally take a deep breath.

"How did I do?" Tali asks.

"Sorry?"

"At your office and taking the T. Did I pass the test?" Tali steps in front of Cyn and keeps talking, walking backward. The gesture is lively and warm, and something about it reminds Cyn that what she mostly feels these days is lonely.

"Not everything is a test," Cyn says. "Although, 'as in stones and in water, you are ceaselessly being changed.'"

"Hey." Tali smiles wide, immediately getting the reference. "You read *The Seagull*."

"You inspired me. I have to say I like it even more now than I did when I read it in college."

When they reach the school, a much shyer Tali pulls a flyer from her backpack. "Opening night's in a week. Maybe you could come."

Without waiting for Cyn to answer, Tali opens the stage door and disappears inside the theater.

18

True Love Lies

THEY'RE USING THE massive window next to Fitz's desk as the Danforth investigation board. Their motley crew doesn't rate enough to take over the conference room. With Zeke Carrington in custody, everyone but Fitz thinks this thing's in the bag.

One side of the glass is covered in press-and-stick easel paper, blocking out all traces of sunlight. On it, Fitz is listing evidence they have and questions they don't have answers to.

"No surprise, early labs have Carrington's DNA on the jacket, along with a number of unidentified hair samples that forensics is still working on. They've confirmed June Danforth's blood on the sleeve. What's nagging me is that Charlie Stockbridge said he found June on her back, when the autopsy says she died facedown," Fitz says. "What else are we missing?"

Ross stands next to him in front of the other half of the window, covered by a compilation of maps, Back Bay to

South Shore. He's drawing red dots and blue lines with Sharpies, plotting the movements of Tali and June from the night they were abducted to the night they were found. Neither of the girls' cells has been recovered from the scene, which means Ross is working from phone records and tower pings. One map is a zoom-in view of the city around the school; the other, a closeup of the location around Watties Beach in Scituate. Each speck and dash bears a time stamp and coordinates signposting the story of two girls missing two days.

Detective Doyle sits at his desk in front of a computer, slurping a milkshake and stacking pencils Jenga style.

"Doyle, did you find anything that stands out on June's social footprint?" Fitz asks.

"Can't say I have," he says.

"Why is it taking so long to get the forensics report on her laptop?"

"Good question."

Ross suggests an addition to Fitz's list, without looking away from his maps. "Do we really believe Carrington got rid of his laptop?"

Fitz stands there, looking at all they've got besides his notebook with its missing posters, duplicate crime scene photographs, and handwritten memos.

"I'd like to know if there's any evidence June did drugs," he says. "Is the reason Tali can't remember anything because she did drugs?"

Fitz tosses a notepad on the desk in front of Doyle. "Make a list. I need you to follow up with forensics on June's laptop and her tox screen. And I need the paperwork to request access to Tali's medical records. I'll put in a call to the team working on what was found at the beach, and requestion Sam Wallace."

The cell phone on the desk lights up, turning Doyle's face a sickly shade of blue. He doesn't look up or say anything as he picks it up to take the call.

"Hang on," he says. His knees and hips are so riddled with arthritis, it takes him a while to extricate himself from the desk chair. His agility, or lack of it, is a constant reminder of why the guy sits around marking time.

Once he disappears around the corner, Ross puts a hand on Fitz's arm. "What's with the tunnel vision? You've got a bee in your bonnet over that kid."

"I'm telling you, he's evasive and his story has holes. I think he knows something."

Fitz has no plans to admit to Ross that Sam is tangled up in his mind with Connor. That his gut tells him there's more to it than just a resemblance to his brother.

"Never decide in advance who's involved, or you'll miss who did it," Ross says.

"You're one to talk. That's what you're doing, focusing on Carrington."

"No, you little shit. Think about what was done and what anybody else had to gain by doing it. The evidence keeps rolling in, and it implicates Carrington."

"Well, I'm not backing off until all our questions are answered."

"When was the last time you read your damn messages or listened to your voicemail?" Ross asks.

Fitz pulls out his phone and taps notifications. He's got two missed calls from the DA's office and a string of unread emails.

"They want to move forward with obstruction and felony drug charges against Carrington," Ross says. "He's admitted to selling for two guys he owes money to. One of them claims Carrington's full of it, though. Says he's the one who's been taking their money but never coming through with the pills. The dealer matches the description of the kidnapper, and surprise, surprise, that guy can't furnish an alibi."

"They're waiting on us before indicting him?"

"Exactly. DA wants us to button this up and pass everything off to prosecutors tomorrow. Monday at the latest."

Fitz checks the time, remembering his meeting with Cyn. "I hate to do this, but I've got to go."

"You better not be leaving me and Doyle to do the dirty work so you can feed your obsession with that kid."

"I'm not. I'll be in first thing tomorrow to help pack it up."

On the stairs, out of view from Ross, Fitz skims his unread email, stopping on one with the Danforth name and case number in the subject line. He opens it and reads:

Prelims on the pill bottle confirm it contains a mixture of drugs. Specifics of the toxicology are pending, but we put a rush on pulling prints. Will try to call you by five.

Fitz clicks on the attached jpeg to find a close up of the bottle found at the beach. Oxycodone, eighty milligrams, one hundred tablets, no refills. The pharmacy that filled it and the patient name don't ring any bells.

When he finally makes it to The Bean on Stuart Street, it takes him a while to spot Cyn at a table by the window. Seeing her there, all back to business, her hair pinned high and her suit buttoned up, Fitz realizes that he'd hoped to see her the way she looked that night at The Beehive, her hair brushing her shoulders, blouse open to reveal her slender neck. The way those damn heels accentuated the shape of her legs.

Fitz makes some noise as he maneuvers between tables in this hipster spot. Kids from the high school and other artsy types sit drinking their high-priced coffees and eating their sandwiches without meat. She's a jumpy person, so Fitz is careful not to startle her.

Cyn has her back to him, facing the brick wall lined with the work of local artists. She's lost in an oil abstract of something that resembles either a field of poppies or a crime scene. Fitz wonders what she sees.

"Hey," he says.

Her hands cup a wide-bellied mug a little bit tighter. "There you are," Cyn says.

Fitz can't tell if she's happy he came or pissed that he's late.

"Sorry. I got tied up with a case." Fitz motions to the waitress that he'll have a cup of coffee. "Thanks for meeting me."

When he slides into the leather banquette across from Cyn, his butt makes a loud squeaking sound. He's been here all of two minutes and he's already embarrassed himself.

"You said you had questions about parents and teenagers."

"I do. Not everything at that school is on the up and up." Fitz reaches into his pocket, pulls out his wallet, and slides a dollar bill across the table to her. "I'm not being cheap here; I only want to make it official."

Cyn slides the bill back in his direction. "I'm not a lawyer. I don't work on retainer."

"I don't have authority to get you under contract as a consultant with the BPD. I'm just a detective who needs to catch a break."

"I didn't say I wouldn't help you. If you want to talk to me as a forensic psychiatrist, I'm fine with that. But I'll save you the trouble about asking anything about Tali. You won't be able to charm me into talking about her."

"You'll let me pick your brain about my theories of the case gratis?

"Consider it a professional courtesy."

"Keira's right. You're a sweetheart."

At the mention of Keira's name, Cyn sits up straighter and looks away, the paintings on the wall a convenient escape. *What the hell, Keira? What did you tell her?* After the waitress drops off Fitz's coffee and refills Cyn's mug, he gets to it. "How often do stage mothers cross the line into murder?"

"Wow. When you say you have questions, you have questions. I assume you're talking about Sam's mother."

"What makes you think I'm talking about Ana and not Nell?"

"You told me the other day you think Sam knows something. And because, even to a lay observer, Ana shows all the classic signs of maternal narcissism. Nell does not."

"You're telling me 'stage mother' is a disease?"

"Competition among parents is definitely a thing, but it's typically not diagnostic. The profile is exceedingly rare, and even then the majority of the time it doesn't involve murder. The media eats up the dramatic cases. Like Wanda Webb Holloway. The cheerleader's mother who hired her brother-in-law to murder the rival's mother. Her twisted logic was that the girl would be so overcome with grief over her mother's death that she'd drop out of the competition."

"What happened?"

"The brother-in-law couldn't go through with it in the end and went to police. Then there's the Ramsey case. A friend of mine from grad school lives near Boulder and was one of the investigating forensic psychiatrists. Patsy fit the stage mother archetype to a tee, but there's a difference of opinion on whether or not that translated into murder."

"Would a kid protect his mother at all cost? Like some say Burke Ramsey did or like Sam might be doing?"

"Family bonds are like no other. People will hold onto all kinds of horrible secrets for the people they love."

Now Fitz is the one who can't look her in the eyes.

"Okay, let's say Ana had the girls kidnapped," Fitz says. "She wanted Sam to be the standout star. From what I hear, both Tali and June had potential to steal the show. The stakes on opening night for these kids, with talent scouts and Hollywood agents in the audience, are through the roof. Ana wanted Robin Chandler to get the part, a kid who's good, but not great. Maybe, like Wanda, she hired someone to kidnap the girls. She's got the money. If the thing went down before casting, once Tali and June were found, they'd be too distraught to be in the play. No harm. No foul. Except June died."

"You think Sam is acting guilty because he knows his mother orchestrated this? And now she's forcing him to cover for her?"

"That's one of my theories."

"What's the other one?"

"The director bothers me too. What if Normand was trying to drum up attention for his play? What if he kidnapped the girls as a stunt, and things went terribly wrong?"

"Even if he had nothing to do with it, that part worked," Cyn says.

"What do you mean?"

"Tali says there's so much attention around the play that the director had to move it to a bigger theater. And it's still selling out."

"Really?"

"I'm not breaching confidentiality. You could've found that out without my help." It's like Cyn is weighing her potential conflicts of interest out loud.

Fitz doesn't want her ruminating so long she stops helping him. "Sam says the director made a point of sending him and the accompanist home early, leaving him alone with the girls."

"Wouldn't Tali and June have recognized their director if he was the one who abducted them?" Cyn asks.

"Not if he had someone else do it. Or if he wore a hat or hood or something. And not if he drugged them before they left the school."

Fitz takes out his flip pad and makes a note to ask forensics to compare Normand's DNA against what's on the jacket. More than ever he needs to see the toxicology reports on June and Tali.

"After the girls left, Normand could've slipped out the Comm Ave exit, come at them from behind, and shoved them into a parked car without Tali or June knowing what hit them. It's the only side of the school without surveillance cameras. He would have known that."

"That sounds far-fetched," Cyn says.

"Maybe, but Tali told us she didn't get a good look at the guy. All she said was that it was a man who pushed them into the car. After that she can't remember anything."

"Fair enough."

"If I listen to my gut, what nags me most is Sam and his mother. My theory is no crazier than the one everybody else is working from."

"About Zeke you mean? Or can't you tell me?"

"No, I can. It'll be all over the news soon enough. Carrington confessed to doctor-shopping for opioids and selling drugs to gamble. He gave up two dealers to prosecutors. They'll deny everything related to the girls. But the drug charges will stick."

For a fraction of a second, Cyn looks right at Fitz, then crosses her arms.

"You don't seem surprised that Zeke sells drugs," he says. "I suppose if Tali told you, you wouldn't be able to say so."

"That's right. I wouldn't. But she didn't. It's because there's not a lot about what men do that can surprise me anymore."

"I know you can't divulge what she's told you. But you've been doing this work for a while. Am I wrong to be looking at Sam and what he might be able to tell me about his mother?"

"I wouldn't dare weigh in on your job, but in my professional opinion, there is reason to worry about Sam. All I will say is that sometimes appearances can be deceiving. Think about the last time you saw him. How did he seem to you?"

"Irritable and agitated. Distracted. He was sweating like crazy. Wait, Sam does drugs?"

"You didn't hear it from me. But maybe those symptoms aren't signs of guilt."

Fitz feels like an idiot. Did he concoct a story around a kid who's a pillhead? All of this because the cocky son-of-a-bitch reminds him of his brother.

When his phone vibrates, he pulls it out of his pocket to see who's calling. "State lab," he says to Cyn. "I've been waiting for this."

A CSI tech Fitz has never met makes a good first impression. "One set of prints on the pill bottle belongs to Zeke Carrington, the other sets remain unidentified," the guy says. "The chemical residue inside contains a mix of opioids, ecstasy, and ketamine."

"You'll send all that to me in a report? Great." Fitz thanks the tech and ends the call.

"You don't look happy. Is it bad news?" Cyn leans toward him, her face inches from his. God, she is mesmerizing.

"Look, there are things I'd love to share with you too."

"I get it. You can't." she says, trying to hide her disappointment.

Fitz reaches out to take her hand. "I'd like to see you again, though. Take you someplace nice."

Cyn draws back, adjusting the sleeves of her blouse. "What, you don't like the place I picked?"

"I'm talking about a real date. No work talk."

"I don't think so."

"If you're worried about that night at The Beehive, when I indulged in a little too much whiskey, well, given everything, I want you to know I don't usually drink like that."

"What do you mean, 'given everything'?"

"Keira probably told you. Our father was a mean drunk."

"Oh. Yes. She did." Cyn pulls her sweater tight around her.

"I'm not like him. I take whatever's bothering me out on pianos, not people."

"You seem like a nice guy, Fitz, but sorry, no."

"Why not?"

"It's not a good time. I'm dealing with a lot right now." Cyn unhooks her purse from the back of her chair and stands. "I've got to go. Good luck with the case."

"Wait. That's it? I have more questions."

Cyn keeps walking. Next thing he knows, she's out of there, and he's sitting with his back against a wall.

19

Brief Encounter

WALKING DOWN MARLBOROUGH Street toward Peter's house, Nell makes a mental note to do something nice for Ana, offer some token of gratitude for yet again looking out for her girl during rehearsal.

Nell can't say when she stopped thinking of Ana as a schemer. It's hard to pinpoint exactly when she started to see the woman's actions as a type of odd generosity, albeit self-serving. When, days after June's death, Ana ushered Nell out of Peter's house—as nice as the offer to drive her home was—it had a whiff of calculation about it. During the short trip, Ana asked in as many ways as a nosy person can if Tali remembered anything about the kidnapping.

On the night of June's wake, Nell was too preoccupied by the scene Zeke was making to fully appreciate Ana corralling the kids out of the funeral home so Peter could grieve in peace.

It's possible she came to trust her motives only days ago, when Ana picked up on Nell's reluctance to let her daughter out of her sight while she went to visit Zeke in jail. Ana's promise to keep an eye on Tali, and her uncanny ability later that day to recite a detailed account of Greg's notes to the cast—proof she'd kept her word—forced Nell to admit she'd misjudged her. It's not that Ana isn't obnoxious at times, driving parents and kids crazy with her endless demands for special treatment of Sam, but who is Nell to talk? She's desperate for others to take exceptional care of her child too.

It's twilight, and though the street is busy with traffic, it's no longer crowded with news vans; there's no police presence. Despite being lost in a sea of tall, narrow brownstones, the flagstone path leading to his door is familiar, lined with yellow and rust dahlias. Nell can almost put herself back three weeks, to a time when there was a world of possibility between them. Dependable, compassionate Peter. A man she can trust. Nell knocks on the door.

It's been a few days since she last saw him, but Peter looks even more unlike himself. Hair tousled, days of stubble, and his shirt untucked and wrinkled. Only his voice, deep and steady, confirms it's him.

"Thanks for coming," he says, opening the door wide.

"Of course. I want to help."

The entry way teems with overflowing black plastic bags. Every table within view is covered with dirty plates, half-filled glasses of water, cups of untouched coffee. Nell's never seen the place like this.

She gestures to the heap of what must be June's things and bends down. "Mind?" With a nod from Peter, she peeks inside the bags. Mostly they are filled with the detritus of life with a daughter. Pairs of sneakers in shades of pink and lime. Lone gloves, sparkly headbands, outstretched scarves. The same board games that could be found in her own spare room at home—Clue, Risk, Life—pull at her heartstrings.

"I can't do her room by myself," Peter says. "Maybe I can't do it at all."

"I'm glad you called me. We don't have to throw a single thing away if you don't want to. We can store it all for now; then, if you change your mind, it'll all be right there. How does that sound?"

"Good. That sounds good." Peter's hand is on her shoulder; the warmth and pressure of it sends a small shudder through her body.

"I think I have a bottle of that shiraz you like," he says. "Want a glass?"

"Sure." Using one of Mei's pretty lacquer trays, Nell collects the plates and cups and glasses, and in two trips manages to get everything to the kitchen and into the dishwasher. Peter goes for the wine.

The bottle he said he had is already open. He pours what's left of the red wine into two glasses and then stands motionless, seemingly unable to figure out where to put them in the face of a kitchen table overflowing with unopened bills and piles of condolence cards. June's laptop, covered in flower power stickers and indie band decals, sits squarely in the middle of the mess.

"I'll get that." Nell moves it aside, thinking she should come over more often. Peter needs her, and it feels good to be attentive to someone who deserves it. She sips the bold red, letting her mouth fill with the bitter taste of wild black fruit. Unearthing a notepad and a pen from under the laptop, Nell begins to make a list. "Which rooms have you gone through already?"

"There's nothing of June's in my room, the master bath, or my study. I checked. All I could bring myself to do was empty the back hall closet."

"That's a start. I can go through the other rooms—the den, the living room, her bathroom—on another day, if you want."

Peter traces the outline of a bright pink daisy stuck to the lid of June's computer. "Her Facebook cover photo is that one of her with me and Mei in Jurong. Want to see it?" Without waiting for an answer, he opens the laptop.

"How did you figure out her passwords?" Nell asks. An image of Zeke's desk with its hidden drawer flashes through her mind.

"Tali told me. I texted her to see if she had any idea what June's might be. Turns out they used each other's laptops all the time."

Nell didn't know they'd been texting. She isn't sure how to feel about Tali not mentioning it.

He clicks the photo of him with his family. June must have been around eight back then. It's one of the last pictures he has of Mei.

Nell wonders how many times a day Peter does this, scroll down June's page. He points out the newest posts. Nearly all of them contain the letters *RIP*.

"Do you want to show me her room? What do you think you might want to do in there?" Nell feels terrible that she can't keep looking at pictures of his daughter and his wife. How in the world is she going to help him clean that room?

Peter pats her hand. "You're good to me, Nell. I should've asked you by now: How's Tali?"

She doesn't move or say anything, willing him not to pull his hand away. But he does.

"It'll hurt me more if you tell me everything's perfect," Peter says. "I know it's not. I know it won't ever be. For either of us."

Nell takes another sip of wine and closes her eyes. Peter is the only person in her life she can be completely honest with, except this conversation is a minefield. The truth about Tali collides with Zeke. And the subject of her husband is without question undiscussable.

"Tali's different. Less upbeat. She's not doing much schoolwork, that I know. She skips classes, and everything she does centers around that damn play. When I'm not with her, I'm anxious all the time. Worried about where she is, even if she's down the hall in the theater. I can only handle being here now because Ana is being Ana. And for once, her obsession with Arts High benefits me."

Nell tries to smile. The topic of Ana used to serve as a wellspring of levity for them. Oddly enough, the woman acted as both point and counterpoint to the oppressiveness of their daughters' school.

"Maybe it won't always be so bad," Peter says as a kind of a wish.

"In some ways we're closer." As Nell says this out loud, she realizes this is only partially true. Their relationship isn't better or worse because of what happened; it's merely altered. They talk about different things.

"Remember when Tali was little and she used to make those faces whenever I'd hold her too long or if I went overboard on rules before letting the girls out to play? Now she lets me hug her. She lets me fret a little. Except the reason I'm needy hangs between us. It's like I got her back and I didn't."

Peter swills the rest of his wine. Devoid of emotion, he stands. "Let's do the room."

"Oh God," Nell says. "I wasn't thinking. That's a terrible thing to say to you of all people."

He slams the glass down on the table. "Maybe you're trying too hard not to talk about Zeke."

Peter moves down the hall toward his daughter's room, and she follows. Outside his bedroom door, he stops abruptly, as if the laundry basket overflowing with sheets and towels is a fallen tree in the middle of a road.

"I managed to wash them," he says. "But I didn't have the energy to fold them or put them back on the bed."

"Here, let me." Nell takes the basket into Peter's room and rests it on one of the side-by-side chairs near the window. Peter stands by his bureau, its surface cluttered with his key ring and wallet, strewn with the ties he wore to the wake and funeral. Mei's jewelry box anchors the disorder, sitting where it's always been.

Nell remembers the lotus pin. The lovely piece placed in and out of that jewelry box so many times, first by Mei and then by her daughter. A treasure never again to sit inside the velvet drawer.

Peter stares at her staring at him. She breaks their awkward connection by making the bed. As the smell of laundry fragrance fills the air, she smooths out the fitted king sheet and turns back the top one. Before she can plump the pillows or adjust the duvet, Peter sits on the edge of the bed, and wrinkles arc out from the impression his body makes. He's in a trance.

Nell sits next to him and places her hand on his knee. "I'm worried about you."

At first, Peter doesn't move or speak. Seconds feel like minutes until she is brave enough to lace her hand in his, sending a tingle up her arm. The last time they were alone— days before half the school's mothers were parked in his kitchen—their bodies were close, and Peter had kissed her. It was the beginning of something, and her longing for him was urgent. It still is. Nell turns to him to caress his face, and he leans into her hand, briefly closing his eyes.

"I saw a future for us," he says. "You and me—and the girls. I truly loved Mei, but I was ready to love again. Because of you."

"We can still be together." Nell squeezes his hand for assurance, a promise that things will get better.

"Dealing with Mei's death was agony. I missed her with every part of me, and I thought rallying for June would be the hardest thing I would ever have to do. But this, this is different. I'm destroyed over losing her."

"You won't ever get over it. But I can be here for you. I'll love you."

"I wish it were that easy. I do. I just can't get past Zeke's involvement. He put our girls in harm's way. We were friends. We took trips together, for heaven's sake. I trusted him." Peter stands like he did in the kitchen. His ability to harness what's left of his energy seems only to come when he's disgusted.

No one knows better than Nell the perils of placing faith in Zeke. The last trip the two families took together, to Paradise Island, had been perfection. Despite trays of tropical drinks everywhere they went and resort casinos around every bend, Zeke drank temperately, and he completely resisted his compulsion to gamble. Nell was flying high. Even Peter and Mei agreed she should be hopeful that his troubles were in the past. Two weeks later, in the dead of a Boston winter, he relapsed. Zeke lost more than the balance of their savings in a single night, leaving her no choice but to sell Parker's Cottage.

All Nell wants now is to be fully free of Zeke, though no part of her wants him to be guilty.

"No matter how we feel about him," Nell says, "we need each other now."

"I can't." Peter is pacing. "I don't know."

"I'll give you all the time you need. But no one can help you through this like I can. I know grief too. We have history." Nell moves toward Peter, though she resists the urge to touch him. "You should know, I cut him off. For good this time."

"Don't be naive." Peter's voice is louder than it's ever been. "This is completely different. It's not about Zeke behaving irrationally or cheating you out of your own money. It all points to him. Don't you see? His recklessness and complete disregard for anyone but himself got my child killed."

This conversation is unlike any other time the two have sounded off about her husband. So why is it that in this terrible, horrible moment, Nell recognizes hope? She's already ended it with Zeke. For herself and for Tali. She will go back to his hiding place and scour his computer. When she finds something that proves once and for all that he did not do what he's been accused of, Peter will come around.

As if to mark the clarity of her purpose, to emphasize that she is on to something, a bell rings.

It's the back door.

Afraid to let him out of her sight, Nell all but drags Peter toward the kitchen. Once there, he drops into the chair she pulls out for him. Within seconds, he's lost once again in June's Facebook page, hitting refresh over and over to see any new posts.

At the door, Detective Jameson looks puzzled to see Nell standing there.

"I came by to give Mr. Danforth an update."

"I'm right here," Peter says from behind her.

Fitz reaches out to shake his hand. "Mind if Mrs. Carrington stays? I have some questions for her too."

20

The Innocent One

I T'S THE FIRST thing Fitz sees when he enters the Danforth kitchen. June's father is tuned out, lifelessly staring at her computer. All this time, he believed the girly-looking laptop was already in evidence.

While Fitz is making small talk, his mind is trying to work out how to ask the father of a dead girl for procedural details. Did Doyle ever confirm it was collected, or did some dipshit in forensics give it back to Danforth before the case even went to prosecutors? Just what he needs, another hitch in the chain.

During the momentary silence, he nervously rejects thing after thing he could say because all of it makes him look like a town clown. No way around it, there's no acceptable excuse for it to be here.

"You've finally come for it, have you?" Peter grips the sides of the laptop as if he expects Fitz to pry it from his hands.

"I'm afraid it's time. Things are falling into place with suspects, but we need to cover all our bases."

At the subtext reference to Zeke, Peter and Nell lock eyes, and a telepathic shorthand passes between them. Fitz might've expected an expression of apology or kindness from her to him, maybe anger from him to her, but both are devoid of emotion.

"It won't be easy to part with it," Peter says.

Despite the house being bigger on the inside than it looks from the street, the kitchen is tight, with barely any clearance between the table and the imposing chairs that surround it. Fitz unhooks the backpack from his shoulder and reaches inside for an evidence bag, then walks behind Nell and drops to one knee beside Peter.

"I know it can be a comfort to look through past pictures and posts. I promise you'll get it back."

"Unless there are surprises." Nell's voice trails off as she staggers back a few steps. She is stopped by the hip-high edge of the counter.

"Sorry. I missed what you said."

"Nothing. June wouldn't have done anything to shock us," she says.

Fitz rethinks bagging the laptop, tucking the plastic pouch under his arm. Peter will be calmer in the presence of photos of his daughter. In the seconds it takes him to straighten up, Fitz looks back and forth between the pair. "I wonder if I can speak freely to the two of you. Together."

Without pause, Nell says, "Sure."

Peter says, "It depends."

Fitz plows ahead. "I'm worried about Sam."

"How so?" Nell pulls out a chair and sits, gesturing for Fitz to do the same.

"Look, I'm no psychiatrist, but I've seen my share of grief-stricken people. I think there's more going on with him."

"Dr. Rawlins says with teenagers the swings can be wild. That's what's happening with Tali. But every time I see Sam, he's very, very down."

Take your time, Fitz tells himself. He's got Nell on the line, but he needs Danforth. Trying not to overplay his curiosity, he brings his hand to his mouth.

"What is it, Detective?" Peter lowers the lid of the laptop enough to focus his attention squarely on him.

"Could Sam have been in trouble before your daughter's death? I thought you'd know because they spent so much time together. Did you ever overhear him talk to her about family problems or see any out-of-whack behavior?"

Danforth is looking at Fitz like he's speaking Gaelic.

"I heard they were dating," Fitz says.

"June and Sam?" Peter asks. "Who told you that?"

Fitz hates being the one to blindside the poor guy.

"It's common knowledge at the school." Fitz looks toward Nell. "Did Tali tell you about June and Sam?"

Peter looks at her, willing her to say she hasn't kept this from him.

"You know what they say about teenagers." Nell looks away. "Parents are the last to know."

"Did she tell you?" Peter presses her.

"I overheard kids talking only after June died. Ana mentioned Sam is taking this hard because he'd fallen for her. Apparently, they were going out or about to be going out."

"Tell me about the mother," Fitz says. "She strikes me as a bit much, you know what I mean?"

"Ana can be high strung," Nell says, "but she's only looking out for her child. There's nothing wrong with that."

Danforth opens the laptop and angles it so Fitz can see June's Facebook page. "There isn't a single picture of her with Sam. He's in a lot of group shots, but most of the time he isn't even standing next to her."

June is a living doll in photo after photo, which makes it hard to believe her page acts as a balm to her father. But then Fitz's mind briefly substitutes Maddie's face for June's, and he is reminded about the photos he keeps. Without them, he might be tempted to let go of her for good.

"Why did you ask about Sam's behavior?" Nell asks.

"I don't know," Fitz says. "Blame it on the things I see day in, day out, but when I think about teenagers, I worry about drugs."

"You think Sam does drugs?"

"Do *you* think Sam does drugs?" Fitz asks.

"I have no idea." Nell crosses her arms and leans back hard, telling him this is not the first time she's wondered about what's going on with him.

"I have to ask the questions," Fitz says. "There's another reason I stopped by."

Peter looks at him with a pleading stare, begging Fitz not to drop another bomb.

"In her statement to Detective Ross, Tali said she didn't remember anything after she and June were forced into the car. I've got to rule out that they weren't in some kind of altered state. We're waiting on June's toxicology results. I was wondering if you'd release Tali's emergency room records to me."

"My daughter does not do drugs. Except for the medication Dr. Rawlins prescribed for her. She doesn't even drink."

"I'm not accusing your kids of anything. But if their lab work is positive for things like sedatives, or say, Rohypnol, we need to know."

"If you're not saying the girls took something on their own, are you suggesting someone could've given it to them? Without them knowing?" Like someone slapped Peter awake, he is wholly out of his stupor, making connections Fitz didn't think he was capable of making.

"Let's take this one step at a time," he says. "I'd like to see June's results—and Tali's—before I put any more puzzle pieces on the table."

"I'm sure Nell will give you permission to see Tali's records." Peter speaks as if she isn't sitting right there. "We need answers."

"Absolutely," she says, moving her chair back, readying to stand.

"Good, good." Fitz reaches into his backpack for the release form, sliding it across the table, along with a pen, before Nell can change her mind. Then he taps the side of the laptop. "I'm afraid I need to take this now."

Peter kisses his fingers, then presses them to the most colorful image of his daughter on the screen.

Nell wipes quickly under each eye before rising from her chair.

"One more thing. Your husband told us he disposed of his laptop. Any idea where he might have chucked it? You haven't seen it, have you?"

Rigidly Nell stands there, silent. Fitz can almost hear her internal debate over whether or not to plead the fifth or assert spousal privilege. In that moment, he knows she has it.

"Nell, did you hear him?" Peter asks. "Do you know where it is?"

Nodding heavily, she says, "No, but I'll talk to him. And I'll turn the house upside down when I get home."

With reverence, Fitz closes June's laptop, slips it into the evidence bag, and marks it with her name. Peter watches intently as it disappears inside his backpack. The three of them say their goodbyes, and in minutes Fitz is back on the street.

It's windy outside, and the air feels good against his face. He decides to leave his car parked where it is and walk the few blocks to the school. Without thinking twice, he tightens the strap on his pack. There's something comforting about the weight of evidence on his body. Maybe it's because he knows he can remove it whenever he wants. Pass it off to another cop or forensics, something Fitz has never been able to do with what he knows about Maddie.

A few days after she died, before cops moved on from questioning his brother, Fitz tried to get everything off his chest. His first mistake was confiding in Keira.

Close in age, Keira and Fitz grew up like bookends. Saturday morning in the house on M Street, Ma would hand them a stack of hardbacks and park them in the same chair, a wide-seated rocker with gray fabric dotted with little brown houses. She'd tell them to take turns reading aloud. Without really needing to, she'd order them to behave. When Ma circled back to her ironing or went upstairs to change the baby's diaper, they'd sneak cups of juice into the den, resting the tumblers on the wooden arms of the chair. Pretending to drink the way Da did, they never got in trouble for watching forbidden cartoons or for deepening the pale white rings on the furniture. Keira and Fitz so enjoyed the warmth of their sides touching that for years, before meals, they would push two kitchen chairs together to form a bench, claiming they were making space for baby Connor's high chair and later his big boy booster seat.

Back then Fitz's wild Irish twin was everything you'd want a sister to be. And right from the start Con was odd man out. It didn't help when Fitz and Keira abandoned him for school, even landing in the same first-grade class. Keira was fierce and fiery in the way she stood up to the kids who made fun of Fitz for his music, but she knew when to leave him alone too. When to let him fight some of his battles without her. Except for when Fitz played piano, he was his most confident when Keira was around. He hated that the older Connor got and the more outrageous he acted, especially once he hit high school, the more protective Keira was of him. Increasingly, Fitz was on his own.

Less than two weeks after Maddie's funeral, Fitz put together a plan. He'd skip school and show up at the Townsend's house to spill his guts about what his brother had done, and confess his own role in lying about it to Maddie's parents. Fitz figured no one would notice him hanging back from the pack of Southie kids who took Telegraph Hill to the high school like they did every morning. But the wider the distance got between them, the more often Keira looked over her shoulder. Fitz knew something was up when she grabbed Connor by the arm and whispered something to him. His brother shot him a menacing look, then took off toward the front of the high school. Keira stopped right where she was and waited for him.

"You okay, Fitzy?" she asked when he caught up. "You don't look good."

He hadn't expected Keira's kindness to hit him hard. Blame it on the lack of sleep, his Catholic guilt, or missing Maddie, but in that moment, Fitz was so messed up he didn't know whether to shove his sister away or pull her into a hug.

Keira moved to his side and put her hand on his back. "He said he had nothing to do with it."

"If you don't think Connor did anything terrible, why did you ask him?"

Keira shook her head. "After he met with police, you two were acting awful to each other. I figured something else was going on."

"Did he tell you he was there? And that he kept that little detail from police?"

"Look Fitz, whatever happened on Castle Island had to be an accident."

"You don't believe that. You and I both know Connor is not a good person."

"He can be awful to us and his friends, but he'd never do anything to hurt someone. Not like that."

"Easy for you to say. I saw him right after. Now I'm stuck with his horrible secret. She was my friend, Keira. I can't do this."

Fitz walked away from her, heading in the direction of Emerson Street.

"Where are you going?"

"Mr. and Mrs. Townsend deserve to know what happened to their kid."

"Fitz. Stop. Please, listen to me first. If you want to go there after you hear me out, I'll go with you."

The street was too crowded to keep going at it out in the open. Without saying anything, Fitz and Keira picked up the pace, turned on to East Broadway, and made their way to a favored bench inside Medal of Honor Park.

"Here's what happens if you tell," Keira said. "Connor gets locked up. Unless Da kills him first. Ma spirals into her black place. Again. We both know that I'll have to take care of her. I can kiss Holy Cross goodbye. And the Townsends? They're gonna grieve either way. But starting now they get to do it in peace. If you start pointing fingers at Connor, there will be a trial, and this whole thing gets a lot worse for everyone. Most especially the Townsends. Do you want to be responsible for that?"

"You want me to do nothing?" Fitz popped off the bench. With one foot, he stamped the pavement hard, sending a flock of pigeons scattering. His remorse for unnerving even these dirty birds was crushing and immediate. "I'm supposed to live at M Street with Connor walking around as if nothing happened? Come on, Keira. If it was an accident, he would fess up. We're letting him get away with murder."

"What if we make him pay? Come up with an excuse to send him away, back to Ireland. Make him swear he'll never come home and never talk to us again."

"He's sixteen. How would you ever make that happen?"

"Don't underestimate me. It's not penance if it isn't hard."

"Detective, stop!"

Fitz comes back to the present to the sound of shouting. He pushes aside his jacket, puts a hand on his concealed carry holster, and whips around to see who's behind him. He never goes through with pulling his weapon.

Ana Wallace halts where she is nearly toppling off her mile-high shoes. "Jesus, don't shoot me," she says.

"It's a reflex, ma'am. Didn't mean to frighten you."

"I'll use that thing on you if you're planning to go anywhere near my son." She swings her shopping bag in the direction of the main building of Arts High. Under an overhang ringed with klieg lights, a group of teenagers dressed in crimson gowns and ruby capes are rehearsing a scene. Or maybe they're dramatic in real life too.

In a different circumstance, Fitz would tell Ana that threatening an officer is a bad idea, in some cases a crime, but he doesn't want to tick her off.

"Actually, I'm here to see you," he says. "I have questions about Mr. Normand. Nell tells me you're here twenty-four/seven and that no one knows the school and the people in it better than you do."

"Nell said that?" As she gets nearer to the entrance, the kids recognize her and surround her. They exchange hugs and kisses all around, as if they haven't seen her in weeks instead of hours. Fitz takes advantage of the parting Red Sea to pull open the front door, holding it for her till she's ready to step inside.

"You know I don't always approve of your tactics," she says. "But you are polite."

"My ma will be happy you said so."

"Do me a favor? Don't tell Nell we bumped into each other on the street. I promised her I'd keep an eye on Tali, that I wouldn't leave rehearsal. There's just a lot to do before opening night. Sam tells me you did theater once upon a time. I imagine you understand."

"I played a little piano. That's all."

"Come with me," she says, linking arms with him. "There's a corner of the atrium where we can speak in private."

Without Sam in the room, Ana has no trouble sharing her gift of gab. She dives headlong into the case against Zeke. "I'm not surprised he's in deep, deep trouble. His ruin has been brewing for years. Poor Nell. And Tali—I feel so bad for her. Though I hate to be the one to say it, because no one would ever want this to be true, but this could have a strangely positive impact on her career. You can't get noticed if you haven't been seen."

The alcove Ana leads him to is perfect for spying on kids coming and going from practice studios and class-rooms, while also letting any lingerers stay mostly out of sight. In one smooth motion, she drops onto the couch and crosses her legs. Her showiness and the shortness of her skirt suddenly has Fitz rethinking being alone with her. Instead of sitting across from Ana, he parks himself on the high arm of a chair.

"Seems the consensus around here is that Normand is . . ." Fitz pauses.

"An ass?" Ana smiles pretty as you please. "The prob-lem is, he's contemptible but also a genius. If you come to the play, you'll see what I mean."

"He doesn't strike me as terribly compassionate. How was he the day after the girls went missing? Did he get involved in the search?"

"I can honestly say I don't know. I was focused on the children. It was pandemonium around here the day after we got the news the girls disappeared. Right from the start, I had a horrible feeling something awful happened. I positioned myself in the theater so that anyone who couldn't handle being in class would have somewhere to go. Some of their friends sat in the audience in a stupor, texting and crying. For the ones who needed to keep busy, I put them to work organizing the costume closet and tidying backstage."

"Nell's right. The school sure is fortunate to have you."

Ana waves off the compliment, even though she waits a few seconds to see if there's more where it came from.

"Sam was born under some lucky star," Fitz says. "So talented, and with this place right in your backyard."

"Actually, we're from LA. Most of the families with a child enrolled here are transplants from all over the country," she says. "Tali and June—they're the exceptions. Boston born and raised."

"What about the teachers? I doubt they can afford to live in Back Bay."

"The majority are commuters who live in Cambridge, Allston, Brighton. A handful drive in from the South Shore—Cohasset and Hingham. Greg takes the T in from Winthrop."

"He doesn't own a car?"

"Not that I know of. Why do you ask?"

"I heard it through the grapevine that he has a thing for the ingenues. It's probably just talk, but if I were a parent, I wouldn't want my girl in a car with that one."

"I'd be pushing for the school to let him go if I had a daughter. There are many more inspiring directors who'd give anything to work with these kids. On their craft." Ana raises a quizzical brow.

"Are you saying he's more than a flirt?" Fitz asks.

"He likes one sweet cherry in particular, but you didn't hear it from me. I'm not one to gossip." Ana runs two fingers over her lips the way Ma used to when she was telling Fitz and Keira to zip it and stop tattling on Connor.

"You wouldn't be dishing dirt," Fitz says. "You'd be helping with a criminal investigation."

He barely finishes his sentence when Ana abruptly looks away. She's up off the couch, rearranging her skirt in the time it takes Sam to crest the atrium stairs. Either she's guilty of something or she felt her son's presence before she saw him.

"Well, I hope I've been helpful. Must go now. Costume fitting," she says, raising her shopping bag.

"No worries. Thanks for taking the time. Maybe we can connect again?" Fitz waits till Sam is within earshot. "Before you go—do you happen to know a guy named Roger Davis?"

"Not in real life." Ana's laugh is a tinny little bell. She's preoccupied now, staring at her kid like he's some mythical god. Fitz is looking at him too. His pupils are pinpoints, and there's sweat on his brow.

"Sam played the part of Roger in *Rent*. Brilliantly, didn't you, honey?"

If Ana is wrapped up in this, she's a much better actor than her kid. The simplest explanation for the color draining from Sam's face is that his mother embarrassed the shit out of him. What Fitz chooses to believe is that the kid is thrown off because Roger Davis is the fake patient name listed on the pill bottle found at the Scituate beach. Feet away from the body of June Danforth, the leading man's alleged girlfriend.

Act Three

That the powerful play goes on, and you
will contribute a verse.

—Walt Whitman, "O Me! Oh Life!,"
Leaves of Grass

CHAPTER

21

Little Fears

UNACCUSTOMED TO THE knocks and whispers Campion Hall makes late at night, Cyn is on edge. Her classes have been prepped. Course texts ordered. The orchid watered. There's nothing left to do but wait for him.

All her energy goes to listening for Detective Mick Doyle's footsteps on the stairs. But it's the shrill whine of the elevator that startles her. She's over the threshold of her office before he makes it down the hall.

"Thanks for meeting me." Cyn watches him amble toward her, and it's easy to imagine his bones crumbling to dust with each step. His arthritis. Of course he skipped the stairs.

"No problem. Like I told you, I was gonna be in the neighborhood. Took my granddaughter to Legal Sea Foods for a well-deserved study break."

"Is she liking BC? The nursing program here is pretty tough." Cyn rarely enjoys making pleasantries, but Mick deserves every ounce of her patience. Ten years ago on her first reunification case, this man set the bar for how compassionate cops should deal with traumatized kids. Mick Doyle is a pleasant reminder that there are some detectives far and away better than that horrible Dave Ross who was on duty the night Tali came into the emergency room.

"Sorry I couldn't talk when you called," Mick says. "The less said at work these days, the better. Retirement can't come soon enough."

"Make sure I get an invitation to your party, okay?"

"You bet. And bring a guest, or whatever it is you call it nowadays."

"No plus one for me, Mick. Noah ruined me for a while."

Mick collapses into one of her guest chairs, a sleek modern thing perfect for students, not built for a big guy like him. Low and narrow, she wonders how in the world he'll get out of it when the time comes. She sits beside him.

"I have a favor to ask," Cyn says. "I'm coming to you because it's something I know you can find out, and you won't judge me. I need to know where he is."

"Aw, little lady." Mick reaches out to pat her arm. "After all the cases we've worked together, I consider us friends—you know that. So I'm gonna come right out and ask: Why are you doing this to yourself? You gotta move on. Find one of the good guys."

"The other day I thought I saw Noah on the T. I lost it and I was with a client. I'm tired of waiting to be blindsided."

There was a time not long ago when Cyn put confidence in her instincts. She built a life around her ability to tune into the emotional subtleties others miss. Then Noah cheated and lied, crashed her practice, and flatlined her bank account, all while she was supposedly awake. Once, she had been a woman of unwavering resilience, but Noah took that from her too. The cord he left tied around her heart is tangled. Unknowingly and even from a distance, he can yank it at any time.

"I kinda figured when you called that you'd want to know where he landed," Mick says. "I put a PI friend of mine on it, and she found him in Connecticut. Said he's living with his sister, not working, awaiting trial. And if you're looking for a bit of sweet revenge, my friend says McDreamy looks like shit."

"It's not that I want him to be ruined," Cyn says. "If I'm honest, I don't know what I want where Noah's concerned."

Mick looks down at his swollen hands, splaying them, then forming fists, trying to work out the aches with movement.

"Why does it feel like there's more?" Cyn asks.

"Not about Noah," he says. "Look, I'm only saying this so you can call to mind what you already know."

As Cyn suspected, Mick had purposely cut their phone call short, using the proximity of his granddaughter at BC as an excuse to meet her in person.

"You're not the only one who's misjudged a person. No matter how hard you try, you can't get inside someone else's head. Even if you're the psychiatrist. All you've got to go on is your instinct. Think of all the girls you've helped and how they came to you because they got it wrong with someone. Maybe more than once. You would never tell one of them not to trust anyone again."

"Are you sure you want to retire?" Cyn asks. "I see a future for you in counseling."

"No, no, no, you're the expert. I'm just an old man who wants you to know we've all done it. Guessed wrong.

Trick is to take people as they are, even if you get punched in the gut a time or two. Cuz it beats the alternative. I'd hate to see you choose bitterness."

Mick grips the arms of the chair. He's wedged in good, and it takes time to work his body out. Before taking a single step, he arches his back and stretches his legs. In the dim light of the office, the pain on his face is thrown into sharp relief.

"Do you still see her?" Mick points to the rain drop art piece displayed on Cyn's bookcase. The one Tali thoughtfully placed there.

"I get a Christmas card every year. But I'm not Allie's therapist anymore."

"Is she making do?"

It strikes Cyn then, the way Mick asks about the girl—now a woman—who brought them together all those years ago. Making do. Maybe that's all anyone ever does. We try to make do.

"She's a social worker in an after-school program for homeless children. She has a beautiful two-year-old son."

"Glad to hear it. No doubt she got through that horror show because of you. Speaking of survivors, how's the Carrington kid doing?"

"Tali's only at the beginning of treatment, and it'll surely be complicated by whatever's going on with her father."

"I'm afraid it's about to get worse. Carrington failed his first polygraph spectacularly. On a second sweep of the crime scene, we found an Oxy pill bottle with his fingerprints all over it."

"Poor Tali. And Nell. I don't know how completely he's wrapped up in this, but it sounds bad."

"Worse than bad. To put pressure on him, the DA is damn near probable cause on conspiracy to commit kidnapping, maybe even negligent homicide."

"That's terrible. Can you give me a heads-up when he's about to be charged? Tali and Nell will be devastated."

"Will do—if you promise to take some advice from a friend. Put Noah Clarke in your rearview, you hear?"

For the first time since Cyn's known him, Mick gives her a peck on the cheek. His grandfatherly kiss calls up tears she holds back until he's in the hall, waving, heading back the way he came.

It's late and she has class in the morning, but the idea of taking the T home to her barren apartment fills her with emptiness. If ever she deserved a stiff drink, it's tonight. Cyn springs for a cab.

The Beehive on a Monday is as she expected to find it. A handful of singles line the bar; a lone bartender stands behind it. Fitz is at the piano, his back to the door.

Cyn orders her liquid courage in the form of scotch neat and takes a table behind him. There's something indecent about scrutinizing him when he hasn't noticed she is here.

The first time she heard him play, over a week ago, there was no denying his talent. After he got over Keira's tricking him to perform, the pieces he chose were flashy, almost bawdy. He was showing off for her. Tonight, watching his hands let loose an almost violent explosion of motion, Fitz is a different musician. Moody and reckless, he's focused only on the keys and the dark music he can seduce from the instrument. He transitions piece to piece unendingly, each one full of the whorls and ridges of regret.

When Cyn takes the last sip of her drink, she considers leaving, imagining future Mondays. One scotch and one set without Fitz ever knowing she's been there.

The bartender comes toward her holding a glass of something whiskey-brown in one hand and a bottle of Chivas in the other. On his way to her table, the man catches Fitz's eye by raising the glass and cocking his head in Cyn's direction. The music stops. Annoyed, Fitz swings his body over the side of the piano bench. Then from across the room, she sees him smile.

Before Cyn can refuse the bartender or cover the rim, he's completed a heavy pour of her scotch and put the whiskey glass on the table for Fitz. "Keira's friend," he says, "Round's on me."

"Hey, there you are." Fitz says this as if he'd been expecting her to show. Like he knew, despite her refusal to go out with him, Cyn would change her mind. He rests those hands on the back of the chair facing her.

"Hard day. Not many places open this late in my neighborhood," she says.

He laughs a little. "Oh, okay."

Cyn takes the first sip of her second drink. The smooth burn at the back of her throat urges her not to make this complicated. "You play better on Mondays."

"What can I say? These are my people." Fitz opens his arms like he's referring to a crowd, but he never takes his eyes off her. "Mind if I sit?"

"No. Please."

"Anything on your mind?"

"Everything and nothing," she says.

"Sounds about right. If we wanted to sleepwalk through life, we definitely should've picked different professions."

"Why didn't you study music? You're amazing."

Fitz looks into his drink for a second. He hasn't taken a sip. "I gotta say. I never know exactly how much Keira's already told you about me and what you might not know."

"Tell me whatever you want. Just make it the truth." Cyn comes off sounding harsher than she meant to.

"I got into Juilliard. After a friend of mine died, I ended up not going. I've been playing here Mondays ever since."

Cyn doesn't tell him she already knows about the girl who died when he and Keira were in high school. It could be the scotch or the story, probably both, but she doesn't overthink it. "I'm sorry." She slides her hand across the table. Pushing aside his drink, Fitz puts his on top of hers. Long fingers, veins visible, their genius. The contact is almost too much for her.

"How long will you play?" she asks.

"If you're speaking generally, then forever. If you're talking about tonight, thanks to you, I'm done."

"Do you want to leave with me?"

Such is the terror and apprehension Cyn feels at the impulsiveness of her proposition, she suggests they go to her place. Better to reveal what little fills her apartment than to deal with the hollow aftermath of a one-night stand in his. Won't it be more of a triumph to be with someone new in familiar surroundings, to stick it to Noah in their old bed?

Brisk weather has been known to kill the mood, except there's something hypnotic about walking Back Bay streets side by side with Fitz. She's tempted to lose her footing, to list to the left, to see if he can be counted on in this one small way to shore her up.

With her key in the lock, Cyn hesitates. They should've gone to his place. If he says anything about her sparsely furnished rooms—if she has to talk about why it is the way it is—she won't be able to go through with it. Cool autumn air on her skin is a memory. Already her head hurts from too much scotch, and even to her, this is taking too long.

With impatience that isn't coercion, Fitz takes over turning the knob, pushing open the door. They aren't inside before he touches her face, lets loose her hair, unties the bow on her blouse. The first thing she notices is that Fitz is easy to kiss. His lips are soft, not rough. There's no straining her neck to reach him. Base notes of his after-shave, more woody than leather, are unfamiliar, though pleasant.

They move as one body down the hall to her bedroom. She likes the idea of his talented hands playing her back, gliding across her hips. What a fool she'd been to think he'd care what Noah took. Fitz wants her. This is about sex.

Then as if to contradict her, to prove she was right to worry all along, he steps back and surveys the room.

"Help me," he says, pulling one end of the bed toward the window.

"What are you doing?"

"It'll be better over here," he says.

It's hard to see his face in the darkened room, but there's something light in his voice. She grips the frame and lets him lead the way.

When the bed is positioned under the window, Fitz twists the wand on the blinds a little and moonlight spills across her peony sheets. "I want to see you," he says.

She needs to see him too. To stop comparing him to Noah. Cyn is tired of thinking about how he left her and what he left her. Sick to death of what's left of her, she steps out of her skirt.

After, when her body feels lighter than it has in months, freer than it's felt for years, Cyn registers that being unloved is a different kind of choking vine. A heart deprived of touch doesn't stand a chance against intrusive thoughts and dark feelings.

Fitz traces her lips with one finger. "You look happy."

"Tonight turned out better than I thought it would."

"What changed your mind about going out with me?"

"We didn't go out. I went out for a drink and there you were. And here we are."

"That's as good a story as any."

"What do you mean? That's what happened."

"You can spin it any way you want. But after that Saturday night at The Beehive, I knew you'd be back. Then seeing you again at The Bean, I figured it was only a matter of time."

"Look, I've got a talent for overthinking things," she says. "Can this be this for right now?"

"What, you don't want me calling up Keira to give her the details?"

"Please, no. I love your sister, but she'll have us walking down the aisle before the weekend."

"Sorry, I've got plans. There's this hyped-up show I'm planning to see."

"Did you go see Sam?" As Cyn rises up on one elbow, she lets the sheet slide down a little.

He plucks at it, teasingly, coaxing it lower.

"How about Ana?" she asks.

Fitz doesn't say anything. Her powers of seduction are rusty. His definitely aren't.

His mouth is busy kissing her neck.

"No work talk, okay? Not here."

"Did you really move the bed because you like the light?" she asks.

"The better to see you," he says, running his fingers through her hair.

"You're not a wolf, are you, Fitz Jameson?" Cyn leans into his hand. "Because of a certain someone, I imagine you know a lot about my past too."

"Sometimes a person doesn't need to be told certain things. I figured I could make this easier for you, that's all."

"If only starting over was as simple as rearranging or replacing some furniture."

"Tonight you moved your bed. Who knows? Tomorrow you could buy yourself a couch."

It's hard to reconcile that the brooding man who plays piano the way Fitz does can also be a master of the light mood. Suddenly she has no interest in pressing him about whether or not he can be trusted. For now, Cyn relaxes against the pillow, noticing how, from this angle, her bedroom is pretty. Wide open and full of moonlight.

"I've looked around," she says. "I can't find anything I love as much as the one I've got in storage."

"Hey, you brought me here when you were ready. There's hope for your couch."

22

A Steady Rain

THE HEAVINESS OF his backpack reminds Fitz that he hasn't scoured June's laptop even a little, and he's already late to the precinct. He's supposed to be helping Ross get the case file ready to present to prosecutors.

None of this stops him from leaving Cyn's place, swinging by his apartment to shower and change, so he can head back to Arts High. Whatever this is—an unhealthy fixation or finely tuned instincts—the place has its hooks in him.

The receptionist barely looks up when he flashes his badge. She taps the visitor's log and he signs in. First stop, Nell's office. Twice in the last few days, he stopped by the house to press her about Zeke's computer, but no one was home. Now her door is closed, and there's no light sneaking through the slits in the blinds.

He knocks anyway. When no one answers, he starts walking in the direction of the theater. Time to pin down Normand.

Once and for all, Fitz has to rule him in or consider him out. He needs to find out who Ana was referring to when she said the director had his eyes on one girl in particular. Whoever it is, if she's a minor, Fitz might arrest Normand just because he can. He'll consider the morning a raging success if he can corner Sam again without his mother putting in an appearance.

The closer he gets to the theater, the quieter it is in the hallway. He puts his ear to the door. No voices. No movement. He steps inside. The lampstand and bare bulb center stage confirm he's alone in the black box. Fitz scans row after row till his eyes hit the pit and the piano.

The ebony grand has seen its share of abuse. Even in shadow, he can see the dings and divots that mar its body and legs. The action and the case take a beating in a place like this. Obsessive conservatory types, like Fitz used to be, pound on these beauties for no less than ten hours at a stretch. He tries to remember if this one's soundboard produces good tone in spite of its heavy use. The only time he's heard it played, during Tali and Sam's rehearsal, he hadn't been giving the piano its due.

The dozens of spiral smudges left visible on the fallboard would be a detective's dream if the instrument were involved in a crime, and Fitz wasn't tempted to add his own fingerprints to the mix.

He should get to work. Instead, he exposes the keys. Without taking the bench or breaking the line between elbows and wrists, he lets his hands dazzle. Broken chord after broken chord, in this school where anything is possible, he loses himself to the music.

"Who's there?"

It isn't until a girl materializes from behind the curtain that Fitz stops playing. Tali's dark hair fades into the black backdrop, and the ghost light casts her face in other-worldly shadow.

"It's Detective Jameson. Sorry, I got a little carried away."

"Oh, hi. Sam told me you played. But I didn't think you'd be good."

The kid pulls no punches, and her delivery is refreshing. She's sarcastic and magnetic at the same time.

"I do okay. Hey, where is everybody?"

She clutches a familiar notebook to her chest. It's the one Normand threw on the stage to accentuate how pissed off he was at her for needing a session with Cyn during rehearsal.

"We have academics in the morning," she says. "Run-throughs in the afternoon. I'm rereading yesterday's cast notes."

"Who knows you bailed on class?"

"Leads can get away with anything the closer it is to opening night."

"What about Sam? Is he here?"

Tali comes to the edge of the stage and sits, letting her long legs dangle over the proscenium. That's when Fitz notices she's got one of the director's signature pencils, bite marks and all, threaded through her hair and tucked behind one ear. Another reminder he needs to follow up on Normand's DNA.

"His mom is running lines with him." Tali gestures backstage toward the warren of hidden rooms where Fitz interviewed Sam a couple of weeks ago.

"Those two are weirdly inseparable. That must have driven June crazy."

"She and Sam took it as a challenge. Sneaking around, stealing time together without his mom knowing. It wasn't easy because she's always lurking. It was pretty funny. Until she found out, I guess."

"What did she do?"

"I heard she went ballistic. Right here on stage. Screamed at Sam for lying to her. In front of everybody." Tali pauses, placing the notebook beside her. "I wasn't in school that day."

Fitz moves away from the piano and toward her. "I've never had the chance to say I'm sorry about June. I know she was your friend. It has to be hard. Dr. Rawlins will probably have my head for asking, but how are you handling everything?"

Tali's legs are restless. She taps her heels, one and then the other, against the side of the stage. "I'm not sure. Acting helps. The way you play piano, you probably know what it's like. When I'm in the zone, it gives me a break from being me. Ask me again when the show's over."

"There will always be more plays. If that's what you want."

It's the first time Fitz has seen sadness wash over her face. Her own emotion, not the by proxy kind she borrows from characters.

"I didn't mean to bring it all back. I lost a friend when I was your age, under super strange circumstances. I just want to say it gets better."

If he wasn't trying to get her to talk, Fitz would have said things don't get better as much as they become a terrible kind of normal.

"Yeah, but was your dad in jail and all your friends acting weird around you?" Tali gathers her hair in both hands, twisting and twisting the mass of black curls. When she lets go, her hair falls down her back, landing exactly where it was before she touched it.

"You've got me beat there." There's no way Fitz is comparing asshole fathers with anyone, never mind this girl.

He moves in front of the piano and plays his favorite jazz lick. Then he closes the lid and asks, "Is Sam one of your friends who's behaving differently?"

Tali shrugs. "He and I are fine. We've been friends a long time." She looks at Fitz, waiting expectantly for him to ask another question.

"Do you talk about June?"

"Sometimes. Mostly we talk about the play. There's a lot of pressure on us to nail our parts."

"From Mr. Normand?" he asks. "I need to talk to him. You wouldn't know where he is, would you?"

"In his office. But you probably shouldn't bother him. He's with someone."

"He's not doing anything I wouldn't do, right?" Fitz fakes a laugh.

Tali is silent but it's clear she knows what he's asking. She flips open the notebook next to her on the stage, letting the pages flutter. After they settle in a way he can read them, she angles the point of the pencil under one character's name. Ilsa Neumann.

His phone rings, startling only one of them. Fitz wracks his brain but comes up empty. He has no clue who plays that part.

"I should go," Tali says, picking up the notebook.

Raising a finger, Fitz mouths, "Please wait."

It's Keira. In the time it takes him to tell his sister to hang on, Tali disappears through the wings.

"Drop everything," Keira says. "It's Ma."

Getting to M Street from Exeter is a clusterfuck. Now, no matter where he stands on the porch, raindrops escape the leaky gutter, hitting him on the head and trickling inside his collar, down his back. "Come on, Keira—hurry up."

"Are you kidding me?" From the minute she opens the door, she's giving him face. "It takes you forever to get here, I finally have her settled, and now you're laying on the doorbell?"

"I was at the school, and my car's at The Beehive. I left Ma's house keys at home because I didn't think I'd need them today. She okay?" Fitz pushes his way into the house and closes the door.

"Why did you leave your car over on Tremont? How did you get home last night?"

Jesus, Fitz is only seconds into his first contact with his sister since being with Cyn, and already her senses are tingling. Damned if he'll be the one to tell her.

"What's with Ma?"

Keira brushes the rain off his shoulders and backpack. "I only called you because I couldn't calm her down. I thought I might have to resort to calling an ambulance. She's fine now. Sleeping. You can leave."

"What the hell, Keira? I came all the way over here for nothing?"

His sister pulls him by the elbow into the front parlor. "Be quiet. If you wake her or go ballistic on me, I'll kill you."

"Can everyone stop using that word?"

The large room is crowded with odds and ends of furniture collected from generations of Jamesons who've lived in the three-decker. Brother and sister sit side by side on the old couch. The cushions have so much butt memory, that no matter where you park yourself, you end up tilting to the middle.

"I want to tell you and I don't," she says.

"Go ahead. I won't be an ass." Fitz braces himself. Ma and Keira can only be losing it simultaneously over one person.

"He called shit-faced. Said he's in trouble and needs money."

"It isn't Sunday. I take it you weren't here?"

The deal sixteen-year-old Connor had no choice but to take was to move in with relatives in Ireland and stay lost for good. The only exception was phone calls to Ma, when he was to keep things light and tell her everything was peachy. Early on, the calls were regular, short and sweet. Several years in, they started coming sporadically, but always in the wee hours of the morning. No matter the time, Con was smashed. For days after, Ma would be inconsolable. Finally Keira put her foot down. She slept over M Street for two weeks straight, angling to intercept his next drunk dial. If Connor didn't want to be turned in to police, he could call once a month when Keira was here. Sunday afternoon, not drunk, or not at all.

"Now he's blitzed on a weekday?" Nothing in Fitz wants to know where his brother is now or what new mess he's landed in. He's never asked before. Why would he give a shit now?

Keira's bottom lip starts to quiver. Fitz hasn't seen her cry since Maddie's funeral. She didn't lose it when Connor left. Or when Da died. Fitz throws his arm around his sister and kisses her hair. There isn't a person on this earth who drives him as crazy as Keira does. There's no one he loves as much either.

"There's absolutely no reason for him to stop doing this," she says. "He knows I'll never turn him in."

"He doesn't know you won't. He's a prick. Like always, he wants what he wants when he wants it."

Keira squeezes his arm till it hurts. "Tell me you won't ever do it, Fitz. Turn him in. It will kill her. You know that." This time his sister uses that word on purpose.

He shakes her off. "You said Ma's good now. We'll think of something. Don't you have a class to teach? The psychology of maniacal siblings or something?"

Keira rubs his arm by way of apology. "It's two hundred freshmen in an intro class. I can call and cancel. Before I left the office, I told Cyn to warn the dean I might have to. The kids will love me for it."

"No, you go. I can stay till you get back." Fitz yanks his backpack free of his shoulders and drops it at his feet.

"Won't you get in trouble with Ross the boss?"

"I told you, he's not my boss. And I've got work I can do from here."

"Okay. If you're sure."

Like he used to do when they were kids, Fitz pretends to push her away. "Go. And Keira, you promise not to tell anyone about Connor either, right?"

"Who would I tell?" His sister gets up and moves through the maze of downstairs rooms, fully expecting Fitz to follow behind her.

"I left the door to Ma's room open a crack so you can peek in on her without making any noise. Even if she wakes up, she'll be fine once she sees her Irish prince. I'll be back in time to make dinner."

Keira leaves and Fitz checks on Ma. From the doorway, he sees her diminished body curled up facing the wall. Even in the dim light from the hallway, he can make out her breathing, slow and regular. Standing there, making sure she's okay, Fitz figures this is what it must feel like to be the parent. If you're capable of being the parent. If it wasn't for this fragile woman, Fitz believes he would've come clean about Connor. That's the story he tells himself. At least it's the one Keira refuses to let him revise.

Back to business, Fitz brews a cup of tea, grabs his backpack, and sets up shop at the dining room table. A walk-through of this place feels like a bloody crusade. There's the Sacred Heart of Jesus painting on the wall in the kitchen. The Infant of Prague statue in the parlor. A Celtic cross above the archway to the dining room. Growing up Jameson, Fitz never had to ask what would Jesus do? The guy was always front and center, staring at him wherever he went. Maybe if he'd been a few feet further away, Fitz would've been forced to ponder existential questions. And things might've turned out differently.

When June's laptop refreshes, he clicks on Facebook and picks up where Peter left off, scrolling status updates, reading posts. The pictures he comes across are mostly selfies. The poses exaggerated freeze frames Fitz wouldn't have been caught dead doing when he was her age. The ones of her with other people all seem to be taken with her in motion. Dancing here, leaping there—the kid's vivacity practically bursts through the screen. He doesn't know how her father can endlessly do this. At times Fitz has to look away.

It doesn't help much to stare out the window, watching the drizzle become a downpour either. Thanks to Connor, since Maddie died, the mood of this house on the inside is a magnet for the gathering storm clouds on the outside. He can't remember a time when he's visited M Street when it hasn't been raining.

He returns to the screen. In a stroke of luck not usually found in the Jameson household, Fitz lands on a photo that's a game changer. Maybe, like he'd hoped, his redemption turns on lively June, because there she is with Tali in the costume closet. It could be their smiles or the presence of pretty outfits and stage makeup, but these girls with their faces cheek-to-cheek already look like stars. That isn't what's slamming him, though.

Normand is there too, in the background, holding court with a group of teenagers. He's showing off what he's wearing. A faux fur bomber that's either an exact replica of Carrington's one-of-a-kind jacket, or it's the same one Fitz found in his coat closet with flecks of June's blood on both sleeves.

23

Fame

NELL IS DRAGGED from sleep by a rumble of voices, deep, high, and terse. Above her racing heartbeat, a voice calls out, "Tali!" As she wills the life to come back into her limbs, she realizes this shrill one belongs to her.

The pins and needles in her legs can't stop her. Nell runs toward Tali's room, using the wall as a prop. When she finds it empty, her heart is a Roman candle. The night of Tali's disappearance is replaying itself, except this time Nell is home, not Zeke. She's the one responsible for losing their daughter.

"Wake up," she chides herself. "Let this be a nightmare."

The voices get louder and more real the closer Nell gets to the stairs.

Then she remembers. Sam is here. Nell agreed to let him sleep over last night. Tali and Sam camped out in the living room. As pleased as she was with the normalcy of it, it frustrated her too, because it made it impossible for her to get at Zeke's computer.

Though the relief is overwhelming, by the time she gets to the bottom of the stairs, she's confused all over again. Greg and Ana are standing with Sam and Tali. Having been ripped from sleep, Nell's mind isn't clear enough to register if they're acting or arguing.

"What's going on?"

"Oh good, you're up," Ana says, grabbing the blanket from the back of the couch. "Great news. Arts High—and our little darlings—are going to be featured on *Boston Live*. They're filming today."

It's only when Ana drapes the throw around Nell's shoulders like a shawl that she realizes her threadbare nightgown is nearly see-through. Sam knows enough to look down. Greg doesn't bother to.

"I don't think it's a good idea for Tali."

"This isn't about her. It's about the school," Ana says, "and all the talented children who deserve the exposure." No surprise Ana thinks this is a break-out moment for Sam.

"If it's such good news, why are you arguing?" Nell pulls the blanket tight around her chest, reinforcing the firmness of the gesture with crossed arms. Only then does Greg look at her face.

"I'm with Mrs. Carrington." Sam moves closer to her, as if it's safer to disagree with his mother from a distance. "I think they're only saying it's about the school. If it weren't for June, they wouldn't even know about us."

"They promised not to go there." Tali looks to her director for confirmation. "Right?" She's practically bouncing as she speaks. Her daughter is desperate for this to be about talent over tabloid.

"I've spoken to the producer," Greg says. "She knows the subject of the kidnapping is off limits. And even if they were to ask about it, I can show Tali and Sam how to pivot. Spin it back to the play and the program. Sink or swim, live television is something they'll have to learn to roll with if they want to make it in the business."

Sink or swim? Did that asshole really use that phrase in this house? In the presence of her daughter?

"Go ahead and showcase the school. Focus the interview on Sam and Robin if you want," Nell says. "Tali's not doing it. There will be other times, honey." She reaches out to rub her daughter's back.

Tali flinches. "I can handle it. Dr. Rawlins says I'm doing great. You said from now on you'd listen to what I want. That we'd talk about how things affect me before you make decisions."

"Maybe you'd feel better about this if you *did* speak with Tali's doctor," Ana says. "And I'm sure Greg could arrange for you to connect with the show's producer if that will give you peace of mind."

Nell's outnumbered three to two. Her daughter will never forgive her if she says no. Ana will hound her until airtime and then throw this in her face for all of eternity. Greg will go forward with or without her daughter.

"What about you, Sam? Will this be too hard for you?" Nell's been worried about her daughter's friend ever since Detective Jameson brought up his suspicion that Sam does drugs. Then last night, like old times, Sam and Tali watched some of their favorite movies, eating pizza and reciting the lines. They were overly silly for the first few hours, as if they'd been storing up their good humor and finally had permission to release it. However fleeting their laughter was, it was a balm to Nell, and it convinced her they'd both be all right. Now she's not sure.

"It's to be expected that he's trepidatious," Ana says, making it clear to her son and to the rest of them that Sam's position on the interview is moot. "He'll be fine."

Ana is convincing, not because she's letting her child do this, but because she isn't listening to a word Sam is saying. Her domineering ways make Nell want to treat her daughter differently.

"You can do it," she says to Tali. "On one condition."

"What's that?"

"I talk to Dr. Rawlins. Get her thoughts on how to prepare you in case they ask you difficult questions. I'll pick her brain about how to help you if it doesn't go as planned."

"I like it," Ana says. "'Expect the best, but prepare for the worst.'"

The rest of the quote is "capitalize on what comes." Quintessential Ana leaves out the part of the motto that best describes her.

Nell ushers all four of them out of her house, and despite the fact that they're going to Arts High together, she makes Tali promise to text her when she gets there. At this point her girl will agree to anything.

Feigning trouble with Zeke—though it's never a lie to say Zeke and trouble go together—Nell calls in sick. Again. Worrying about losing her job is something for another day.

She looks through her phone contacts to find Dr. Rawlins's listing. Scrolling past the number for the call service, she hits the private one the doctor gave her after that disastrous trip to the beach.

Nell doesn't say much before Tali's psychiatrist invites her in for a session to sort through the television appearance.

The Boston College office looks miles better than it did the last time Nell saw it. Without the stacks of boxes and cluttered table tops, the unassuming space is a respite. Maybe Nell should ask if she can see Dr. Rawlins more regularly.

"I'm glad you didn't mind coming to Chestnut Hill," she says. "Have a seat."

"Thanks for squeezing me in. I think you're right; there's more to this than we could get into on the phone."

"Media requests are inevitable in situations like yours. Fill me in."

"Turning down all the national stuff was easy," Nell says. "Mostly I ignored producers' emails and didn't return phone calls. This is local, and it came through the director. *Boston Live* doesn't do exposé-type pieces, and they say it's not about the kidnapping or June's death. But I don't trust they're being honest."

"I take it Tali's excited to do it."

Nell smiles. Dr. Rawlins knows her girl. It's a relief to sit across from someone who knows what she's doing.

"She says she can handle it. And that if I asked you, you'd agree. Imagine if I put my foot down, and then the whole thing turns out to be this great big wonderful deal for the kids. It would hurt Tali unnecessarily to miss it, and I'd feel awful. This play is everything to her right now."

"Her acting is more than a positive outlet. It's possibly the most effective way she has to compartmentalize the trauma. It seems to be how she's channeling her anger toward her father too."

"How can I be sure they won't ask her anything, especially about him?"

"You can insist they steer clear of it, but there are no guarantees. The good news is that it's not that kind of show. And Tali's not the only person they plan to interview, right?"

"Last I heard, they plan to grab footage of rehearsal this afternoon and then go live tonight with Sam, Tali, Robin, and the director. I'm not sure why Robin's included. The part of Ilse is more of a featured singing role than lead actress."

"That's a lot of people for this kind of interview. Live segments tend to be short. It isn't likely the anchor will highjack it. That said, if you want, I can come to the studio with you and Tali. Sometimes they behave better when I'm in tow."

Dr. Rawlins is more relaxed than Nell's seen her. Loose auburn strands of hair surround her face, making her look younger, brighter, less tense.

"You'd do that for Tali?" Nell asks. "What about your other commitments?"

"It's pretty obvious my life has changed of late. If I didn't have the time or thought it wasn't appropriate, I wouldn't offer. Tali's my patient. I'd like to help."

Nell tries to focus on her generosity and not the flicker of irritation she hears in her voice. "I'd appreciate it. I have no trouble admitting I've hit the limit of my abilities as a mother."

Dr. Rawlins relaxes again. She leans in as if Nell is her only care in the world. "Is this a new feeling?"

"Everything's magnified lately, but I think I've always felt out of my depth to some degree. It has less to do with Tali and more to do with the fact that nothing is easy when your husband acts like the bigger child."

"That sounds stressful."

"At times it's been unbearable. Whenever Zeke would lose a ton of money, he'd become irrational if I got upset.

He'd say I was melodramatic. That all I wanted to do was to control him. Off and on, I worried about the effect all of this was having on Tali, but she seemed unfazed by our turmoil."

"Or maybe she learned to work things out through her acting."

In the space of a few weeks, Dr. Rawlins is grasping things it's taken Nell years to comprehend.

"I think her love of theater started back when she was a very little girl. I remember when she was five, Zeke got her this beautiful antique dollhouse. I told him it was more for a collector than a child, but he insisted on refurbishing it for her, no matter what I said. Night after night, I'd find her out of bed curled up next to him, watching his every move as he glued back the scalloped trim at the edge of the roofline or replace missing pieces of wood and molding. I didn't think he'd follow through and finish it, but he did. After it was sanded and painted, she played with it for hours. Delicately. I've never seen a child play more carefully with a toy."

Dr. Rawlins slides the tissue dispenser across the nearby table before Nell knows she needs it.

"Tali had this one storyline where she'd pretend to move the family out, furniture and all. I'd overhear her tell the dolls on move-in day, *'In this new house, everyone is happy. Lower your voice. Shh. No yelling. No crying.'*"

"But then the little family would start to argue about something silly or have some ridiculous misunderstanding, and she would act out their fight, only to stage an elaborate apology with lots of hugs and kisses. Tali entertained herself with some version of that play for years."

Nell rips a tissue from the box and dabs her eyes. Even to her own ears, her laugh is pitiful. "Maybe she still is."

"Tali's got a lot going on under the surface. I think counseling is a good idea, now more than ever. She's slowly opening up to me, and I'd like to see her a few more times; then I might want to do some psychological testing."

"What exactly are you worried about?"

"Projective assessment is another way I have to uncover hidden emotions and internal conflicts Tali may have. I've only known her a short time. We're not there yet. I only ask you to think about it before we mention it to her."

Should Nell have done this years ago? Find someone like Dr. Rawlins for Tali? Women like Ana are consumed by mothering as a cure for what's missing in their own lives; Nell always had enough to do to manage Zeke. Back when Tali was young, Nell remembers feeling grateful to her for needing so little from her. What a fool she'd been to think Tali had been unaffected by his addiction, her parents constant arguing, and the childish way Nell could sometimes behave because of Zeke.

"I've ended things with my husband," she says. "I've talked around it with Tali, but I haven't come right out and told her."

"What's holding you back?"

"She's had so much to deal with lately. It feels like I'd be piling things on. When I tell you I've barely had enough energy to deal with Zeke all these years, I'm not exaggerating. If I could do things over, I would've asked for help from someone like you. I would've paid more attention to what Tali and I needed."

"I'm sure you did the best you could. You weren't concerned about her before the kidnapping. I see both of you making progress. I remember you telling me you had trouble leaving her at school, and here you are."

"The Tech Week schedule helps," Nell says. "The kids are in classes all morning, and then from lunch till ten at night they're in rehearsal. Someone's with Tali at all times."

"It sounds like you're less worried about her these days?"

"I wouldn't quite say that. Right before the wake, Ana told me June and Sam had been dating. I work at the school, and I didn't know. June's own father didn't know. Then the other day, Detective Jameson asked Peter and me if the girls ever used drugs. He thinks Sam's into pills. It's all so overwhelming to think I missed things. Do you ever feel that kind of panic? Like there's this big horrible thing right in front of you and you can't see it?"

The look on Dr. Rawlins's face is pure recognition. The tautness of her jaw looks almost painful.

"You would tell me if Tali's doing anything I should know about, right?" Nell asks.

"What has Tali told you about using drugs or about what Sam might be doing?"

"Except for what you prescribed, and her telling me she isn't drinking, I haven't asked her straight out. I'm trying to respect her privacy. I don't want to be the way I was with Zeke with her. And I won't be the kind of mother who sneaks around or goes through her child's things. I'm not Ana."

"There might be something between hovering and trusting Tali to make good decisions on her own you could consider. Maybe you'd like to meet again, and we can dig a little deeper into that."

It's Nell's cue that the session is over. They book another appointment, and she collects her things and looks around the office one more time. Nell is calmed by the ordinariness of the space, how the lack of anything overly decorative leaves room for her to pay attention to herself for once. Everything seems simpler here, clearer. "I'll see you tonight at the studio?"

"Be sure to tell Tali I'm coming," she says. "I don't want to blindside her."

Nell stops at the threshold. "Dr. Rawlins, she's okay, right? Tali's going to get through this?"

"If I didn't think she could handle the interview, I'd speak up," she says. "And please call me Cyn."

At the top of the stairs, Nell considers dashing back to the office to tell Cyn she wasn't talking about tonight. She should have been clearer and pressed her more forcefully about when she thought Tali might fully open up to her. Then like clockwork, Nell's phone rings.

"What did she say?" Tali asks. "Can I do it?"

"She thinks you'll do great. I invited her to come with us. Is that okay?"

"That's fine. And Mom? Do you have time to stop at Chestnut Hill Mall? There's this peasant dress at Anthropologie. It has a Wendla vibe without overshadowing my costumes. Mrs. Wallace said she'd buy it for me. Isn't that nice?"

"Of course I can pick it up for you. But we don't need Ana to pay for it. I'll get it and bring it to you around six. That'll give you plenty of time to change before we head over to the studio."

WFXT is a state-of-the-art glass and chrome newsroom. Their gaggle of studio virgins walks through the place with their mouths in varying degrees of open. The producer is a pip of a thing, blonde and bubbly. She ushers them around the anchor desk, past the giant weather map, and when the group lands in the green room, she drops the bomb.

"The b-roll we took at the school has plenty of the director. We only plan to interview the kids."

Nell wishes she could enjoy Greg getting bumped off camera, but she's panicked he won't be with Tali to steer the interview in the right direction.

"Don't worry, Mom," the producer says. "I saw them perform today. They'll be great."

In a flurry of activity, the three actors are prepped on the mechanics of a two-shot live interview and mic'd up. The rest of their group is parked at a distant desk the producer promises won't be on camera.

The anchor is nowhere to be found until the kids are positioned on stools that have been lined up on the metal landing under a galaxy of lights.

With her viciously high heels and impossibly tight dress, the woman manages to slide onto her stool as the stage manager counts down—three, two, one—and a finger wag that takes the place of the word *live*.

Nell is comfortable at first, telling herself it's a four-minute segment. Even without Greg, given the lead-in and the closer and needing to pay attention to three kids, how much damage can the woman do? Plus in the preinterview, Ana angled for the anchor to start with Sam.

"My character has a close relationship with his mother," he says, "but during the play, he realizes that not everything he's been taught is right. He starts to question things. He's a critical guy."

"Bordering on arrogant, wouldn't you say?" Tali lightens the mood of Sam's answer, and the anchor laughs.

Sam keeps going as if he'd better get those talking points in or his real mother will have his head. "I have a desire for control. As I discover this, my explosive temper begins to frighten me."

"So, as you can imagine," Tali says, "my character is attracted to him."

The anchor laughs again and swings her body in Tali's direction. Nell's daughter is as natural on camera as she is on stage. Nell is in awe of how commanding Tali is, especially since she's never done this before.

"Keeping in mind that *Boston Live* is a family show," the anchor says, "what can you say about the mature nature of the play?"

"It's not that we're doing anything that shocking," Tali says. "We're just brutally honest about what it's like to be a teenager. Trying to direct our own course despite the opinions and mistakes the people around us make. We're trying to love ourselves, even if that's a hard thing to do."

"What kind of trust has to be established between actors to work through the more intimate scenes?"

Suddenly it's as if the conversation is between the anchor and Tali. Ana sighs. And though it's impossible for Tali to have heard her from this distance, she knows enough to include the others. Or at least Sam.

"We've been friends a long time. And we've been through a lot together." Tali reaches over to take Sam's hand. As if they've rehearsed it, they lace them together and squeeze tight. "We have each other's backs. We protect each other. Emotionally."

Unfazed by being left out, Robin sits perfectly still with a frozen pink smile plastered to her face.

"This has to be a hard time for you specifically, Tali. I'm sure our viewers remember you were one of the girls kidnapped from the school. How are you coping with the death of your friend June. And your father's alleged role in all of this?"

Nell doesn't know whether to keep watching the monitor or rush the landing to pull her daughter from the interview. "Make it stop," she whispers.

Cyn whispers back. "She's got this."

Slipping her hand from Sam's, Tali folds hers onto her lap. She looks demurely at the anchor. "I won't say it's easy. I try to stay in the moment. Appreciating the people who love me—and experiences like this one. Being here with you."

Disarmed by Nell's daughter's vulnerability, the woman who speaks for a living is nearly speechless.

"Would you like us to sing a little something?" Tali asks, filling the void. As she scootches forward on her stool, Sam leans back hard.

"Oh dear, Melchior's gone a bit pale," the anchor says. "How about you?" She looks to finally include Robin, but before the girl can respond, Tali is singing.

"Just too unreal, all this. Watching the words fall from my lips. Watching his world slip though my fist."

Nell grabs Cyn's arm. "It's that horrible song. Why is she singing this one here?" And then as if Tali has performed this version a million times before, she stops mid-verse, before the lines about bruises and bodies.

"That's all I'm giving you," she says, flashing a camera-ready smile. "For more you'll have to come see us on stage."

The anchor turns to the center camera. "Sounds like it's a show that shouldn't be missed."

24

Proof

Fɪᴛᴢ ʜᴀᴛᴇs ᴛᴏ use Ma's downward spiral as an excuse to keep working a nearly closed case, but he will if he has to. It's not a lie to say she's out of commission, even though the situation is under control and Keira's on watch.

His plan is to hike the back stairs of the precinct, grab a copy of Charlie Stockbridge's statement, and then head down to Scituate to ask the old man some new questions. All before Ross can grill him about what he's up to.

So that's exactly who he bumps into.

"Where the hell have you been?"

"I've got a whole family song and dance I'm sure you don't want to hear."

As Fitz drops his backpack on the desk, June's laptop hits it hard.

"Here's the thing," he says. "All along, my gut's told me Sam knows something, that he's covering for someone. Turns out, I'm right. We need to keep working the case."

"Convince me."

Fitz lays out what he knows about the director and Sam, and how they might be mixed up in this. "Zeke Carrington's prints are on the prescription bottle found at the scene. He's admitted to dealing. I think at the school. The fake patient name is a made-up character the kid played. Expertly if you listen to his mother. I've seen Sam recently, and I think he's into opioids."

"So what? The kid's a pillhead and he gets his stash—or at least he did—from his friend's dad," Ross says.

Fitz unzips his backpack and opens June's laptop. "Ana says she picked Sam up after the audition that night. We have witnesses who saw him get into her car. But here's the thing—Normand directed that other play and he could've picked that fake name. And look at this. He's wearing Carrington's jacket." Fitz clicks on the picture and zooms in on the director to prove to Ross he's right.

"On a hunch, during one of my early visits to the school, I picked up something with Normand's DNA on it. Forensics is running the unidentified hair and fibers found on the jacket against it as we speak."

"Okay, the kid and the director get their drugs from Zeke, and they're tangled up in ways that go beyond the typical teacher–student relationship even for that school," Ross says. "Why should we care?"

"Sam could've figured out that Normand was involved when Tali and June went missing, or possibly after the fact. I don't know yet. Maybe Normand wanted to amp up publicity for the play, and things went sideways. It's common knowledge he's intimately involved with at least one student. He's not a good guy."

"Why would the kid cover for him?"

"Have you met his mother? She's a barracuda. He's screwed if she finds out he does drugs. Speaking of mothers, I got permission from Nell to pull Tali's Emergency Room records to check her labs. I plan to pick them up now. June's tox is due back any minute. If both girls had drugs in their system, that would explain why Tali can only remember being in the car and then much later at the beach. I'm heading to Scituate. June and Tali were gone for over forty hours. Where were they all that time? I think if I can look at the Glades property with this theory in mind, and talk to the caretaker, things might come into sharper focus. Charlie Stockbridge, as forgetful as he is, knows the place inside and out."

"Fine, go," Ross says. "Take Doyle. I can't stand watching him become part of his chair. I have zero interest in taking that drive. I'll stay here and push prosecutors off another day."

As Fitz heads back through the cubicles, he's trying to come up with reasons to go it alone. Doyle in tow isn't exactly how he envisioned this.

Both men sigh the whole way from precinct to parking lot, but for different reasons. By the time Doyle finally makes it to the car, Fitz feels bad for him. All he's got the energy to do is lean on the passenger side door and fan himself. At the point that Fitz resigns himself to a day played in slow motion, Doyle asks to be dropped off at the hospital.

"I'll pick up Tali's ER records," he says. "Then cab it home and do follow up calls from there."

Turns out it's pretty easy to ditch Doyle. Arthritis and long walks on the beach don't exactly go together.

When it takes forever to drive from Boston to Scituate, Fitz gets why Ross and Doyle bailed on coming with him. Between the bird-flipping, crazy lane changers and the continuous, meandering, single-lane road that takes him from the off ramp through Hingham and Cohasset to the Scituate town line, Fitz wonders who in their right mind would put up with this commute to Boston. Then he comes to the end of Glades Road. The sunbeams above the razor-sharp horizon. He's never seen this color blue—or this much of it—in his life. Fitz wishes Cyn were here to see it.

Driving toward the old Glades Club, he has a hard time keeping his eyes on the road. To his right, below the seawall and beyond the rock ledge, the sandy beach stretches for miles in both directions. As beautiful as it is in daytime, these roads must be treacherous at night. It makes him wonder why Normand would pick this place, and whose car he used to get here.

At the entrance to the property, there's a gate stretched across the road. Despite the "No Trespassing" sign, Fitz gets out to open it; then he's back in the car to keep driving.

Beyond the gate, the road narrows, and it feels like nature is closing in around him. Down go his front windows. Fitz needs the air but could do without the sound of waves crashing.

He remembers Charlie talking about the thick stone lighthouse that sits in the middle of the sea, and he knows it's his marker for how far out on the point the estate goes. As picturesque as this place is, the longer it takes to get to the caretaker's house, the more he can't imagine Charlie living out here alone.

Black birds and large birds and seabirds fly high, then dip into and rise from the ocean. Fitz has no clue what species these are. There are no birds like these on Castle Island.

His tires screech as he pulls into a circular drive covered in crushed shells and packed sand. He's barely out of the vehicle when his phone rings. It's Doyle.

"June's tox screen pops on ketamine and ecstasy," he says. "Tali's is clean except for the Ativan she was given by paramedics at the scene. The guy at the lab says you can't rule out she was dosed with Special K though. It's notoriously short acting and could've been out of her system by the time she was tested."

Fitz can't believe his suspicions—one right after another—are being confirmed. "Okay, I'll call you when I'm twenty minutes from Boston. We'll head back to the precinct to fill Ross in together."

There is high-pitched yipping coming from somewhere close by. Because of the swells, Fitz can't pinpoint exactly where the dog is before it jumps him, and his phone goes flying.

"Daisy, get back here!"

"It's okay. She's okay." Fitz bends down, moving the dog aside to retrieve his phone. He doesn't know his corgis from his elkhounds, but the little thing is cute, and she's definitely happy for the attention.

"Good to see you again, Charlie."

"This here's private property," he says, without a glimmer of recognition. "You can't be parked out here. Beach is off limits."

"It's Detective Jameson. Remember me?" Fitz flashes his badge. "I'm investigating the kidnapping of the girls."

"Oh for heaven's sake, yes. You're that nice fella who interviewed me a hundred years ago."

"That's me. Daisy sure likes it better out here."

"We both do. Gotta be near the sea. Right, girl? You're a good Daisy." Charlie is playful with his dog, rubbing behind her ears, patting her back.

On site, not reliant on photos and secondhand accounts, Fitz can see that the caretaker's residence and the main Glades property are connected in an L shape, making it easy for Charlie to keep an eye out for trouble. It would be a challenge to penetrate the compound, hiding the two girls inside for any amount of time, without him noticing. Plus it's ringed by black steel poles with glass globes.

"Those switch on automatically at night?" Fitz draws Charlie's eyes up to the lights.

"Newfangled things are tripped by movement. They can give you a shock when they come on sudden, and you ain't the one doing the tripping."

"Do you remember them going on unexpectedly the night you found the girls on the beach?"

"Sorry to say I don't." Charlie looks toward the beach, as if he can see June and Tali there the way he found them. "How's that Parker girl doing?" he asks.

"You mean Carrington. She's doing okay. No worries about not remembering things. Some witnesses can call up every last detail, and some none at all."

Daisy is a bundle of joy, romping between the two men's legs. Fitz wonders if Pops might've lived longer if he'd had a dog to keep him company.

"How've you been?" Fitz asks. "Must be unsettling to have had a crime take place right outside your back door."

"Oh, there's plenty a tall tales involving this place, including rum-running and bootlegging. All back before I was born. They called it Strawberry Hill in those days. Wasn't till the rich crowd took over that the name was changed to the Glades. Lots of military history here too."

Charlie's off topic and Fitz is tempted to redirect him. Except that some of the best stuff he ever learned from Pops came when he let his grandfather ramble.

"Did you see the observation tower on your way in?" Charlie points to the woods opposite the water. "Back in my day, I'd climb that beauty once a week at least. The view of the sea from the top is like nothing you've ever seen."

"Could you climb it now—if you wanted to?"

"No, sir. Entrance has been cemented shut since the sixties."

Fitz stifles a laugh as Charlie calls up details from sixty plus years ago like it was yesterday. "So there's no other way in? If, say, a person wanted to camp out around here?"

"No sir. Not inside that tower anyway."

"But somewhere else? Another place where three people could fit to take shelter?"

"Well, there's the cottages. But only townies like me know about those."

"Can you show me?" Fitz asks.

Charlie might not remember what he had for breakfast, but he knows exactly how to navigate the forest canopy that takes them away from the sea. Fitz looks ahead, then down and up again, trying not to lose his footing. Daisy yips and skips over the exposed granite ledges like it's the best treat in the world to head in this direction.

"I've got to thank you, son," Charlie says over his shoulder. "Daisy and me—we haven't walked this way in a long time. I forgot how pretty it is back here."

"You won't come out here by yourself, will you, Charlie? I'd hate for you to get lost."

As if to prove that Fitz is right to worry about the old man's memory, ten minutes in, Charlie comes to a standstill in the middle of nowhere. Fitz thinks he's confused after all, until he sees what the caretaker wants to show him.

The reinforced shells Charlie calls *the cottages* are anything but. They're disguised remnants of two other military towers, with wooden roofs, false siding, and cracked and blackened windows. It's no wonder there's no mention of these structures in the crime scene report. The concrete pylons couldn't be camouflaged any better if someone had staged it.

Fitz pulls out his phone, and it takes three taps of the icon before the flashlight comes on. Inside the smallest structure, there's broken glass all over the concrete floor and barely room for one person, never mind three. It's when he flashes the light inside the second shelter that his blood runs cold.

"Pick up Daisy. Now." Fitz doesn't mean to scare Charlie, but he can't have the dog corrupting the crime scene. Even through the dirty window, with what amounts to a penlight, he can clearly make out pieces of discarded duct tape and a spray of rust-colored splatters all over the slab. Blood. No leaves, no shards of glass, room enough for three.

Anxious or oblivious, Charlie collects his dog and starts rambling again, throwing around words like barracks and northeast elevations. Fitz needs a forensics team down here ASAP.

"Let's back it up, Charlie. Move away from the cottages. Okay?" He takes hold of the old man by the elbow and guides him in the direction of the ocean.

"I been meaning to ask you," Charlie says. "How's that Parker girl doing?"

"Her name is Carrington."

As much as Charlie has been invaluable to Fitz, he's becoming a distraction. Between the sound of the waves crashing against rock and Daisy's yapping, Fitz can't hear himself think.

"Marion Parker was a looker," Charlie says. "Quite a sense of humor too. We used to tease each other about who had the more memorable lighthouse. My Minot Light or her Scituate Lighthouse. I was changing channels last night, and I saw the girl on TV. I said right out loud, 'Well, I'll be. All dolled up, she's the spitting image of her great-gran when she was young."

"Wait—are you saying the girl you found alive on the beach has relatives in this town?

"Not no more. Marion passed away years back. Her daughter was gone already by then. Bless her soul, Lucy died in a terrible wreck, leaving her girl to come live with Marion. The granddaughter inherited the Sunset Road cottage. Word has it she couldn't hold on to it thanks to the husband." Charlie lowers his voice as if someone there might hear him gossip. "Money troubles, if you know what I mean. Sold it not one year later."

"Did your friend Marion ever bring her out to the Glades? Her granddaughter, and maybe her great-granddaughter? They might've walked around here. She could've shared the history of the place with them like you did for me?"

"I can't recall specifics, but I imagine so."

Tali's family has some kind of connection to this town. Being taken here may not be that random. Fitz goes through what he knows and how his evidence syncs up or doesn't to this new revelation.

As Fitz mulls it all over, he's suddenly struck by a lack of evidence where he should expect to find it. While June's blood and hair were found on the jacket, Tali's were not. And the jacket supposedly belongs to her father. Tali's prints are not on the bottle and neither are June's, even though her tox lit up on ketamine. Ana doesn't remember the director being at the school the day after the girls went missing. Did Normand parse out the drugs, bring Tali and June here, and then leave them alone at the Glades? Or were they willing to be left in the cottages?

Charlie lets Daisy jump from his arms, and the dog scampers off in the direction of the sea; he follows behind his dog like it's another one of their walks.

How many times did Charlie tell Fitz that he walks Daisy at the same time every day, at dawn and dusk. If the girls were being held on the property for two days, they may have figured that out. They could have placed themselves by the shore at the right time to be found. Except one of them couldn't weather the wind and tide.

Maybe Tali's the one involved with the director, and she pointed to someone else to throw Fitz off. If Normand wanted publicity for the play and came up with this plan—and then June died—he'd need to cover it up. Maybe he threatened to expose Tali if she didn't stay quiet. And Sam's protecting her.

Is Zeke?

Fitz pulls out his phone. He's not sure he'll be able to convince Cyn to share what she knows about the girl, but he needs to at least try. To refresh his phone, he hits the "Home" button, but thanks to Daisy, and the drop, it won't turn on.

CHAPTER

25

A Father's Secret

Cᴠɴ ᴡᴀɪᴛs ɪɴ the lobby of Suffolk County–Nashua Street. This isn't her first time in jail. Zeke Carrington isn't the only alleged perpetrator to request a visit from her so he can recount his version of events involving one of her clients. Sadly, he's not the only father either.

This place isn't Federal Prison Camp, Yankton, the minimum-security Club Fed where entitled men, who, even while incarcerated, take great care of their appearance and behave in ways that are overtly charming and inappropriately seductive. White-collar types with plenty of money to make even the most incriminating evidence disappear, or at least seem less damning.

This Boston jail is not the eccentric Hazelton Penitentiary. Nor is it the aggressive bully, Rikers Island, where fiery language and blatant violence have been known to send a seasoned counselor to bed for days after traveling with women who think they're ready to confront their attackers.

What this jail is, is an impostor. It's the centerpiece of Nashua Street Park, a showy facade with wide paths along the river's edge and raised lawns filled with flowers designed to distract. The beauty allows walkers and bikers and women pushing strollers to ignore the people locked up inside a few feet away.

To the incarcerated ones lucky enough to get called to the visitors' room, a glimpse of that park through a window is either a taunt or a totem. Cuffed and shackled, awaiting trial or sentencing, whether they admit it or not, inmates at Nashua Street know their odds of getting out of the trouble they're in. Men like these know exactly what they did or did not do to land here.

Every facility has tedious check-in procedures, and this one is no exception. After Cyn finally gets through security and puts her things in a locker, she's brought to a meeting room to wait for Zeke.

Minutes later, when he's ushered in by a guard, the first emotion that finds her is sadness for Tali, for all she's been through because of him. This, despite how diminished Zeke looks, the dark circles under his eyes, his otherwise pale skin. His feral hair.

"Thanks for coming," he says. "I wasn't sure you'd stick by what you said about talking to me now that I'm in here." His handcuffs clang the table, competing with the sound of the chair legs scraping the floor.

"No problem. But after this visit, I'll need to refer you to someone else. There are good clinicians here."

It's not unusual for Cyn to hear someone out, even the person implicated in the crime against her patient. But if she's honest, she isn't sure she should've agreed to meet him.

"How's Tali?" he asks.

"Busy. Her play opens tonight. She was on *Boston Live* last night. You'd never know she was nervous." Cyn brushes the hair from her face to cover her embarrassment. Why is she talking to him about Tali like this?

"You're acting like Nell right now," he says. "I wasn't asking about my kid's schedule."

"You're right. That was insensitive. I came here to listen."

"Well then, let's get to it." Zeke's cadence is slow and his mannerisms sluggish. Unlike the other times Cyn has met with him—always with Nell—he's more subdued then manic.

"You probably know by now that I sold drugs to get money to gamble. I didn't use pills myself until the night of the vigil, and then again at June's wake."

Cyn angles her body toward the door. She had hoped Zeke would be forthcoming, but now that he is, she wishes he'd stop.

"I dealt mostly in opioids. I used character names from some of Tali's plays. Sick, huh?"

A flush creeps across Cyn's cheeks. "Did you sell drugs at her school?

Zeke sits rigid now, and he won't look at her.

"Did you give drugs to Sam?" Cyn asks, raising her voice.

"I supplied lots of people at that school. There's a pocket in the bottom of Tali's backpack she never uses. The bag is otherwise a mess, so I knew she'd never find the stuff in there."

Zeke takes his time to lay out what he did. No excuses. Not much emotion either.

"When the kids are rehearsing, they leave their stuff all over the auditorium or in the costume closet. The people I hooked up knew where to look."

It's getting harder for Cyn to hide her outrage at the selfish things people do to hurt each other. "You used your child to deliver drugs to teenagers at a school?"

"Absolutely not. I used the bag, not my daughter."

"Were you involved in the abduction?"

"No. God, no."

"Your pill bottle was found on the beach."

"Police found it in Tali's backpack, or that one fell out. I don't know exactly what happened."

When Zeke goes to scratch his neck, both hands come together and the sound of metal leaving the table makes the simple gesture jarring.

"Did you ever give drugs to Tali?" Cyn asks.

"No. If there's one thing I taught her, it was to steer clear of addictive things. You could say I was the best kind of bad role model."

"What about June?"

"No, not June. She would never take drugs."

His conviction would be comical if it weren't so misguided. People will surprise you. No one can be absolutely certain of the things someone might do.

"I've known June from the day she was born," he says. "Always a cautious kid. More of an observer than a doer. That's why her talent came as such a surprise to all of us. Over the years when our families hung out together, Tali would create these elaborate plays where she was the star, and poor June had to raise the curtain, move the set pieces, hand her props. She didn't start acting until middle school. But, man, once on stage, she was fearless. When she got accepted to PAHS, I teased Tali. I told her she'd finally rubbed off on June."

Cyn recognizes in Zeke the same ability Noah had for covering his lies with an elaborate story. Except when Zeke talks about Tali, the corners of his mouth turn down, and Cyn has the strong sense that if he starts to cry, he won't be able to stop. Something about his remorse is sincere.

"Do you think people can change?" Zeke asks. "I was an okay kid. And I'd like to think that at least some of the time I was a good father. Do you think someone can be good but make bad decisions? Or if someone does bad things, they've been bad all along?"

How many times has Cyn asked herself some version of this question? Was Noah the kind, funny, competent man she fell in love with, who got lost along the way, or a selfish person who was always capable of taking advantage of other people and betraying her?

"Things that happen in our lives can change us," she says. "Who we are evolves and shifts, and other people's behavior can force us to become different people. I think it's hard for us to admit that we're all a little unstable."

"What if I'd gotten counseling when I was younger?" Zeke asks. "If I go now, will it make any difference?"

"I'd like to think so," Cyn says.

"Will you do me a favor? Meet with Tali for a long time, no matter what she says. Can you promise me that?"

"I wish I could. But Tali gets to make her own choices."

"You mean there aren't any circumstances where you can make someone get help?"

"Not unless the person is a danger to themselves or others. Are you worried Tali will hurt herself?"

"No. I don't know. I do think Nell assumes she's strong, without questioning it. I know I did. Tali's always been able to rise to any kind of challenge. But we—I—put her through a lot. After everything that's happened, can she be doing that great?"

"It's hard to know. Our minds shoehorn the people we love into an idea of who we want them to be. We create the illusion. Just because Tali appears capable and resilient doesn't mean that deep down she's not struggling."

This is exactly how Cyn missed Noah's lies. She wrote the narrative. She chocked his detached behavior up to being tired and overworked because that's what she wanted the distance to mean.

"You should be concerned about Tali," Cyn says. "I'm not at all sure she'll accept support from you, but you're her father, and it's your responsibility to at least keep trying to offer it. What I will do is encourage Nell to keep bringing her to see me. I'll give Tali the same message."

Zeke's eyes lock on to hers. His hands go white from clasping them too tight. "If you were concerned—I mean really worried about them—you'd tell me, right? You would do something."

Cyn adopts the firm voice and confident posture she uses when she needs people to come clean about harm risk. "If you think I need to know something to help Tali, I want you to tell me. Now."

Zeke leans back in his chair. "Never mind. I'm being paranoid. Too much time in here with nothing to do but think. Nell and Tali are better off with me out of the way, that's for sure. They'll be fine."

Their time is up, and Zeke is led out of the room by the guard. Cyn stops at the locker to retrieve her things. Her mind races in fits and starts, doubling back over her conversation with Zeke.

She remembers Fitz saying that none of the girls' belongings were found at the scene—not their phones or their backpacks. And the one Tali brings into her sessions is well-worn and monogrammed—the extra CharlieCard she offered Cyn the other day came from the bottom front pocket.

There's a riptide that hides below the surface of every unsuspecting couple or family, and Cyn wonders if she's finally getting clarity on the schism in this one. A fracture older and deeper than she ever imagined.

Outside, she gives in to the urge to dial Fitz so she can talk through what happened with Zeke. Call it instinct or prescience, but a terrible feeling washes over her when he doesn't pick up. It's dusk and the night air is cool; even free of the jail's confined spaces, it's as if she's trapped in a room without windows. Suddenly she's overwhelmed with urgency to get to the school, to ask new and different questions, to see for herself that Tali is indeed the capable, confident girl she portrays herself to be.

26

Cruel Intentions

THE FIRST POUR is pure need and urgency. Remove the wrapper. Uncork the bottle. Find a clean glass, a pretty one if it won't slow her down. Like so many times before, the initial swirls and sips of something red from a deep bowl are paired with a suspicion of lies. Then the shiraz becomes a pause, giving her a chance to block her husband's actions of their shock waves at least for a night.

Nell closes Zeke's laptop that sits atop the kitchen counter next to the spray of roses and succulents in plum, cream, and green. The abundant bouquet from Peter to Tali came with a simple card that said, "With love."

She should feel better than she does after scouring the computer yet again and not finding anything to tie Zeke to what happened to Tali and June. That was the dream, wasn't it? For once to seek and not find any wrongdoing. In the past, as exhausting as it was, Nell would persevere until she got her hands-on evidence of his deception. Always good at catching Zeke in his lies, with proof she could confront him.

Like all his other stories, this latest one doesn't ring true, but in a completely different way it nags her. If he isn't involved, why is he saying he is?

Nell carries the laptop to the den and secures it back in the hidden compartment under the desktop, wondering if or when she'll have to hand it over to Detective Jameson.

Tonight she can't deal with it. Back to the kitchen for round two. The second glass of wine is the best glass of wine. By the time she's through with it, the hard edges of worry will be blunted, and her laundry list of fears will be transformed into hazy nuisances, or not so bad possibilities, all of which can be tackled another day. For now, she'll focus on the feathery texture of accent grasses layering the showstopper arrangement Peter sent. It's a luxury to be staring at more than one bloom.

As much as she wants to linger on thoughts of him, tonight is Tali's night. It helps Nell to hear her music blaring overhead and the undertone of her daughter singing. The sounds of her safe at home, dashing about her bedroom, getting ready for opening night. Nell's had her share of bad, bad luck. No matter what happens with Peter, her good luck is right upstairs.

Maybe it won't be so hard for her to make small talk with the other parents in the lobby of the Holden Theater before the show. Or pretend people aren't staring, talking behind her back, wondering why she married Zeke in the first place. A question she's no longer able to answer should anyone dare ask. All she has to do is survive till intermission, when they'll be buzzing about Tali—the other person who defines her. That's when it will be easier to stand tall.

Tali is shouting now. How does she expect Nell to make out what she's saying from one floor away? Wine in hand, she heads toward the stairs.

Tali's on the landing, looking impossibly young and beautiful—and pissed off. "Have you seen my dance flats? I know I wore them home from dress last night."

"They must be here then. I'll help you look."

Nell climbs the stairs and finds Tali's room looking like a twister passed through the open window. She didn't think her daughter owned this many pairs of jeans and tank tops. The only clothes not all over the bed and floor or spilling from bureau drawers is the outfit Nell bought her to wear on TV. The care Tali took to hang the peasant dress with tassels on a hook over the closet door reminds Nell of June's room and the way she kept her things neat and tidy. Nell places her glass on the only empty space she can find on Tali's nightstand.

Nell picks up a damp towel and uncovers a pair of ballet slippers. "Are these the ones?"

Tali bats the shoes from her hand. "I said dance flats. They're black."

"Hey, I know you're nervous, but watch it. What about these?" She tries once again to offer a pair of shoes to her daughter.

Tali accepts them. "Sorry. You know how I get opening night. One song in and I'll be fine." She shoves the shoes into her backpack, one compartment away from the baby doll dress and thigh-high stockings she'll wear in the first scene.

"Does Mr. Normand know which scouts or agents might be coming tonight?"

"Way to make me less nervous, Mom." Tali fakes a worried face, then smiles. "American Conservatory and Carnegie are sending people. There's one more I'm too frazzled to remember right now. It'll come to me. Can you grab a few hair elastics and throw them in my makeup bag?"

Helping her girl pack for the theater is something they've done countless times together. It's nice to be doing it the way it's always been done—Tali needing her there while Nell takes her cues to pitch in or stay out of the way. Where her daughter is concerned, she's always been able to read her. Something that's impossible to do with an irrational husband.

Nell tidies the top of the bureau of its unsightly clutter, lining up cosmetics off to one side, hooking earrings and bracelets on to jewelry trees.

"I'd like to take you out after the show. Treat you to Mistral."

"We can't afford it," Tali says. "And a bunch of kids are going to Wallace's."

The arm of her new PAHS sweatshirt hangs limp from a drawer like it's reaching for Nell. She pulls on it. "Maybe you should take this with you in case the temperature drops. You've been so cold lately."

Tali dives toward her, angling her body in front of Nell, shoving the sweatshirt back in its drawer. "Stop adding things. I'm already late. Let's go."

Downstairs, Nell fills Tali's water bottle and reaches for her keys to drive her to the theater.

"You know I can get to the Holden faster if I walk," Tali says.

"Not alone. I'll walk with you."

"Come on, Mom. It's light out. You're being ridiculous. And you need to get ready." Tali unzips the bottom pocket of her backpack and produces a small envelope with bent corners. "Don't miss opening curtain, okay? Here's your ticket."

After smoothing out the edges, Nell peeks inside. She's slammed by the presence of an extra one she can't use, but pretends not to notice. "Wow. Center Orchestra."

Nell kisses her cheek and then watches Tali make her way to the end of the flagstone path. "Break a leg, honey. Text me when you get there."

Tali waves and keeps going.

Back inside, Nell leans against the front door and the tears come. At the top of her voice, she shouts, "Fuck you, Zeke."

She needs her wine. Tali's room. By the nightstand. Inside her daughter's disordered space, she finds the glass where she left it. She takes a sip, and then another. Nell sits down on the bed and looks around.

The messy room is at odds with her daughter's ability to shape things to her own liking with people and things real or imagined. It's like a reverse sanctuary, where Tali gets a break from the perfection that's expected of her everywhere else. Nell is reminded of Cyn's office and how comfortable she felt there.

She gets up to fold her daughter's clothes. Smoothing out her sheets and comforter, Nell wonders if Tali will see her well-intended cleanup as a kind of invasion. How often has she heard her say, "Stay out of my room!" There could be some order to this chaos.

Except Cyn says there's a middle ground between diving in and butting out. Perhaps the most motherly thing Nell can do now is leave everything physically as it is but snoop a little.

The top drawers of the bureau, left and right, are jammed with underwear, bras, and odd socks. Nell's heartbeat ticks up when she remembers Tali blocking her from the drawer nearest the bottom. The sweatshirt is balled up on top of turtlenecks and cardigans. It could be the wine, but Nell's hands shake as she pushes aside the clothing to uncover a stockpile of prescription pill bottles. Ambien, Percocet,

Xanax. Shoved all the way back, is a nearly full bottle of Klonopin with Tali's name on it. The rest of the stash is labeled with Zeke's name and a half-dozen other strangers.

The knot in her stomach tightens; it aches with both sharp and dull pains. When Detective Jameson asked if Tali did drugs, she'd rejected his inquiry outright. Without thinking twice. Without having looked. But if Tali's using drugs, wouldn't Nell be able to tell? And why are all the bottles and pill packs full?

Nell frantically empties the rest of the drawers, looking for some kind of explanation. As if to build to the blow, it's in the very last one that she feels the scalloped edges of a hard object she recognizes. From its shape and glossy finish, before she even gets a good look at it, Nell knows it's the Chinese lacquer box June gave Tali as a birthday gift back when they were girls. There it is. Hand painted in vivid reds and yellows. The picture is of two happy children holding hands and dancing across the top. Nell lifts the lid.

Her face is hot, her chest booming. There's a tightening in her throat like she swallowed the exotic, sharp thing. Her mind can't make sense of the wrongness of her fingers touching the lotus pearl pin. How can this be here? The last time Nell saw the unmistakable treasure, it was pinned to the pretty pink neckline of June's forever dress.

Beyond panic now, Nell needs to know if Tali is all right. Because this does not look like she can be okay.

Get to the theater. No matter what diminished her capacity to do it before, she needs to force a conversation with her daughter now. To find out what's going on. *Put the pin in your pocket. Grab your purse. A coat. The keys.*

Her legs are weak as she moves out into the hall and down the stairs. Despite the urgency her mind registers, her body responds in slow motion. All she wants to do is down the rest of the wine, crawl into bed, and close her eyes. As if sleep would come. As if her mind could ever stop inventing horrible reasons for this pin and those drugs being inside her daughter's room.

Tali will have a reasonable explanation for having the pin. Maybe Peter gave it to her, and neither of them thought to tell her. Oh, God, if Tali unpinned it from June's dress at the funeral home and then hid it in her room, it has to be because of emotional trauma or suffocating grief or something else Cyn suspects is wrong with her.

If Zeke asked her to hide the drugs, that could be why Tali's angry with him. Nell wouldn't put it past him, but that's low. Even for him.

Outside in chilled air, she's able to move faster. It isn't until Nell gets to Newbury Street that she realizes it's because she's unencumbered. No coat. No phone.

Nell's out of breath by the time she lands in front of the stage entrance of the Holden. Thanks to a group of stage crew smokers, she slips in through the propped-open door. Backstage is humming, and because she needs to stay calm for Tali's sake, she slows her walk and scans the place discreetly, all the while praying she won't run into Ana.

Robin is off by herself, marking a dance routine. "Have you seen Tali?" Nell asks.

"She took the underpass back to school. I feel bad she's freaking out. She can't find her shoes for the opening number."

Nell shakes her head at the memory of her daughter packing her backpack.

Robin reads Nell's disbelief as disagreement. "She left a while ago with Sam."

The quarter mile stretch of tunnel connecting the Holden to the high school is dimly lit and dank. She would've avoided the closed-in space with its low ceilings and narrow paths if it weren't the fastest way to get there. The only sound comes from the echo of Nell's footfalls against concrete.

The school theater is empty, lit only by the ghost light. All of tonight's action is taking place next door. If Tali is here, she's backstage. Bypassing the roped-off passageway that leads to the catwalk, Nell climbs the stairs, presses the wall in exactly the right place, and the hidden door opens.

When she turns into the hallway, the only light comes from the dressing room at the end of the corridor. After a few steps, she hears their voices.

"You don't have to," Tali says. "I'll tell Normand. We can figure everything else out after the show. Calm down."

Inside the dressing room night-light floods in from the buildings that surround the alley. Sam has his back against the wall and he's guzzling from Tali's water bottle. They're in full makeup and costume, and her daughter is standing in front of Sam urging him to drink.

"Tell him what?" Nell asks. "Why are you two over here?"

"He doesn't feel good." Tali looks surprised to see her, and she's talking too fast. "We don't think he can go on. We're trying to figure out what to do."

"Is it nerves, Sam? Or did you take something?" Nell looks at him, but he won't look at her.

Sam hands the water bottle to Tali and drops on to the only seating in the room, an oversized upholstered piano bench. With his head in his hands, he says, "I can't do this. You have to tell her."

"It's not a big deal. He took one too many Xanax. Normand can step in for one night."

Sam lies down on the bench, curling into a ball. His costume—dress shorts, suspenders, and wool socks—make him look like a little boy. Whatever he's muttering, Nell can only make out, "My mother's gonna kill me."

"Sam can stay here," Tali says. Turning toward her mother, she outlines the next set of directives. "You and I will go back to the Holden. I'll tell Normand he needs to go on in Sam's place and you can find Ana to send her over here." Tali tries to pull her toward the hall by her elbow, but Nell is immovable.

"Come on," Tali says. "They're probably freaking out not knowing where we are."

"Are you on anything? Who gave the pills to Sam?"

"No. Dad's the one. Dad—"

"Why are all those bottles in your drawer?"

"You went through my stuff? I can't believe it. Why would you do that?" Tali looks over at Sam as if he's the keeper of the explanation.

"Did your father ask you to hide them?" Nell lifts Tali's face by the chin, trying to look straight into her eyes. "Answer me."

"No, I found them. They're Dad's."

Tali backs away from her. Before Nell can register what she's doing, Tali has opened the door to the fire escape and stepped on to the balcony platform. Without pause, Nell follows her.

"Come inside. You're scaring me." Nell wants to reach out to her, but she's afraid Tali will go closer to the ledge. Five floors below them, the alley is paved in stone.

When Tali stops moving, Nell searches her pocket for the pin, hoping this is the thing that will bring her daughter closer.

Palm out, she shows it to Tali, who looks at it a little too long.

"How did you get this?" Nell asks.

"Mr. Danforth gave it to me," she says, her eyes shining with tears. "The night of the wake, when I lost it over seeing June, he said he wanted me to have it. He told me not to tell you because it would hurt you too much."

Nell stands motionless, disbelieving, anchored to the brick wall. This is a twisted version of what June told her when she gave her the pin after her mother died. Nell doesn't stop to wipe the tears from her own face. Instead, she reaches out to brush away Tali's. "Are you telling me the truth or are you acting?"

"That's what happened. Ask him yourself. Why don't you believe me?"

"Once someone lies to you, it's impossible to know when they're telling the truth."

"I need to go. Mom, please. We can talk all you want after the play." Tali looks left, then right, considering whether to push past Nell to get inside or take the metal stairs that zigzag their way down the side of the building.

Her child, who isn't afraid of anything, will choose the stairs.

This time Nell is a step ahead of her, gripping the iron railing, blocking the fire escape steps. "Tali, no."

The wrought iron landing feels precarious under her feet. The building is old, and in this moment, Nell can't remember whose job it is to pay attention to things like the safety of children at school.

Tali follows her gaze to the rusted bolts and the thin space between the collection of brackets and the brick.

At the same time the platform trembles again, there is movement inside the dressing room.

Nell can make out Cyn, with Detective Jameson beside her. She doesn't care how they found them or why they're here. All she knows is that she's never been happier to see anyone. The detective stops at the bench to check on Sam, his fingers at his neck, his cheek near his lips to feel for breathing. He mouths the word *phone*, and Cyn hands him hers. After seeing the detective lift the water bottle to sniff it, Nell looks back to Tali. "Did you give Sam something?"

When Tali notices them there, she moves toward the ledge.

Nell wants to scream, "Get back. Please answer me." Instead, Cyn's voice is a relief coming from the threshold of the fire escape. "I came to see you, Tali. You said you had a ticket for me. To see the show."

"You can't trick me. My mom called you. She told you about June."

"She didn't. I went to see your dad."

"What does all of this have to do with June?" Nell asks.

Gracefully, Cyn raises one hand, a subtle gesture telling Nell to let her do the talking.

"I know you're angry with him for all the mistakes he's made. But he's worried about you. And so am I."

"Then what's *he* doing here?"

Detective Jameson comes to stand beside Cyn. For brief moment, Nell notices him put a hand on her back.

"He's my friend," Cyn says. "I asked him to come." She steps out on to the fire escape. "I'm going to come closer, okay? We can sit right here and talk."

The wrought iron groans at the idea of more weight on the balcony.

"It's unstable," the detective says, grabbing hold of Cyn's arm.

"Both of you, please come inside," Cyn says, retreating to the threshold. Her voice is firm yet kind, and Nell is desperate for Tali to respond to it. She won't move unless her daughter does.

When Tali takes her hands off the railing, Nell realizes she thinks they're exaggerating the risk to get her back into the dressing room.

"I'll throw myself over if anyone comes any closer." Tali looks over at the detective. "You know, don't you?"

"What do you mean?" Nell asks, breathless with fear.

"Not all of it," he says. "I think you left the school with June like you said you did. There aren't cameras on the Comm Ave side of the building, but I think either Sam or Mr. Normand met you there."

Tali stands in the center of the platform now. Above her, the moon is brilliant white, so large it owns the sky. Surrounded by incandescent light, the flimsy costume, more nightgown than dress, makes her look simultaneously nubile and innocent.

"Everyone knows about the cameras. It's the side of school where kids get away with smoking. Mr. Normand and Robin stayed behind. I wasn't lying when I told you they have a thing."

"So it was Sam." There's an odd note of satisfaction in Detective Jameson's voice.

Nell is less able to feel the iron bars under her feet. It's like she's outside her body watching them stand there, hearing someone else say her words. "You weren't abducted?" she asks. "You faked it?"

"It's not like I planned this horrible thing. I didn't. I was mad at Dad for what he was doing to us. And I was angry at you for thinking you could take a new job and move me to another school without asking me. I needed a break from everything, so I convinced Sam and June to go for a ride that night after auditions. I thought if we didn't come home till morning, Dad would be freaking out. And he deserved it."

Nell wants to ask Tali, what about her? Did she want to punish her too?

"At least Ana's up front with Sam. She lets him do whatever he wants as long as he gets the lead in whatever play he's auditioned for. But June didn't want to go at first. Sam was the one to talk her into loosening up. Have a little fun. Try a little pill! I told her to relax. Nothing bad was going to happen."

"You chose Scituate?" Nell asks.

"Parker's Cottage on the water—another thing we lost because of Dad. I love everything about that town. I told Sam and June there was a great place for skinny-dipping in North Scituate. We stopped for snacks and drinks, and then headed toward the point."

Nell hears her daughter's words, but she doesn't understand them. If all of this was teenage mischief gone awry, ending in a terrible accident, why didn't Tali say so?

"At first, we had fun. We parked Sam's car at Minot and walked out to the Glades. It was deserted. We ran around for a while, laughing and joking around. June was pretty out of it, and she couldn't stop falling down. When she kept wanting to call her father, I took her phone. Sam was high too. In the beginning he thought everything she did was funny. He'd help June up, then chase her some more. I hadn't told them yet, but the whole time we were out there, I was looking around for a place we could spend the night. Then June got all panicky and paranoid, and she kept asking to go home. Sam sided with her, saying we had to leave. I warned him that we'd all be in a lot more trouble if we dropped her off at her house like that."

Everyone looks toward Sam now, who's unmoving on the bench. Detective Jameson holds up the phone to Tali. "I'm going to call 911 for him. Okay?"

When Tali nods, he taps the screen and puts the phone in front of his face, though he doesn't speak. Nell swears he already made this call, and she wonders if maybe he's filming.

All at once her daughter looks transformed. Like a character delivering a monologue she's rehearsed so many times her performance is flawless. Nell doesn't expect her to keep spilling the story unprompted, but in this detached way, she does. If Nell weren't in her own fugue state, she'd be begging Tali to stop. Except as unbearable as it is to listen, there will never be a good time to hear the rest.

"When I remembered the tower cottages Great Nana showed us a few times, I knew they must still be there. I told June it would be a good place to lie down for a while.

"Sam and I got her there, but by then he figured out I wanted to stay the night. He tried to convince me to leave. He said June would be fine by the time we got back to Boston. I told him no. Go without us. The story would be even better if we pretended to be kidnapped. Two girls abducted to a beach town. There'd be tons of media coverage, and even if he and June got the leads in the play, we could all be stars.

"Sam said he wanted no part in it. I was still pissed at him for keeping things from me. We were friends and he'd lied to me. I told him I'd tell his mother he got drugs from Dad. That was all it took. He got us the waters and snacks from the car and left us there. I wasn't worried at first because I was sure someone would find us by using the GPS on our phones."

"I don't believe you could hurt June," Nell says. "Not on purpose. You didn't mean to."

"I don't know when exactly, but sometime after Sam took off, being there by myself with June passed out, it all started to feel unreal, like I was acting in a play."

"This is my fault," Nell says. "Honey, I'm sorry."

Cyn takes off her jacket and holds it out to Tali, trying to entice her closer. The only thing keeping the girl warm are the black thigh-high stockings.

"It's cold," Cyn says. "Come inside and you can tell us the rest. I'll help you through this, I promise."

Only an inch or two from the ledge, Tali kneels and grabs the railing, suddenly looking like a small child refusing to leave the playground.

"No, it's Dad's fault. One day I was happy—loving school and my life—and the next day I'm watching Sam pull a pack of pills from the bottom of my backpack, coming clean to me about how my father moves drugs through our school. Using me to hook people up."

"Why didn't you tell me any of this?" Nell asks. "I would've made him leave. You have to know I would've turned him in myself." The look in Tali's eyes tells her everything. Her daughter doesn't believe she would've done that.

"The night you were away, Dad figured out that I had been holding back the pills to punish him. We had a huge fight. He told me I had no idea what I'd done. I didn't care. I had my own stuff to worry about. My first audition hadn't gone well, and June had nailed hers. I could see Norman looking at her like she could carry the show. Everyone knew he was going to give Robin the only other big part. If I choked at the callback, I'd end up with nothing. Dad never even asked me about it. He was too busy trying to clean up his mess; he didn't even notice me leave the house."

"Your father believes what happened to you and June is because of his dealing?" Fitz asks Tali this unimaginable question quietly, tenderly.

As her daughter nods, Nell realizes she has never looked so devoid of emotion.

"Did June go along with what you were planning?" Fitz asks.

"Not really. She slept through the first night because it was warm enough inside the shelter. Everything would've been fine if you'd found us the next day. The more time went by, the colder it got, and the harder it was to keep her under control. She woke up yelling, begging to leave. She kept saying her father would forgive her. I didn't know what to do. I kept feeding her pills to keep her calm and to give me more time to figure out what to do.

"I went back over the whole night like I was blocking a play. Thinking of things to make it look more real. Inside the cottages, there was glass all over the floor. I used shards of it to give myself scrapes and cuts. June already had plenty on her arms and legs from running through the woods high on pills. The windows were duct-taped in places, so I used that to bind our wrists.

"The second night June was seeing and hearing things that weren't there. I knew she couldn't prove that I'd done anything wrong, and Sam wouldn't tell as long as I kept his secret.

"I focused on what would happen after. We'd be found and everyone would be relieved to have us back. There'd be lots of media coverage, and maybe June would be too messed up to take the lead even if it was offered to her."

"Did you put yourself on the beach so the caretaker would find you?" Fitz asks.

"After the next day, when you didn't come for us. I couldn't wait any longer. I buried the water bottles and snack bags, and threw the phones in the ocean."

Fully inside the story, Nell imagines the girls lying on that cold, wet sand. Poor June slipping away, while Tali waits, desperate for someone to rescue her from this out-of-control scene.

"June started shaking and making horrible breathing noises." Tali closes her eyes, the tears streaming down her cheeks. "I turned her over, but it was too late. I didn't mean for her to die."

Nell's mind is flooded with images—Fitz, at the vigil, telling them the girls had been found in Scituate. Zeke hugging her far too tight when they learned Tali was alive. Peter collapsing to the ground when Fitz told him June was dead. And finally, her family at the hospital—Nell sitting next to her husband as they tried to console their daughter. Unbeknownst to her, both of them complicit in completely different ways.

"Did you leave the pill bottle at the Glades that night or did you plant it there later?" Fitz asks.

"Oh, Tali, you did that the day we went there together?" Nell asks.

"You were right there, and you didn't even suspect me."

"Why in the world would I ever think you'd be involved in something like this?"

"Ana would never have missed it."

Tali's words are a knife.

"Sam and June weren't going out, were they?" Nell asks harshly. "That was another lie."

"We needed a way to explain why he was such a mess. After June died, Ana started getting suspicious. I think she knew Sam took her car out again after she drove him home from the audition. He was freaking out that his fingerprints could be on the bottle. And he was wearing Dad's jacket that night; it was still in his room."

"Sam had the jacket this whole time?" Nell asks.

"That jacket had been in the costume closet since I borrowed it for some show. Sam just happened to wear it that night. I told him all he had to do was put it back. Practically everybody in that school had worn it at one time or another. Except he was afraid someone would see him. I promised him that all the evidence on the beach was mixed up and confusing. No one would put any of this together."

"Is that how you convinced him to let your father take the blame? Because he was wearing the jacket?"

"No one needs convincing that my father is a bad person. Sam agreed to put it in our closet. Then after he did and Dad got arrested, he started to crumble. He was going to tell his mother everything."

Tali stands, though her hands are fused to the railing. "Please, Mom. I don't care what happens to me later, but you have to let me go now. It's almost curtain up. When I'm on stage, I don't have any problems. It's like nothing feels real unless it's scripted."

When it came to her daughter, Nell always felt like things would break in her favor. Everything her girl was made up for all that Zeke wasn't. But she's not making any sense. After telling this unbelievable story, Tali wants to go on as if nothing happened? Something is dreadfully wrong with her, and Nell doesn't know whether to turn her own daughter over to the detective or let Cyn take her to the hospital.

It's as if Tali has read her mind. "I'm not sick, Mom. Dad is. Think of all the horrible things he's done to you. And to me. I deserve this one good thing."

For a split second, Nell sees herself taking charge. Ending this nightmare by lifting her arms, extending them out, giving Tali a forceful push and then following her off the edge into oblivion. She pictures the fall, the crashing. Except from this height, their deaths are not certain.

"I didn't mind being in the news for the kidnapping, or even for all that stuff with Dad," she says. "All I did was look out for myself, and now everyone's gonna hate me."

"It's too late to change what you did, but you have control over how you handle things now," Cyn says.

"I'll be famous for all the wrong reasons."

When Tali rubs her eyes with the backs of her hands, Detective Jameson gets down on his stomach and inches out on to the platform. He's going to reach for her.

"Trust me," he says. "No matter what you've done, your family will always love you."

Despite his attempt to spread his weight evenly, the iron squeals like an angry child. Or is that Nell's heart finally bursting free of her chest?

How long the fire escape will hold them, she can't say.

When the detective has no choice but to back up, Nell decides to end this one way or the other.

Closing the distance between them, another few inches and she'll be near enough to pry every one of Tali's fingers off the railing until she has her daughter in her arms.

But Tali's grip is a vise.

"Let go!" she shouts.

"Tali, wait," Fitz says. "Dr. Rawlins and I won't stop you if you come in through this door. Please."

"You'll let me go to the Holden?"

There's a duet of yeses—his and Cyn's. When Tali lets go, Nell breathes for what seems like the first time since she moved toward the metal staircase.

"I totally get that I have to pay for what I did," Tali says, her bright eyes dancing. "After tonight, okay? One more show."

Nell sees Dr. Rawlins and Detective Jameson exchange calculating looks. They're lying. Cyn's face says Tali is ill; his says her daughter is a criminal. A distant siren sings out both realities.

Then Nell looks at her child and hears herself say, "No!"

"No, what?" Tali asks. "They're saying I can perform."

Nell steps in front of her. "This is the end of the lies. No more pretending. We go in and face this together, or we stay right here until this entire balcony gives way. I'll even jump to make it come down faster if that's what you want."

"Mom, no."

"We've all been reckless. What your father did was unconscionable. And as masterful as he is at deceiving me, I missed it and I own that. It's inexcusable that I didn't see you were in trouble. But you did a terrible thing, Tali. You have to take responsibility for it."

There's much more Nell wants to tell her. That she is a mirror of her mother, fragile and fierce. That, although she doesn't know how, they will find a way through this. They will do it together. But Nell does not express these things. Instead, with a note of calm in her voice, she simply says, "We're going inside."

She reaches out to her daughter, and for all the panic in Tali's eyes, her small hand, though alarmingly cold, relaxes in hers. Nell isn't surprised by this. Her approach to the world has always been through saving someone. She knows how to do this.

27

People, Places & Things

CYN VISITS NELL on a late fall afternoon, the time of year capricious New England breaks the day in two, pretending to be summer in the morning, forecasting winter by night.

In a startling arrangement, Nell has been staying at the Wallace's brownstone, and from the look of the sparse traffic on Gloucester, reporters have yet to figure out that both women are holed up there. Ana ushers Cyn in, guiding her toward an airless Victorian great room with showy wallpaper and heavy wood furniture, everything ornate and tinged in amber.

It's hard to imagine Nell comfortable here. This place so unlike her cozy home. But then Cyn imagines Nell can no longer find respite anywhere given her child and her husband are across town locked up in the same county jail.

"I'll tell her you're here," Ana says without offering to take her coat or rid her of the box she carries.

This being Ana's home, if this were a different time, Cyn would've expected her to be in full-on hostess mode.

Yet today she wears dark sweatpants and a pilly gray sweater, and the tiny lines around her eyes give away that she's not sleeping. Subtle changes are more noticeable in otherwise happy people.

"Wait," Cyn says. "How's Sam?"

"We've agreed to ninety days' inpatient treatment in exchange for probation," Ana says. "Sam's going to tons of meetings. He likes his doctor a lot."

"I'm glad. How about you?"

"What's there to say?" Ana looks down and notices a small hole in her sweater near the cuff of her sleeve; she covers it with her hand. "Imagine me without words," she says with a half-suppressed laugh. She goes to leave.

Cyn checks the bottom of the box for dampness. When she finds the cardboard dry, she places it on the floor, drops her bag in a chair, and wrestles free of her coat.

When Ana returns, it's oddly disorienting to see her and Nell together. Whenever Ana's name has come up in their previous conversations, Nell's never made a secret of her dislike of her.

"Don't be silly," Ana says to Nell. "It's all been arranged. It's the least I can do."

Ana excuses herself but the look on Nell's face tells Cyn she doesn't trust she isn't around the corner eavesdropping. Cyn slides closed the pocket doors separating the great room from the foyer, leaving them alone finally.

In the weeks since what would've been opening night, they've spoken often by phone. But this is the first time Cyn has seen Nell since Tali was taken into police custody. The jeans and smock top she's seen her wear before hang a little freer from her frame.

"I don't have the energy to fight Ana over paying my bills," Nell says. Including my health insurance and Tali's legal—"

Nell holds on to the back of a chair and closes her eyes tight for a second, as if this is something she does now to brace herself against waves of overwhelming emotion.

"That's generous," Cyn says, motioning for them to sit.

"I'm out of other choices. I don't have the kind of money I need to help Tali. Or to pay for sessions with you."

"It seems like Ana genuinely wants to help, and I'll bet it's her way to make up for not coming forward once she suspected Sam's story didn't add up."

"Who am I to judge? She's been good to me. Right now I need all the help I can get."

"If your arrangement with Ana changes, as long as you'd like to keep seeing me, we can figure the payment part out," Cyn says.

"When we first met, you laid out all these rules of counseling. Why the exceptions now?"

Cyn feels her face harden when Nell brings up the conflict of certain therapy ideals— refusing to treat more than one family member, discounting rates—ordinary practices imposed for good reason. But not all boundaries are equal. Look what Noah did. Cyn can bend whatever norms she wants from now on, and she won't come anywhere near his iniquity.

"Yours is a special case," Cyn says, reaching down to pick up the box by her feet.

At first Nell shows reluctance to reach for it, as if she needs to locate the energy it takes to simply move her arms. When she struggles to open the top to extricate the plant, Cyn leans over to help her.

"Now you're giving me gifts?" Nell's eyes become glassy as she admires the prettiness of the waxy red blooms.

"I picked it out, but it's not from me."

Nell wipes her eyes with her sleeve.

"Tali told me she gave you a plant like this for Christmas once," Cyn says. "When she was little. She remembers it flowered all winter."

"Tali asked you to give this to me?" Nell traces the outlines of the heart-shaped leaves. "I visited her this morning, and she didn't mention it."

There's no need to point out that there's a raft of unspoken things Tali has yet to broach with her mother.

"It's not easy to apologize," Cyn says.

"I'll never forgive myself for not figuring out what Zeke was doing. And worse, for not knowing our messy marriage was making her sick."

Cyn understands the desire to rearrange the past in order to answer the question: *Am I complicit?*

"You can only operate on what people decide to reveal to you," Cyn says. "Zeke showed you what he wanted you to see. Tali too. And you know family stress isn't the only thing that contributed to what happened."

"Once in a while, when I'm with Ana or talking with you, I believe that. That you can't possibly know someone's in trouble until they're visibly in trouble."

Nell leans in to smell the flowering plant, and Cyn is reminded of the care she took with a little clutch of buttercups set on the kitchen table during her first visit to the Carringtons' house. Tali's offering to her mother—though wholly inadequate—is somehow perfect.

"Most of the time I blame myself for not realizing something was wrong with her," Nell says. "A better mother would've known. You would have."

"You're giving me too much credit," Cyn says. "As Tali's counselor, time and distance let me see her issues run deeper than any one influence. Before anyone is a mother—or a partner—she's a woman doing her best to cope with her own preoccupations. We can't know how I would have handled things if she were my daughter."

"You don't have to tell me if you don't want to," Nell says, "but do you ever want to have kids?"

"You want me to talk about myself now?" Cyn lightens her tone to be sure Nell knows she is teasing. "I think I've made enough therapy exceptions for one session."

They talk more about Tali, specifically Cyn's plans for her treatment. Nell stays calm in this dark place, and Cyn ends the session feeling hopeful she can shoulder what comes next.

After they agree on another time to meet and say their goodbyes, Cyn walks in the direction of her apartment. Not for the first time she thinks about the question of children. Mostly she's grateful she hasn't already made this decision. The relationship between Nell and Zeke is as irrevocable as hers with Noah, but they still have to be Tali's parents.

It's the first time in a while that thinking about Noah doesn't hurt in some deep-down way. As she registers this, Cyn recognizes Fitz sitting on the stoop outside her building.

She sees him before he sees her, and thinks, *This is how it could be. I could feel happy to be home.* Fitz is leaning forward, elbows on knees, content to watch the people and cars fly by. By the time he notices her, she is close enough to hear him say, "Oh, good."

Fitz pats the space next to him. "It's nice out. You okay to sit for a bit?"

Cyn puts her bag down and angles her body to face him. She finds it easy to read his mood. With him she feels like she's in the presence of something good happening.

"I thought we agreed to meet later at The Beehive," she says.

"You said you were going to see Nell today. I took off a little early because I thought it might be hard."

"That's nice of you." Cyn touches his arm impulsively; he covers her hand with his.

"It was difficult and it wasn't," she says. "The whole thing is tragic, and Nell and Tali have a long way to go toward healing, but at least they're opening up to me."

"I heard Tali's lawyer is going to use her age and mental state as mitigating factors to try to reduce her sentence."

"She is. I'm going to be deposed next week. Even though I've been upfront about having to say Tali's responsible. Not everyone with a dissociative disorder commits a crime."

"You told Nell and Tali that?"

"I did," Cyn says. "Whether it helps her or not, they want me to do it."

"Even if it does, involuntary manslaughter plus obstruction—tried as an adult—I'd say she could be going to prison for in the neighborhood of two to four years. Zeke's a totally different story. He's upward of five even with the plea."

The detective-speak Fitz uses does nothing to mask the sense Cyn gets that he's here with something more personal to tell her. But just because she can play the counselor doesn't mean she should. She sits in silence.

"Mind if I confess something?" he asks.

Cyn expects to feel blindsided by that word, given her tendency to attach gravity even to the things she has predicted. Instead, she breathes.

"You were right about Sam," Fitz says. "I shouldn't have come down so hard on him."

"It's big of you to admit that," she says. "Though in a way, your intuition was right. He wasn't there when June died, but he helped Tali cover it up, and he didn't come forward after the fact either."

"True. But I feel bad that it got a lot messier for Peter Danforth. If I had handled things differently with Sam, I might've figured out what happened to June much sooner."

"It was never going to be anything but awful for Peter, no matter the details. June was his child. Forgiving Tali and Sam won't be easy. If it's even possible."

Fitz gets that look again. Like there's something else he wants to say.

Someday Cyn will ask him about his life before they met. About the events surrounding his friend's death when loss brought him low. She will do this knowing full well that only he can choose what to share, what to show. For now she doesn't push. After all, there are things she may never tell him. Experiences that will remain forever hers.

"You ever going to invite me in?" Fitz stands, and his dark mood vanishes as quickly as it appeared.

When Fitz and Cyn stand outside her apartment door, he asks with a gesture if he can have her key to unlock it.

"It doesn't look any different from the last time you were here," she says. "But that doesn't mean I'm not making progress."

"Let me guess. You've quit the search for the perfect couch, and screw past history, you're sticking with the one you love."

"How did you know?"

They look at each other and say in unison, "Keira." Both of them laugh.

"I didn't exactly phrase it that way," Cyn says. "But close enough."

Fitz pushes open the door, and they walk into the living room. The couch from her old office takes center stage.

"How did she do this?" Cyn asks. "I only mentioned it yesterday." Then Cyn remembers the afternoon Keira watched her bury the Castle Island Storage receipt in her desk.

"She might've had some help."

Cyn makes her way around the couch and drops on to it with a bit of a bounce.

"If you're pissed we overstepped, then I had nothing to do with it," Fitz says. "You know Keira. When she makes up her mind, God help anyone who tries to stop her. But if you're happy, then it was all my idea."

"I'm happy. To have it back."

"Some things don't belong locked in the past," Fitz says. "I'm starting to think not much does."

What she should have said is that she's happy because he's here, and because it's been so long since someone did such a kind thing for her. Except she's caught between two dangers—to avoid loneliness, she'll have to expose herself to love. For as surely as she could be wrong about Fitz, she could also be right.

"Hey, where'd you disappear to?" Fitz waves a hand and then sits beside her.

"Oh, sorry. It's been a day."

"I hope bringing up my fixation with Sam earlier didn't make you feel bad somehow."

"No, no. I get inside my head sometimes, that's all."

"Maybe I should teach you to play piano." Fitz leans back and puts his arm around her; she curls into his side.

Cyn has never forgotten what it feels like to be safe with someone. And she wants that again with Fitz. She has no idea how long they will be together, but if she's not careful, she'll ruin the time they do have worrying if or how he might betray her.

"Can I say one more thing before we move off the subject of the Carringtons and on to something like what you're going to do about a coffee table?" Fitz looks at her with an expression that is as sweet as it is sincere. "You have no reason to be hard on yourself about Tali. You figured her out in a matter of weeks. Who else can you say that about?"

"Hopefully you," Cyn says. Then she pulls him in to kiss her.

PLAYS

In order of mention

The Swing of the Sea by Molly Hagan
Curious Vigil by Don A. Mueller
Detective Story by Sidney Kingsley
I Bring You Flowers by William Lang
Good Kids by Naomi Iizuka
Landscape of the Body by John Guare
Next to Normal, book and lyrics by Brian Yorkey, music by
    Tom Kitt
A Doll's House by Henrik Ibsen
Relative Strangers by Sheri Wilner
A Sea of White Horses by Peter Dee
A Mid-Summer Night's Dream by William Shakespeare
Story Theatre by Paul Sills
The Seagull by Anton Chekov
Spring Awakening, book and lyrics by Steven Sater, music by
    Duncan Sheik
Miss Saigon, book by Alain Boublil; Claude-Michel Schön-
    berg, lyrics by Alain Boublil; Richard Maltby Jr.
Six Degrees of Separation by John Guare
Dirty Little Secrets by Jeffrey M. Jones
After by Chad Beckim

Dreams by Tom Sharkey

The Miracle Worker by William Gibson

You Can't Take It with You by George S. Kaufman and Moss
    Hart

The Crucible by Arthur Miller

Rent by Jonathan Larson

Our Town by Thornton Wilder

Finish Line by Joey Frangieh and Lisa Rafferty

The Secret School by John Dilworth Newman

Chicago, book by Fred Ebb and Bob Fosse, music by John
    Kander, lyrics by Fred Ebb

Thrill Me, book, music, and lyrics by Stephen Dolginoff

Mirror, Mirror by Kitty Johnson

An Impossible Cure by Norman Beim

True Love Lies by Brad Fraser

Brief Encounter by Noel Coward

The Innocent One by James Reach

Little Fears by Emanuel Peluso

A Steady Rain by Keith Huff

Fame by Christopher Gore

Proof by David Auburn

A Father's Secret by Alexandra Dennett

Cruel Intentions [a film adaptation of the play *Les Liaisons
    Dangereuses*] by Pierre Choderlos de Laclos

People, Places & Things by Duncan Macmillan

Book Club Guide

The Dangers of an Ordinary Night by Lynne Reeves

Author Interview

Q: *The Dangers of an Ordinary Night* deals with the impact of addiction on marriage and family life. As a school and family counselor, why did you choose to write about those who live in the shadow of the disease?

A: The epidemic of addiction includes waves of loss and trauma that go well beyond what the person with addiction experiences. Understanding this ripple effect, and considering the perspective of the people who care for and about those who struggle, has been part of my counseling work for some time. When it comes to a fictional narrative, I wanted to invite readers to inhabit the lives of women caught up in the care-taking. It's my effort to add to the ongoing conversation about the toll addiction takes on every member of the family.

Q: The through line in your work shows flawed characters navigating different kinds of loss. Why do you repeatedly return to grief topics in your novels?

A: Being a school and family counselor, as well as a novelist, it's my hope that every facet of my work creates opportunities for thoughtful conversation around the relationship issues we find most difficult to talk about. Fiction is a powerful vehicle for examining universal experiences. Personally, I've endured some painful family losses, and like many writers, I find it therapeutic to revisit those themes in an effort to keep learning from them.

Q: The novel includes references to over twenty-five plays. How is the theater setting important to this story? Does this have any personal significance to you?

A: After my father died when I was a teenager, complicated grief triggered substance use and mental health issues in some of my family members that have echoed down the years. Acting in plays became a safe haven for me then, and years later, entering the theatre still brings me great joy. *The Dangers of an Ordinary Night* is my love letter to the theater. And this setting is central to both the way the story is conceived and in the dramatic themes the novel explores.

Q: Writing as Lynne Griffin, your previous novels are categorized as women's fiction. Now you've written a novel of domestic suspense under the name Lynne Reeves. Why did you choose to use a pen name for *The Dangers of an Ordinary Night*?

A: Writers use noms de plume, or pen names, for any number of reasons. Mary Ann Evans wrote as George Eliot because back in the day it was taboo for women to write novels. Rumor has it that Elena Ferrante isn't interested in disrupting her private life in Italy, which means no one knows her true identity. In my case, like a number of writers today, I'm using a pen name to open my work up to different cohorts of readers. *The Dangers of an Ordinary Night* will appeal to readers who have enjoyed my previous book club fiction titles, as well as to those readers who seek out mystery, crime, and psychological suspense novels.

Q: Are you working on another novel? What can readers expect from you next?

A: I'm currently at work on another domestic suspense novel that charts the journey of a woman fleeing the city of Boston for the backwoods of Maine with her sons in order to escape her dangerous husband. This story shares sensibilities with *Sleeping with the Enemy* by Nancy Price and *Last Night in Twisted River* by John Irving. It's a family story about what one mother is willing to sacrifice for the love of her children.

Book Club Questions

1. *The Dangers of an Ordinary Night* is a novel about trust in our most precious relationships. At one point, Nell says, "*Once someone lies to you, it's impossible to know when they're telling the truth.*" Discuss the personal betrayals Nell, Cyn, and Fitz have experienced. In what ways do these breaches of trust interfere with their other relationships?

2. After Fitz's friend Maddie died, he sacrificed his opportunity to go to Juilliard. Years later, every Monday night, he plays piano in a nearly empty bar for tips in coins. Why does he punish himself by disallowing the recognition he deserves given his talent? How do feelings of guilt and regret impact our lives even years after we've experienced a traumatic event?

3. Early in Nell and Zeke's relationship, she sees him as charming, spontaneous, and fun. It isn't until after they're married that Nell can see that his big personality has a darker side. Do you have empathy for Zeke throughout the novel? Does his continued self-sabotage impact your ability to root for him to get well?

4. At one point, Nell reflects on Zeke's cycle of addiction by saying she "*lost all sense of what was normal, entering a state of non-movement, letting his relapses and remissions take center stage in their lives.*" In what ways are women

today letting the needs of other family members take away from their own pursuits? How does this impact their own happiness?

5. Eventually, exhausted by the rush and surge that is life with Zeke, Nell decides to leave him. She feels "*her little boat of a heart is no match for his sea of white horses.*" Is it ever justified to sever ties with someone who struggles with the disease of addiction? Is it a heartless choice or one of survival? Might you feel differently if the person battling addiction is your child?

6. In one of Cyn's early sessions with Tali, she notices that, "*like lots of girls her age, Tali has already learned to bury a request for help in either politeness or sarcasm.*" How do young women get these messages? Is it harder for women and girls to ask for the help they need to cope when they're in the shadow of a family member's illness or addiction?

7. Sam's mother, Ana, is a classic stage mother. Discuss the particular intensity of her parenting. How does her treatment of Sam impact his mental health? Does Ana mean well, or is her over-involvement purely selfish?

8. Fitz and his sister, Keira, are keeping a terrible secret about the death of their friend Maddie Townsend. They've come to believe it's better to hurt themselves trying to live with it than it would be to devastate their mother and the girl's parents with the truth. Do you agree that there are times when keeping a secret does more good than harm?

9. What did you think of Nell's reaction after she learns of Tali's involvement in June's death? Why does Nell feel the most confident when she is caretaking? Can you relate to women who find their voice only when they're advocating for others? In what ways is that easier than speaking up for yourself?

10. Nell says she will never forgive herself for not anticipating *"the dangers that hide in an ordinary night."* What does this phrase mean to you? Why do we sometimes miss the signs of mental illness and addiction in our loved ones? And why, with hindsight, is the evidence that something was amiss seemingly hidden in plain sight?

11. In the end, Cyn says she is *"caught between two dangers— to avoid loneliness, she'll have to expose herself to love."* Why does living wholeheartedly make us vulnerable? Do you think Fitz ever tells Cyn about his complicity in the aftermath of Maddie Townsend's death? If so, does she forgive him? Do you think Cyn and Fitz have a chance at healthy love?

12. If you could invite the author to your book club, what would you want to ask her? What would you like to know about the inspiration for the novel?

ACKNOWLEDGMENTS

THE DANGERS OF an Ordinary Night is first and foremost a love letter to the theater. In my high school and college years, my passion for storytelling was found on the stage. A special thank-you to my sister, Dianne Reeves Veale, for nurturing my love of the art form and for the fond memories I have of our trips to New York to see countless plays.

I came to a new and deeper appreciation for storytelling in connection with Boston's GrubStreet. My friends, colleagues, and students at this welcoming center for creative writing have inspired me to continue to grow as a writer and as a teacher.

For their generous gifts of time and perspective, I want to thank my dear friends and early readers of this novel, Katrin Schumann, Marjan Kamali, and Therese Walsh. My conversations with these amazing writers made this a deeper, truer story. Thank you also to Susan Golomb of Writers House for her thoughtful editorial feedback.

I'm forever indebted to my first and most trusted reader, my daughter, Caitlin Batstone, for her endless encouragement. Every story I write is immeasurably better for her insight.

Special appreciation goes to my son Stephen Griffin for inspiring me with his love of jazz music, and for offering his expertise on the nuances of playing piano.

I'm beyond grateful to be working with the amazing team of editors and publicists at Crooked Lane Books. My thanks to Matthew Martz, Toni Kirkpatrick, Melissa Rechter, Madeline Rathle, Rebecca Nelson, and Jennifer Hooks for the attention and care they've taken to bring my story into the world.

Tremendous thanks go out to Megan Beatie for her thoughtful and tireless efforts to bring this novel to readers. It was my lucky day when she agreed to champion my work.

As always, oceans of gratitude to my amazing family. My love for Caitlin and Matt Batstone, and Stephen Griffin—and theirs for me—is infused into everything I do.

To my sweet Oliver, making his debut in my acknowledgments, I'm over the moon that I get to be his Nan.

And to my leading man—my husband, Tom. I will never be able to fully express my gratitude for his love and support. You're holding this book in your hands because of his unwavering belief in me.